The students li_____ and turned to march i_____ up their feet, legs, and _____ aves crashed down on _____ _dent to gasp from the c_____ y California," Miller said as he sp_____.

"Take yo___ _ats!" Chief Packard bellowed out over the water.

The line of students obediently sat down in the cold surf. Now only their heads and shoulders were above the surface, and those only intermittently, as the waves crashed over them. Muscles warmed from the exercise of only moments ago knotted up.

After an eternity of torture passed—actually only six minutes—the students were ordered back to their feet and in toward the shore. Before they could reach the beach, however, another order sounded out, "Drop!"

In less than a foot of water, the class dropped to the push-up position. With the waves now crashing over them completely, the students of Class 78 started doing push-ups in the shallows. Every time they lowered their bodies, the water would cover their heads.

"I'll tell you what," Inspector Hawke called out, "two more people quit and we'll secure from the evolution. Come on now, you too can be warm and dry. Just ring that bell."

But no matter how much he cajoled and tempted the class, he couldn't get another student to quit.

# HELL WEEK
## SEALS IN TRAINING

**Command Master Chief DENNIS CHALKER, USN (Ret.)**

**with KEVIN DOCKERY**

**AVON BOOKS**
*An Imprint of HarperCollinsPublishers*

This is a work of fiction. Names, characters, places, and incidents are products of the authors' imaginations or are used fictitiously and are not to be construed as real. Any resemblance to actual events, locales, organizations, or persons, living or dead, is entirely coincidental.

AVON BOOKS
*An Imprint of* HarperCollins*Publishers*
10 East 53rd Street
New York, New York 10022-5299

Copyright © 2002 by Bill Fawcett & Associates
ISBN: 0-06-000148-8
**www.avonbooks.com**

First Avon Books paperback printing: November 2002

Avon Trademark Reg. U.S. Pat. Off. and in Other Countries, Marca Registrada, Hecho en U.S.A.
HarperCollins ® is a registered trademark of HarperCollins Publishers Inc.

Printed in the U.S.A.

10 9 8 7 6 5 4 3 2 1

I would like to dedicate this book
to a very close friend & considered teammate of mine,
Kevin Dockery.
Kevin is a true professional
in his own field of work. It is an honor to work beside him.
Thanks Kevin.

# HELL WEEK

## Chapter One
## 2 September 1998

The silver-colored Chevy pickup truck that climbed the highway in the Southern California mountains was more gray than silver. The accumulation of road dust and dirt on the pickup indicated it had been on a long trip, one that would soon end.

For five days, U.S. Navy Master Chief (SEAL) Jeremy White had been literally crossing the country. He was driving from Little Creek, on the Atlantic coast just next to Norfolk, Virginia, to his new assignment at the Naval Special Warfare Training Command in Coronado, on the shores of the Pacific and just across the bay from San Diego. His personal possessions were in the covered bed of the pickup. The bulk of his limited household goods were being shipped courtesy of the U.S. Navy, and he expected to be at his new assignment well before they arrived.

Following Route 8 from Phoenix, White had spent a night in Yuma before setting out early on the last leg of his trip. As he climbed up the mountain pass, he noted that he was passing through the Cleveland National Forest, a place he had last seen twenty-five years before, during his training days at Basic Underwater Demolition/SEAL school. Every hopeful frogman and SEAL had to successfully complete BUD/S in order to join the Teams, which was what the men in the SEALs called the Navy SEAL Teams. The huge national forest was one of the places where White had been afraid he would fail to complete that grueling course.

During the last phase of BUD/S training—Third Phase, where the students learned land warfare and demolitions—compass courses had been laid out by the instructors in the national forest. At each of a number of different points, the students would find an ammunition can containing a slip of paper with a set of grid coordinates, directing them to another point on the course. Following a map and using a compass, White and his partner had to locate the first coordinate, and the box, on their own.

It had been a long, harrowing hour of traveling through the forest, over trails and through brush, only to have to search for over another hour to locate that precious first ammunition can. Until they found the coordinates, they couldn't go on to the next objective. Both White and his partner were certain they would be dropped from the class for performing so poorly—a terrible fate, within weeks of finally graduating the twenty-six-week course.

White laughed as he remembered how panicked the two of them had been so long ago. They must have looked like desperate idiots, he thought, crawling around and searching for that damned can. But they finally found it, and the next, and the next, completing the compass course in satisfactory if less than record time.

Coming over the final mountain pass, White had his first view of San Diego some miles in the distance, and the wide, blue Pacific stretching far off to the horizon beyond it. It would still be an hour or so of driving to get to the base at Coronado, but in spite of a rising haze, he could make out the white curve of the Coronado Bay Bridge, which connected San Diego to its small suburb to the west.

The gray ocean haze made the city appear as if it was rising up from a storm cloud. But his view was soon blocked by a turn in the road. He liked the mountains; it was one of the reasons he'd wanted to drive across the country. And he was sure he would be back up in them soon enough.

The morning traffic wasn't too bad, and White made good time as he drove down into the San Diego area. On the outskirts of the city, he turned off Interstate 8 and eventually onto southbound I-5. The gray haze he'd noted earlier was thicker now that he was closer to the cold Pacific water. In fact, most of his view of the city was blocked by the low-lying blanket of moisture. But the haze usually burned off quickly from the heat of the sun, giving way to the blue skies and sunny days Southern California was so famous for.

A few miles after getting onto southbound I-5, he saw the exit for the Coronado Bay Bridge. The ramp was a long twisting turn that climbed up to the bridge, which connected the city with the island of Coronado on the Pacific side of San Diego Bay. The bridge arched high above the blue waters of the bay, high enough so the largest oceangoing ships could easily pass under it.

Usually, the view from the top of the bridge of the surrounding sea and city was spectacular. But the panoramic view of the San Diego skyline was partially blocked by the ocean haze as White drove his truck across, though the towering buildings downtown rose above the haze. He could see the Pacific beyond Coronado, but Point Loma on the north shore of the bay was only a dark line against the gray. Navy warships, also gray, lined the San Diego shore. And in the waters below the bridge, tugboats moved civilian traffic to berths at the piers or started them on their way out to sea.

Passing the crest of the bridge and beginning the descent to Coronado, White saw the Naval Amphibious Base (NAB) past Glorietta Bay, to the south. The Coronado shore to either side of the bridge was lined with brightly colored civilian boats and yachts, and the yacht club at Glorietta Bay contained row upon row of them. But Navy ships could still be seen off to the north.

To the north of the BUD/S compound and Special Warfare Command, the Coronado skyline was dominated by a dozen multistory condominiums. The orange roof tiles of the famous Hotel del Coronado could be seen north of the dull glass and steel condos.

Following the bridge down, Master Chief White remembered a story told to him by his sea daddies—the older petty officers who showed the new men the

ropes—when he'd been in training here. The Teams—
both the UDTs and SEAL Team One, back in the mid-
1970s—conducted public demonstrations of their
abilities as part of the city's Fourth of July celebra-
tions. These took place in Glorietta Bay and on the
land surrounding it, so the public could view it from
the beaches. But during one of those demonstrations, a
condominium that was under construction became an
unwanted part of the show.

The condo buildings had huge cranes on top to
move construction materials into place. One part of the
demonstrations conducted by the Teams involved a
static line parachute jump into the waters of the bay, a
uniquely UDT and SEAL skill. But on that day, the
jump master badly miscalculated the release point for
his parachutists. The jumpers exited the aircraft on
command, and the crowd oohed and aahed at the sight.
Instead of landing in the water of Glorietta Bay, however, directly in front of the appreciative audience, one
of the jumpers landed on top of one of the condo buildings, tangling his parachute in the crane.

Though no one was hurt, it took some time for the
men on the ground to rescue their Teammate. The story
of that jump made the rounds of the Teams for quite a
while.

Now, as White's pickup truck approached the end of
the bridge, the wooded streets and parks of Coronado
drew his attention. The town had become an upscale
community, including both artists and retired Navy
personnel, since he'd last been there. Because he was
alone in the pickup, he had to stop and pay the toll.

Had there been two people or more in the vehicle, he could have passed through the free lane to the right of the booths.

"No advances without costs," White said to himself and he dug into his uniform pants pocket for change. Tossing a dollar's worth of change into the gaping basket, he waited until the bar blocking his way lifted and then continued on his way.

At the first major intersection, the silver pickup came to a red signal light and stopped. If anyone noted the Virginia license plates on the pickup, they also saw the truck turn left when the traffic cleared and head south on Orange Avenue. Master Chief White hadn't been in Coronado for a number of years, but he had spent a long time here over two decades earlier, and the route he was following was one he remembered well.

Orange Avenue consisted of blocks of hotels, smaller motels, and town houses. There were tiny lawns in front of some of the town houses, and concrete in front of others. Palm trees lined both sides of the road, their rough trunks extending up to a spreading crown of spiky green leaves.

Entering the Coronado business district, White saw a number of buildings that evoked memories of the past, in spite of all the changes. The Village Movie Theater was still there, though by its rough appearance, attendance must have been down. A bit farther south on Orange he saw the Day/Night Cafe, where he had eaten many an early breakfast while out on liberty. Farther south, at the corner of Orange Avenue and C

Street, he saw the green cupola of McP's, a hangout for the men of the Teams for years. He resolved to drop in on it at the first chance he got.

As Orange Avenue curved and sloped downhill, he passed Glorietta Bay, with yachts and large watercraft docked at the marina's piers. Across the road to the west was the wall that surrounded the Hotel del Coronado. More than a hundred years old, the building was a monument to a lifestyle long past, and a beacon to those who wanted to return to a slower, easier time. But though the hotel was little changed, the area around it had changed considerably. In contrast to its old-world charm, the huge condominiums of Coronado Shores were at least a dozen stories tall, obscuring the Pacific, only a few hundred yards away.

The military base that held the Navy Special Warfare Center and Training Command was just past the Coronado Shores. Unlike the old days, the command area was now surrounded by a tall cyclone fence, topped with strands of barbed wire. Strips of material woven through the links of the fence blocked any view of the compound area. The beach couldn't be seen from the road anymore.

The main entrance of the SpecWar Command area was a short distance from the beginning of the fence line. A right turn off Orange Avenue put the pickup truck onto Tarawa Road. The armed Navy guard at the gate rarely stopped vehicles during normal times of security activity, and he allowed the truck to continue on its way. Following Trident Way, the pickup passed BUD/S Alley and stopped in front of the Phil H. Bucklew Special Warfare Training Center, which dominated the right side of the road.

Jeremy White had arrived at his new assignment: Command Master Chief of the Navy Special Warfare Training Command. Anyone who intended to become a SEAL and join the Teams had to come here first. All sailors had to complete the Basic Underwater Demolitions/SEAL course, BUD/S, that was only taught here. This building was called the "Schoolhouse" by many of the men who had successfully gone through its doors and joined the Teams. And Master Chief White knew that the enlisted men of this command would soon be under his direction.

But first he had to figure out where he could park his truck. Finding an open spot marked "Visitor" seemed a pretty safe bet for a parking space.

Entering the double glass doors of the training center, he came to the Quarterdeck of the Training Command. An intent-looking youth sat behind a desk, one of the BUD/S students who had pulled the duty. He sat up sharply when he saw White walk up.

"Can I help you?" he asked.

"Yes," White said. "I'm Master Chief White, reporting in."

"Yes, Master Chief," the student answered. "I have instructions to call the Command duty officer immediately on your arrival. If you could wait just a moment, Master Chief."

At White's nod, the young man snatched up a telephone and punched a few buttons. After a brief conversation, he hung up and looked back up at White.

"Mr. Beckman is the CDO today, Master Chief," he said. "He's over at the Amphib base right now and will be back in just a few minutes."

"No problem," White said. "I'll wait."

He turned away from the student before the young man could see the grin spreading on his face. Had he ever been that young and serious? After a moment's thought, White realized that he probably had been.

Gazing around the Quarterdeck, he peered at the double glass doors that led to the training compound and the grinder just beyond, where he could see a number of students running about. As with the young man at the front desk, they appeared younger to White than he recalled. Or, he thought with a wry smile, was it just that he was now much older?

Around the Quarterdeck itself were a number of trophy cases, as well as framed photographs on the walls. But it was the glass doors and the view of the inside of the compound that drew his interest. Stepping up to the doors, he could see the blacktopped central courtyard, the infamous grinder where the BUD/S students were exercised, ground down, and built back up by their merciless instructors.

Today, there were painted pairs of swim fins lined up along the blacktop, each pair facing north, where a low stand could be seen. White knew that the instructor would stand there as he led the class through PT. And that's something he would take a hands-on approach to, he told himself.

Throughout his years in the Teams, White had made a point of keeping himself in even better shape than the average SEAL. The results of his personal exercise regimen could be seen in his narrow waist, broad chest, and muscular arms, which were partially exposed by his short-sleeve khaki uniform. Pushing open the heavy glass door, he stepped out onto the edge of the grinder area.

He could now see that almost the entire area was surrounded by buildings, several of them two stories high, giving it the appearance of a penitentiary exercise yard. The white-painted fins stood out in stark contrast to the black surface of the grinder. There were a number of podium platforms around the circumference of the area, besides the much larger one close to the north wall, so that different groups or even classes could be exercised or watched easily by instructors.

The old grinder surface had been rough and uneven blacktop, only about half of it rolled and compressed down to the consistency of an asphalt road. The rest had been left mostly untamped, only lightly pressed down before being left to cure under the bright California sun. There had been no fins to guide the students to their proper positions then. Everyone had to join in the scramble to space themselves out properly before the wrath of their instructor rained down upon their heads—which always seemed to happen, White recalled, no matter how hard they tried to reach perfection as students.

White would be the Command master chief here at BUD/S for at least three years. He had completed a good run of duty on the East Coast, in SEAL Teams Two, Four, and Eight, as well as pulling a tour with

SEAL Team Six. Being here at BUD/S would give him the chance to give something back to the community that he felt had given him such a satisfying career over the years. Afterward, there might be the chance of going to Florida and a tour of duty with USSOCOM (United States Special Operations Command), or other opportunities he could take advantage of. But only here would he be given the chance to set an example and help lead young men into the world of the Teams.

His train of thought was interrupted by the arrival of an earnest but harried-looking ensign. His name plate read BECKMAN and his young face was covered with freckles and topped with a short-cropped thatch of brown hair. Damn, it's Beaver Cleaver, White thought as he realized that this must be the CDO.

"Master Chief White?" the young officer asked.

"Yes, sir," White answered.

"I'm Ensign Beckman," he said, a big smile on his face. "Sorry not to have met you on the Quarterdeck, Master Chief."

"That's okay, Mr. Beckman," White said. "I imagine they have you wearing a lot of hats as a junior officer here."

"At last count seven, Master Chief," Beckman said. "I've just been made the assistant morale officer and assistant safety officer, among a few other assignments. But I hope to be leaving for an assignment to a Team soon."

The young officer's enthusiasm was infectious, and so was his big smile. White found himself liking him already.

"Can I show you to your office, Master Chief?" Ensign Beckwith asked.

"Sure," White said, with a smile of his own. "But where's Master Chief Jensen? I was expecting to meet with him first before I reported to the CO."

"Some family business came up regarding Master Chief Jensen's transfer, and he moved out early last week," Beckman said as he began walking toward the south side of the compound. White followed. "So we've been without a Command master chief for about ten days now. Some of the senior chiefs have been filling in, and Captain Kopecni—he's the commanding officer—decided that since you were already on your way, he would just let the chiefs handle it. Here we are, Master Chief."

They stopped at a door halfway along the outside wall. Ensign Beckwith opened it and entered a short hallway. The first door on the left, not more than a few feet away, was marked COMMAND MASTER CHIEF in large black block letters.

Ensign Beckwith looked back and noticed an odd expression on White's face. "Is something wrong, Master Chief?" he asked.

"This is the Command master chief's office?" White said.

"Yes," Beckwith answered. "Something the matter with it?"

"No, just an odd moment for me," White said with a smile, and shook his head. "This used to be the medical department back when I went through training. The last time I was in this room was during Hell Week.

The chief corpsman had me on his table and was checking out a bad ankle I had. He tried to talk me into going to the hospital over at Balboa."

"Did you go?" Beckwith asked.

"If I had, I wouldn't be here now," White said with a laugh. "After I told that chief to go fuck himself, he sent me right back out to join my boat crew. Ankle still hurt like a bitch, though."

Beckwith laughed as he opened the door to the small office. "Same thing still happens now," he said as they entered the room. "The only thing that's changed is they moved Medical over to the far corner of the compound."

The eight-by-fifteen-foot office had a large, double-pedestal, gray steel desk along one side; a pair of glass-fronted gray steel bookcases on the wall opposite the desk, the cases filled with black notebooks; and an office armchair on wheels in front of the desk. Three upholstered steel chairs made up the rest of the room's furnishings. Light came in through chest-high windows on the west wall of the room, which were covered with half-open horizontal blinds.

"Be it ever so humble, Master Chief," Beckwith said, his irrepressible smile showing.

"Finely decorated in traditional Navy chief style, I see," White replied with a smile of his own. "At least there's no examination table."

"Nope," Beckwith said. "Usually the master chief would just roast students while they were in the standing position. All of these sumptuous surroundings are yours for the taking. Please make yourself at home.

Captain Kopecni is planning to meet with you at 1330 hours. Do you need a hand with any of your gear, Master Chief?"

"No, I think I can handle everything, thanks," White said. "I'll just spend a little time making myself familiar with the compound."

"No problem, Master Chief," Beckwith said. "Class 217 is out at San Clemente Island in Third Phase right now. Class 218 is undergoing pool training in Second Phase over at the Amphib base. And the First Phase instructors are running Class 219 through the sand on the Strand. For myself, I better get back to the Quarterdeck."

"Thanks, Mr. Beckwith," White said as the young officer headed out the door.

"No problem, Master Chief."

Smiling at the ensign's good humor as he left, White turned back to look at his new surroundings. Master Chief Jensen had already removed any personal items he might have had in the office. Sitting at his desk and leaning back in his chair, White thought about the office being his home in the Teams for a three-year tour. He'd spent his time in much more spartan surroundings than this Command master chief's office.

But in a few minutes, White had seen just about all he wanted to of his office. It would be several hours before he met with Captain Kopecni, and there wasn't an exiting Command master chief for him to meet and talk to. So he decided to take a look at the compound and start getting his bearings.

Outside, the sun was shining. The haze he'd noticed

a short time before was gone. He had taken pains to be sure his uniform was spotless and in proper order, but the general uniform of the day seemed to be khaki shorts, blue T-shirts with gold trim, and boots with heavy socks pulled up and folded back down over the tops.

There were a few other khaki uniforms around, much like the one he was wearing, most of them sporting a bright gold Special Warfare insignia high up on the right breast. Below most of the tridents there were, at most, a line or two of ribbons and a set of jump wings. They made his own five full rows of ribbons seem almost garish in comparison. The few times he'd seen instructors in khaki or dress uniforms back when he'd gone through training, it seemed they must have been sluffing off while in the Teams if they didn't have five rows of ribbons or more.

But that had been almost twenty-five years ago, he reminded himself, and most of the instructor staff at BUD/S then were combat veterans of Vietnam with multiple tours of duty behind them. White had seen action in most of the hot spots of the 1980s during his time in the Teams. Grenada, Panama, the Persian Gulf, Desert Storm, and Somalia had all added up to create the display on his chest. Those same experiences were part of the reason he was at the schoolhouse now: to stand as an example to the BUD/S trainees as to just what a SEAL could be and what a career in the Teams could give you.

As White pondered these thoughts, he walked back in the direction of the Quarterdeck and beyond it.

There, on the far northeast corner of the grinder, gleaming in spite of being in the shade, hung a brass ship's bell with a knotted white cord dangling from its clapper. Along the ground, stretching back toward where he stood, extended a line of green-painted helmets; relatively lightweight helmet liners, really. Each liner was set with its brim pointing out into the grinder, a class number painted across its front and back.

White stood and looked at the helmets for a moment, each one a mute symbol of an individual who hadn't been able to meet the demands of BUD/S. To quit, all a student had to do was ring that bell three times. Then he was done, DOR'd—Dropped on Request. Within hours, a day or so at most, he would be gone, back to the Navy to complete his enlistment. All that would be left behind was a fading memory among his classmates, and a growing line of helmets.

Master Chief White walked up and past the bell. To walk up and ring it had to have been the longest trip some of the young men at BUD/S ever faced. But the Teams weren't for everyone. Standards were kept high, in spite of an average forty percent dropout rate among BUD/S classes. And White knew that those standards wouldn't be lowered on his watch.

He was glad to see that the bell was still standing in its accustomed corner of the grinder. For a short time some years earlier, the bell had been removed. The theory was, the threat of it had been demoralizing to the person who had to ring it in order to volunteer out of the program. Such were the problems when you had outsiders watching BUD/S, White thought, and trying to study it without having passed through its trials themselves.

Everything had a reason at BUD/S, and those reasons had been well proven over time. The ease with which someone could end the pain and struggle of the course—just ring that bell and it was over—was part of the challenge to the individual who had it in himself to stay: if he had the "fire in the gut" to stick things out, overcome any obstacles, and join the Teams. And the sound of that bell ringing through the compound had another effect: it raised the morale of the men who were still in training. It reminded them that they were still there, while someone else had quit along the way.

As White stood near the bell, contemplating just what it had meant to him, a group of students were coming across the compound. They were wearing sharp, crisp, green uniforms. Their clothes were freshly starched and their black boots brightly spit-shined and gleaming in the sun. The green helmets they wore marked them as First Phase students, and the shine on the paint told White that either they had been freshly repainted or this class hadn't been in BUD/S very long yet.

The new students' uniforms brought a smile to his face. Back when he'd gone through training, their uniforms had been reissued over and over until they were almost rags. Ragged edges and tears had to be sewn closed and repaired by their new owners. And the Vietnam-era jungle boots they had been issued were not much better. But times had been different back in the mid-1970s, when money was in short supply after the Vietnam War ended.

It was good to see that the Navy and Department of Defense had begun to recognize the tremendous contribution to the overall defense of the United States that was offered by the Special Operations Forces. Some additional funds coming to the SEAL Teams and their training was a worthwhile thing. Besides, White hated having to work on budgets and allotments, though that was something he would have to do a lot of as a Command master chief.

A lot of money had gone into the buildup of the training center facilities. Past the graveyard of helmets, he walked along the north wall of the compound. In the far corner he could finally see the beach, though a large sand berm blocked his direct view of the cold Pacific waters. The old barracks were still there, but a new medical facility was now in the area that he remembered as the student lounge. The new students in First Phase had met the "old-timers" then—those who were into the Second or Third Phases of training.

The size of the training center now, and the number of students who ran through BUD/S every year, had demanded a larger medical facility than the one that had been housed in his new office. But the barracks beyond the medical center were much the same.

The quarters for the pretrainees—students whose class hadn't started training yet—and those students who were already into First Phase, were on the first floor of the concrete barracks structures. The second deck, or floor, of the building was for the Second Phase students, and the third deck for the Third Phase students. Each floor had the same number of rooms, though as you went up in floors and class, the size of the student population went down dramatically.

When White had started training, they began with six or more men assigned to a room. Now, entering the barracks, he immediately felt himself in familiar territory. The first room on his right was where he'd spent his first months at BUD/S, both in pretraining and as a student in First Phase.

The temptation to look into the room compelled him to push the door open. The steel-framed double bunks were all still there, including the one farthest in the corner to the right, facing the ocean, which had been something that he had liked a lot.

The lockers where they kept their gear and uniforms had all been replaced. But there still was just a bare linoleum floor, no carpets in sight to catch the sand that students would track in constantly. At least some things didn't change.

Farther down the hallway, the laundry room had several new washers and dryers—a small luxury over the single dusty and old washer and dryer shared by White's entire class. They had never been able to keep the laundry room completely clean, at least not enough to foil a sharp-eyed instructor conducting an inspection. You could never keep all of the sand out of the building anyway, especially not on the first floor, with its doors almost opening onto the beach itself.

Three students entered the hallway as White was

walking through. They stopped and said, "Good morning, Master Chief," almost in unison.

Noticing that none of them carried a helmet, White asked them what phase of training they were in.

"None, Master Chief," one of the students said in a flat voice. "We just rang the bell."

With that statement, the trio bowed their heads. A short period of uncomfortable silence echoed through the hall, then the students moved on and entered one of the rooms.

Slowly, White walked on. The ringing of that bell had motivated him while he was going through training, and he assumed it had the same effect on the students today. But he had never given a lot of thought about what might have been going through the heads of the students who had rung that bell. Now, in his position as Command master chief, knowing what those students thought would be important to him.

So he did an about-face and went back to the room the students had entered. He knocked on the door and went in. The students, sitting on their bunks, snapped to attention and shouted out in unison, "Hooyah, Master Chief!"

That shouting reflex was going to be with them for a while yet, in spite of their present situation. And the stark nature of that situation was evident in the tears running freely down the face of one of the three.

These young men had probably accomplished a lot back in their high school days, maybe even in college, White thought. They could have been athletes who excelled on the field or in other activities. Even getting into BUD/S was something only four out of a hundred volunteers could do, with all of the screening tests they had to pass. Quitting training could be the first major failure of these young men's lives. Their disappointment in themselves was obvious.

Quietly closing the door behind him, White looked at the dejected young men who had jumped to attention. He sat down on a bunk, looked up and told the three to take a seat. As the students sat down, he began to tell them a story about when he'd gone through training.

"First of all, I've got to tell you gentlemen something," he said. "I haven't been in the position of Command master chief here for even a full morning yet. I just arrived from the East Coast and haven't settled in at all. You are the first students I've talked to, and the first ones I have ever talked to who have rung out.

"I noticed you three seem very disappointed in yourselves. If you're willing to tell me, I would like to know what went through your heads. Back when I went through training, I never asked anyone who rang out why they had done it. Back then, I used the sound of that bell as an encouragement to keep going myself. That helped to give me the power and will to get through anything I had to during my career in the Teams."

The three young men blurted out their stories, almost all at once. And their reasons all sounded the same. Listening to them, it seemed to White that they didn't know why they had quit, beyond the fact that the training was just too hard. Maybe if they'd prepared more, had better known what to expect, or if the instructors hadn't been so hard on them, he thought, they wouldn't have quit.

Getting up from the edge of the bunk, White thought about what he could say to these young men. They'd made a decision that was going to stay with them for years. But they had a chance to come back to BUD/S and try again someday. He thanked each of them and said, "My office is just on the other side of the grinder. I'm just checking in now, but if there's anything I can do for you, I have an open door policy. Please come by if you want to talk about what happened. You will all be fine. This program isn't for everyone, and there's nothing wrong with that. It's a big Navy and you can still find a lot of adventure in it."

The three students who had brightened up a bit, thanked White, and he left the room. He knew this was something he would have to learn to deal with as a Command master chief. Students who rang the bell were unique to the SEALs and BUD/S, and this was the only place to get any experience in dealing with young men who had found that BUD/S just wasn't for them.

Walking out behind the compound, White moved onto the beach. A large berm of sand had been built up, and it stretched out along the beach, between it and the compound. Broken in places by paths wide enough for a small truck, the berms at least blocked the wind from blowing the worst of the beach sand and salt spray into the compound. Off to the south he could see a group of students being run into the water by their instructors.

After the students were good and wet, they were told to roll in the sand. The "sugar cookie" effect—being wet and covered with scratching, irritating, sand—was a standard of BUD/S training that had been maintained by generations of instructors over the years. Rather than a means of torture, as it appeared to outsiders, the sugar cookie taught the students that they could function almost blinded by sand and salt. That situation had been faced in combat by many a SEAL and UDT operator before them, ever since the first frogman had landed on an island beach during World War II.

Seeing that the instructors had the situation well in hand, White moved along the back of the compound and returned to his office. He knew this was going to be quite an assignment for the next several years.

As he sat reflecting quietly in his new office a short while later, there was a knock. Not knowing who it might be, he quickly got up and answered the door. The short, stocky SEAL standing in the hallway had a dark blue T-shirt stretched across his muscular chest, the words UDT/SEAL INSTRUCTOR printed in gold letters on the upper left breast. Steaming in his hands were two dark blue coffee cups with NSWC, for Naval Special Warfare Center, printed in block gold letters. On his tanned face, the man had a broad grin.

"So, Master Chief," the SEAL said, "figured out where the coffee mess is yet?"

"Damn, Dave." White broke into a wide grin too. "You under my command again?"

Chief Dave Johnson entered the small office and handed White one of the coffee cups. "Yup, looks like," he said. "But this place isn't much like Sixth Platoon back at Team Two."

"No, it isn't," White said with a shake of his head and a wry smile. "It looks like someone let the local high school kids take over this place."

"Yes, they do seem a bit young when you first get here," Johnson said as he sat down in one of the chairs. "But soon enough you'll feel just as old as the rest of us creaky old instructors."

" 'Instructor,' " White said as he sat down at his desk again. "That's going to take a little getting used to. So, anyone else of the old crew around?"

"Do you remember Nick Holmes?" Johnson asked.

"The name's familiar," White replied with a puzzled frown. "But I can't remember why. Wasn't he in your class?"

"Yeah," Dave replied, and took a sip of his coffee. "But he had rolled back from an earlier class. He originally started up First Phase when your class was in Third."

"I still can't quite place him," White said.

"Okay, how about this," Johnson continued. "Remember how one of the new guys just out of boot camp over by the airport came here to the base?"

"Not really," White said.

"Well, it was Nick," Johnson continued. "He had just graduated boot camp and wanted to get over to the island in the worst way. So the silly bastard went and bought a cheap little inflatable boat at some sporting goods store. He got down to the shore near Point Loma and paddled all the way across the inlet to the North Island Air Station without getting swamped or run over by any shipping in the channel."

"Damn!" White exclaimed. "That must be over four miles."

"More like over five miles," Johnson said. "And he got all the way to the beach not a hundred yards from here before his luck ran out."

"Luck ran out?"

"Yeah," Johnson said, his wide grin returning. "The silly bastard had come all that way wearing his blues and carrying his duffel bag in that damned little boat with him. No trouble at all, and he stayed dry all the way. But just as he was coming up to the beach, the surf got hold of him. A big cruncher smacked down on him, tipping his boat and dumping him and his duffel into the water."

Laughing now, White asked, "Was he all right?"

"Oh yeah," Johnson said. "He left that deflated piece-of-crap boat of his on the beach and reported in to the Quarterdeck sopping wet. The instructors then just couldn't quite believe what they saw. Here was this student, soaking and covered with sand, kelp, and dirty foam, his duffel bag and himself dripping all over the floor. They finally told him to get over to the barracks and then report back in wearing a proper uniform."

"And he's one of the instructors here now?" White asked.

"Oh, you betcha," Johnson said. "First Phase, of course. He really gets into surf passage."

"I can believe it," White said with a laugh. "What a way to start your first day."

"Well," Johnson said, as he leaned toward White, "here's to your second first day at the schoolhouse." He reached out and clinked his coffee cup with White's. "May it be almost as memorable as your first."

And both men laughed.

## Chapter Two
### 29 January 1974

It had been a short bus ride in an uncomfortable gray Navy bus to the Naval Amphibious Base in Coronado. Jeremy White was a brand-new bosun's mate, having only graduated from the three-week training class the day before. But now he was finally getting to where he wanted to be in the Navy—BUD/S training, where he would learn to become a SEAL.

Jeremy had been in the Navy all of three months, most of that time spent in boot camp at the Navy Recruit Training Center near the airport in San Diego. He found it an interesting city, though almost anyplace would have seemed interesting to a young man raised in the farm country of central Ohio. But everything he wanted to be was centered on the shoreline of Coronado, facing the wide Pacific Ocean.

His adventure had begun after watching a 1950s vintage movie on television, *The Frogmen*, starring Richard Widmark and Dana Andrews. In the old *Sea Hunt* TV series, Mike Nelson, the main character, had been a Navy frogman, but it wasn't until Jeremy saw the movie that he understood who the frogmen were. They had been a lot more than just underwater swimmers. They blew things up, examined beaches for landings, and later on became a commando group called the SEALs. Their name stood for the three areas the SEALs operated in: sea, air, and land.

There wasn't much available to read about the SEALs and their missions in Vietnam and other places. The organization was so secret that when he went to the Navy recruiter's office, the recruiter hadn't been able to talk to him about them. Instead, he was ushered in to an inside office where an officer had spoken to him about what he called the "Teams."

When Jeremy had convinced the man that he was serious about becoming a SEAL, the officer had shown him a movie called *The Men with Green Faces*. It was the first time Jeremy had actually seen what the SEALs and the UDTs had done during the Vietnam War. It confirmed for him that he wanted to be in the SEALs.

Though the U.S. involvement in the Vietnam War had ended a year earlier, and enlisting in the services was not popular among people his age, the recruiter told Jeremy that he couldn't guarantee him a shot at completing BUD/S, which was the only way to get into the SEALs or the UDTs.

The only thing that Jeremy could get was a guarantee for boatswain's mate school. He would be given a chance to volunteer for BUD/S while at boot camp, told more about the program, and given a physical screening test. One of the other recruiters in the office managed to get him a set of recommended exercises he could do, as well as a list of what he would have to do to pass the screening test.

So at boot camp, while his fellow enlistees thought the limited physical training was a lot of work, Jeremy spent his spare time working out to make sure he could give the screening test his best shot.

The UDT-SEAL physical screening test was given on a regular basis at the Recruit Training Center, but each class of recruits only had one opportunity to try out. Four hours were set aside on a Thursday during their fourth week of boot camp for the volunteers from Jeremy's class to undergo the screening test.

On that day, Jeremy met his first real SEAL. He was the only SEAL chief attending the screening test, but he was easy to pick out. He was huge, his muscles looked like they had muscles, and he didn't appear to know how to smile. If this was what it took to be a SEAL, Jeremy knew he was in trouble. To him, the guy didn't look like he swam up under ships to plant charges, but just bit through the steel hull or tore the props off with his hands. Assisting him were several other instructors, whom Jeremy knew were Navy divers, since they'd conducted classes at the pool. At least they looked like normal-sized people.

The swimming pool had been used in boot camp to learn lifesaving drills and take swimming tests. But what they did over the next few hours was anything but a regular swimming test. Out of the 125 students who originally volunteered to undergo the screening process, only Jeremy and two others were still there after the push-ups, pull-ups, swimming, running, and everything else was completed.

After they graduated boot camp four weeks later, Jeremy's fellow recruits had gone on to their respective A-schools to learn their Navy job skills. But he attended a three-week indoctrination course into what it meant to be a bosun's mate in the Navy. The course, which taught him a lot about a wide variety of subjects, was given at the Recruit Training Center, and Jeremy had merely reported to another section of the base.

Boatswain's mates were the most all-around sailors in the Navy. In fact, they had to be familiar with the complete operation of a Navy ship. Along with chiefs, they were looked on as the leaders of the enlisted community of the Navy. And Jeremy was proud to be in their ranks. But what he still really wanted was to be a SEAL.

The Navy detailer at boot camp had given Jeremy his orders, so he had his shot at BUD/S immediately after leaving bosun's mate training. Everyone, including the detailer, had told him that BUD/S was the hardest possible choice to make as a job in the Navy. But now he was in Coronado and would have his chance.

He'd already seen the training compound once, or what you could see while driving by as a passenger on a city bus. A few weeks earlier his curiosity had gotten the better of him and he wanted to see the place where the goal that he had signed over four years of his life for would bring him. Like all the students in his class, he was given liberty and could leave the base whenever he didn't have other duties. So he took a bus to Broadway in downtown San Diego, transferred to another bus, and rode out to Coronado.

Initially, he'd intended to get off the bus at the stop in front of the base, but his plans changed as he approached. The base area was open, and he grew more excited as he saw what must have been students, and maybe SEALs, walking around. But as they pulled up alongside the base, he realized that he had no idea what he would do if he got off. Suddenly scared, he settled back in his seat, and the bus moved down the road toward its final stop in Imperial Beach.

The main drag in Imperial Beach was well-stocked with local bars, hangouts, and shops. Jeremy picked a spot and got off the bus after asking the driver which bus to take for the return trip. A handy bar looked like a good enough place to have a beer or two and think about heading back, and this time maybe actually stopping and taking a look at the training base.

The bar had a raised walkway where some dancers could come out and entertain the patrons. Jeremy was just eighteen, and was surprised when the bartender didn't ask him for any ID. He took the glass of beer when it came up and turned to look at one of the dancers who had just come onto the stage.

The lady was easy to look at, especially in a short skirt, halter top, and calf-high boots. Her long dark hair swayed as she moved, though Jeremy was watching other parts of her move rather than her hair. She also had a pretty smile that drew the eye, until he noticed just where she was smiling.

There were four men seated around a table near the

stage, and the dancer was smiling at one of them. But he wasn't returning her smile as much as he was looking at Jeremy.

The short haircuts, tanned skin, and short-sleeve shirts exposing arms where the skin was drawn across bulging muscles told Jeremy that these guys were probably SEALs from the base just up the road. Hell, they could be instructors for all he knew. Even though he was wearing civilian jeans and a shirt and had let his mustache start to grow back in after boot camp, he knew he looked like little more than just what he was—a very junior sailor who had strayed into the big dogs' yard.

Not that these big men scared him. He just thought that leaving the bar might save him some time getting back to the base. So he finished his beer, left his money on the bar, and moved out of the bar. Jeremy heard a round of laughter before the door closed behind him. But leaving still struck him as the best thing he could do. Getting into trouble with what could be a group of SEALs before he even got to training himself couldn't do him any good. Besides, maybe the BUD/S training compound looked better coming from the other direction.

That little adventure had only taken place a few weeks before. Now, Third Class Boatswain's Mate Jeremy White was arriving at the BUD/S training center again, only this time he didn't have a whole lot of choice about not getting off the bus.

The BUD/S training compound, part of the UDT

and SEAL base, was across the street from where he'd been dropped off at the main gate of the Naval Amphibious Base. It was the same two-lane street he had taken past the base. Now, as he approached the front gate, he had time to take a closer look at where he would spend the next six months of his Navy service.

The place looked unimpressive. There were several buildings around the area where the gate guard had told him the BUD/S Quarterdeck could be found. Off to his right, a few hundred yards away, a much smaller building held a small exchange he would soon learn they called the country store. To the south there was a confusing collection of logs, nets, chunks of telephone poles, and pipes that he assumed was the obstacle course. Beyond that there was a beach with a scattering of old hulks of landing craft, helicopter hulls, and what looked like a rusty armored box on treads with a big, square door for a back end.

But there weren't any mobs of screaming students. The place looked quiet as he walked up to the only door he could see in the main building. A strange site stood near the door, telling him he had to be at the right place, and making him wonder just what the hell he was letting himself in for.

It was a life-size statue of the Creature from the Black Lagoon. The webbed hands of the statue reached out, the claws spread to rend anything that came within reach. Hanging around the creature's waist was a web belt with a large sheath knife attached, the number 63 painted on the sheath. Jeremy knew he was in the right place because if the wooden sign hanging from the creature's neck. Carved into the wood were big block letters: SO YOU WANNA BE A FROGMAN.

Welcome to BUD/S?

Stepping through the doors, he walked along a short hallway and into the inside courtyard of the compound. The blacktop court was surrounded by low buildings on three sides. The open western side faced the ocean. He could see the quiet Pacific lapping at the beach a few hundred yards away.

There was a badly rusted chain-link fence between the compound and the ocean. The salt spray had to be hell on the metal, he thought. The fence looked about ready to fall down, and the racks of equipment near it didn't look a lot better. One large wood rack held what looked like ugly, flat lumps. They were the rubber boats, IBS—Inflatable Boat, Small—he remembered from his recent training in such things. But these must be spares that were being kept for some reason, Jeremy figured, since they looked flat and unable to even hold air.

The rack of wooden paddles he saw next to the boats weren't much better. Faded yellow paint, or maybe shellac, covered what looked like a bumper crop of splinters waiting to be harvested by an unwary hand. Even the surface of the courtyard looked worse than the outside basketball courts back home. It appeared that asphalt had been spread out on the beach sand itself.

As he looked at the area he had worked so hard to get to, Jeremy wondered if he hadn't made a mistake and was in the wrong place. He soon found out that he was indeed at the right place—but he was doing the wrong thing.

He stood there a moment, then walked toward the fascinating sound of the ocean waves crunching down on the shore, a sound he had never heard before. As he moved toward the water, his bags hanging down from his hands, he heard another sound, one he would become very familiar with, and received his first real introduction to the ocean.

As a lone figure just walking across the grinder, Jeremy had drawn the attention of an instructor who had glanced out the window of an office in the far corner of the grinder, next to the brass ship's bell hanging from a post. All the instructor had seen was an apparent student walking across the grinder.

The first sign Jeremy had that something was wrong was when he heard a bellow: "What are you doing, maggot?"

Realizing that he was the only person in sight, and that the bellow had to be directed at him, a sudden tightness gripped Jeremy's chest. He turned and saw an awesome human being charging toward him. Jeremy thought it was a Roman gladiator come to life. But all a gladiator could do was kill him. And this was his first introduction to something far worse—a BUD/S instructor.

"I said, what are you doing, maggot?" the instructor demanded as he closed to within inches of Jeremy's face. "You're supposed to be running!"

All Jeremy could see was a tanned face wearing

sunglasses, topping off what looked like a pair of tan shorts and blue T-shirt that had been painted over a gladiator's set of muscles. Even as he tried to open his mouth to speak, to tell this apparition that he didn't know where to run to, unless it was away, it was far too late for him to do anything to save himself.

"You drop!" the instructor snarled, the volume of his voice not one bit diminished.

Confused, Jeremy did the first thing that came to mind. He opened his hands and dropped his bags to the ground.

Now the instructor was even more enraged. He loomed over Jeremy and sprayed spittle in his face as he shouted. The tan of the man's face was being replaced by a ruddy red tone. And Jeremy was sure that the man was about to knock him down and beat the crap out of him—and there wasn't a thing he could do to stop him. It was like being a deer frozen in the glare of the headlight of an oncoming express train.

"Are you trying to be funny, maggot?" the instructor bellowed, now within an inch of Jeremy's face. "This is what drop means—I want you to drop down into the push-up position."

Jeremy fell to the ground between his bags. He snapped his legs out behind him, his knees locked and the toes of his polished shoes down on the blacktop. His arms held his chest up off the ground and were so stiff they quivered.

Without lowering the volume of his voice, the instructor said, "Now, count them out!"

Jeremy didn't know if the instructor meant to do

four-count pushups or two-count ones that involved just a single up-and-down motion. But this blue and tan demon shouting at him couldn't possibly want anything easy, he decided, so he started counting out a cadence as he raised and lowered his body by just the strength of his arms.

"One-two-three-ONE!" he called out. "One-two-three-TWO . . ."

The instructor bent down and shouted in Jeremy's face again, to stop what he was doing. "Recover!" he barked.

Again Jeremy didn't move, shocked into immobility.

Suddenly, the instructor put his boot-shod foot on Jeremy's shoulder and slammed him down onto the blacktop.

"You are an idiot!" he snarled. "You are less than a maggot! I will give you ten seconds once I lift my boot to follow these directions exactly. You will get up, and run, RUN, to that ocean. You will get all wet, from the top of your empty head to the bottom of your feet. Then you will get up on the beach and roll in the sand and become a sugar cookie. Then you will jump up and run right back to me here. And you had best be a very well-covered sugar cookie, maggot."

Jeremy didn't spend time wondering just what the hell a "sugar cookie" was. He felt the pressure leave his back and he took off as if from a starter's block on the most important race of his life. Maybe if he followed these insane directions, this obviously deranged individual wouldn't kill him outright.

So he ran out of the compound and across the beach

sand. The tide was going out, so it was well over a hundred yards from where the instructor had been holding him down to the water's edge. But he dashed that entire distance and crashed into the waves as they pounded down on the shore.

The sudden shock of the cold water almost took his breath away. For a sunny day in Southern California, this water was anything but warm. But he rolled in the icy waves and turned to run back up to shore. Going past the beaten-down sand left behind the outgoing tide, he reached the softer, dry beach and dove head first down into the sand.

Digging down into the beach, Jeremy actually plowed his head through the sand for almost a foot before he stopped and started rolling about. As he rolled and rubbed against the sand, no thought crossed his mind. There was just too much confusion going through his head about what the hell he was doing for there to be much room for a cohesive thought to form.

When it seemed he couldn't get covered in any more sand, and not wanting the instructor to have to wait for him any longer, he leaped up. Through his tearing eyes he spotted the instructor still standing next to where he had dropped his bags what seemed like an eternity earlier.

Running back—the term "walking" wasn't going to be in his vocabulary for much longer—Jeremy stopped at a position of attention in front of the instructor.

The man had calmed down considerably. Even though he was still sharply muscled, it seemed he had deflated a bit and wasn't as tall and huge as he'd appeared moments before. Or maybe his vision was suffering from the streaming tears in his eyes, Jeremy thought, as they tried to wash the gritty sand away. The sand was in his hair, eyes, nose, and ears, as well as sticking all over his well-soaked uniform. To a half-blind cook, he may have even appeared as a sugar cookie, the baked dough crusted with sugar crystals.

The instructor appeared satisfied with Jeremy's attention to his instructions. Incredibly, a smile appeared on the man's face, something Jeremy wouldn't have thought physically possible a few minutes earlier.

"Now I hope you understand for next time," the instructor said. "You do not walk through this compound. 'Double time' is double time and it's all the time. 'Drop' is get down into the push-up position, and 'recover' is to smartly get back to your feet. And when you count them out, you count by ones.

"Now, pick up your bags and come with me," and the instructor turned and headed back to the door Jeremy had just stepped out of. Scrambling to catch up, Jeremy grabbed his bags and stumbled along as quickly as he could.

Time blurred as Jeremy was run through the check-in process at BUD/S. He was assigned a room and sent over to the students' barracks, on the north side of the compound, to change uniforms and move along in his processing.

Jeremy quickly found the room he would call home for the next several months. All pretrainees like himself would be sharing rooms on the lower deck, which was the first floor of the building. A number of pre-trainees were already assigned to various rooms in the barracks, but Jeremy didn't meet any of them when he first arrived in the building.

Doors on either side opened onto a center hallway. The room he was assigned was the first one on the right as he entered the building. As far as comfort went, well, it was functional. There were three sets of gray steel double bunks in each room in the concrete building. Several of the bunks—correction "racks" Jeremy told himself—already had owners, judging from the fact that they were made up. One of the unmade racks was on the right, farthest from the door and facing the ocean. He chose that one, tossing his bag down onto the lower mattress.

He still was wearing a clammy, wet, and thoroughly irritating uniform as a souvenir of his arrival. There were a number of double-door metal wall lockers in the room, and an empty one by his chosen rack. He quickly dumped out his bag and began tossing items either on the rack or into the wall locker.

Quickly dressing in a fresh uniform, Jeremy stowed the balance of his gear in the wall locker. There would be time enough to properly arrange his gear later, when he learned what the wall locker inspection layout should be. It was probably the same as back in boot camp, but he didn't want to make wrong assumptions now.

Once again appearing like a properly uniformed sailor, Jeremy grabbed up the folder full of paperwork he'd been given back at the bosun's mate school in the

RTC and he rushed out the door. There would be no more walking for Jeremy White, even if he only had a vague idea of where he was supposed to go next.

The personnel at BUD/S were used to confused young men arriving at the facility. Jeremy soon found that most of the administrative support for BUD/S was at the Naval Amphibious Base across the road. That was also where he found the mess hall and lunch. The food was good, but he had little time to enjoy it, given his level of excitement.

The balance of his first afternoon at BUD/S was taken up by turning in and registering pay records and meeting other Navy administrative requirements. A trip to Supply got him an issue of clean bed linens, and he was able to return to the barracks and properly make up his rack.

While Jeremy was working, a tall, black-haired young man who appeared to be a few years older than him, walked into the room.

"Hey, fresh meat for the grinder," the new arrival said as he walked up to Jeremy, who stood by his rack.

"I guess so," Jeremy said with a grin.

"Jim Alex," the man said in introduction, and put out his hand.

"Jeremy White," he answered as they shook hands.

"Well, you have the harried look of a brand new arrival," Jim said, moving to a rack and sitting down on it.

"Shows that well, does it?" Jeremy said.

"Actually, yes it does," Jim replied. "Something like an expression of stunned disbelief mixed with a touch of wonder."

"Yeah," Jeremy laughed. "Like I wonder just what the hell I've let myself in for."

"Well, enjoy these days while they last," Jim went on. "For you, at least, they won't be very long."

"Oh, so you've been here a while?" Jeremy asked.

"Months," Jim answered. "I'm a rollback from Class 77."

"A rollback?" Jeremy said questioningly.

"Yes," Jim said. "That's what they call someone who couldn't finish with an earlier class but who they didn't want to drop from the program."

"So what happened to you?" Jeremy asked.

"I took a real wallop during rock portage," Jim said. "That's a wonderful little sport they have here where you get to be part of a fun group of guys trying to paddle a rubber boat through a pounding surf and over a pile of rocks. I took a tumble from the boat during our first try and cracked my head on the rocks. The corpsman said I had a concussion, and the doctors agreed with him."

"But they didn't send you back to the regular Navy?" Jeremy asked. "I thought that was what they did to everyone who didn't complete the course."

"No," Jim said. "That's really just for the guys who ring the bell and quit, or who the instructors performance drop."

"Performance drop?"

"Yeah, that's what they call it when you can't learn how to complete an evolution, a task, or are just so bad a screw-up that they don't want you in the Teams."

"But they rolled you back?"

"It was what they call a medical rollback," Jim said. "Personally, I think it was just that they found out I knew how to type and wanted me to work in the Admin office filling out forms and typing reports. Now that a new class is starting up, the corpsman says I'll be able to join up with that one and finally get back to training. I've been working hard enough just to get here."

"It was tough getting here to BUD/S?" Jeremy asked.

"Tough?" Jim said. "It was hell. I was assigned to yeoman's duties on a tin can for the first year of my illustrious Navy career. They didn't want to let me off that destroyer, no matter how many times I put in a chit for BUD/S. Finally my paperwork went through, and I got here last year."

"All I did was volunteer to take the screening test at boot camp," Jeremy said. "The recruiter told me that was the only way for me to get to BUD/S. Enough people said the same thing that I believed him."

"You got here straight out of boot camp?" Jim asked.

"Well, I had to go through bosun's school first," Jeremy answered. "Why?"

"Man, you were lucky," Jim said.

"What do you mean?" Jeremy asked.

"The Navy's real short of personnel right now," Jim said. "So just about everyone who volunteered for BUD/S in Boot has been sent out to the fleet first. That's why I had such a hell of a time getting here. Other guys had to reenlist just to get the hell off their ship and finally get a chance to come here. BUD/S has a pretty low priority as far as personnel goes, so the regular Navy comes first."

"Well, that should change," Jeremy said. "If you pass the screening test, you should be allowed to come here. Otherwise, why would they be giving it at boot camp anyway?"

"Well, that might change someday," Jim said. "But the way it is now, the detailers want you in the Navy to serve in your rate before you come here." He turned and looked at Jeremy more intently. "Did you take your screening test from Master Chief Hunsacker?" he asked.

"I have no idea," Jeremy said. "Who's Master Chief Hunsacker?"

"He's over at SEAL Team One right now, getting ready for his retirement," Jim said. "A real big guy, looks like a boulder with arms and two tree stumps for legs."

"That could have been him, yeah," Jeremy said. "Why?"

"Apparently, he saw some student over at boot camp that he liked for the Teams," Jim said. "While I was working in the office, I heard him talking to one of the instructors about someone he saw who was doing all this PT on his own time after classes. That you?"

"It could have been," Jeremy said. "I had to work out a bunch on my own. The PT at Boot was a joke compared to what I was told we would face here, and I wanted to be ready. But why should that matter?"

"Because Master Chief Hunsacker wanted that student to be here and told the detailer so," Jim answered.

"So if that was you, the instructors already know who you are. In case you haven't noticed, this is not the place you want to be singled out for attention from the instructors."

"Oh," Jeremy said. And he couldn't think of a lot more to add to that.

## Chapter Three

Jeremy wondered more than a little about what he may have let himself in for as he continued to square away his room and personal appearance. The instructors told him he had to have a haircut and be clean-shaven by the next day. Having already seen what an instructor would do to a student who was just standing around, Jeremy certainly didn't want to find out what they did to one who didn't follow orders.

The haircut was easy enough, though at least he didn't have to get his head almost shaved like a raw recruit at boot camp. The mustache he'd been growing wasn't big enough to be worried about, and a quick shave took care of that. Then there was the matter of his equipment issue.

Supply was little more than a relatively small room at the compound, and Jeremy had been issued his uniforms, boots, and other gear for his upcoming training. None of the uniforms had name tags on them, but it was obvious that they had seen some hard wear. The green fatigue uniforms were the same as those throughout the services. Jeremy's issue was clean, but it needed patching and sewing in a number of spots before it would be presentable.

It would take some time to have name tags made after Jeremy ordered them. For the next several days his swim trunks read WOODWRIGHT, apparently the name of the last individual who had worn them, and turned them in with a large rip in one seam. BUD/S was going to be an adventure; he'd known that well before he volunteered. And there would be a number of new skills to learn. But he hadn't thought that his first learning experience would be trying to man a needle and thread.

You got it, you patch it up, was the general rule from Supply. That also extended to the several pairs of boots Jeremy was issued. These weren't the heavy boondockers used in the rest of the Navy, but well-worn Vietnam jungle boots with green canvas sides and uppers attached to a rubber sole. Slits had been cut in one of the sides of a boot—to relieve pressure on the blisters of the last student who wore them, according to Jim Alex.

What needed cleaning, Jeremy cleaned. And the boots received polish and care no matter what they looked like. All of his white T-shirts had to have his name stenciled on them. And once all of the uniforms and gear were prepped and cleaned, they had to be properly stowed in the wall lockers in the barracks. Only during his first day at BUD/S did Jeremy wear a regular Navy uniform. From his second day on, the green fatigues and jungle boots were the normal uniform of the day.

The bulk of Jeremy's regular Navy uniform and boondockers were packed away carefully. His sea bag was always kept packed and ready. One regulation Navy dress uniform, complete with footwear, was kept clean and hung up in the wall locker of each student at BUD/S. When a student quit—or Dropped on Request (DOR), as it was formally called—he would turn in all of his issued gear and immediately put his regular Navy uniform back on.

That packed sea bag and uniform was a constant reminder of just how easy it was to quit BUD/S. Once you said you wanted out, you were gone that day. There was a barracks on the other side of the highway, at the amphibious base, that was ready to accept any student that quit BUD/S. And within a short time of arriving at that barracks, those former students would be shipped out to wherever the Navy wanted to send them.

It was a unique aspect of BUD/S that it was hard to get to the school but very easy to leave. All a student had to do was say "I quit" and he was gone; that, and adhering to the BUD/S tradition of ringing the brass ship's bell.

Jeremy had seen the bell at the northwest corner of the grinder. Pulling the white knotted rope hanging from the clapper, a student rang that bell three times and he was gone. Later, when they classed-up, every student would have a helmet liner with their names painted on the back. The liner would be set on the ground among the others in a line that led away from the bell, that one more person had tried to pass the trial of BUD/S and failed the test.

From what Jim Alex and others in the barracks had said, a line of helmets could easily stretch thirty feet or more away from the bell. The word was that at least forty percent of a class normally quit during the First Phase of training. Often, that number could be eighty percent.

Jeremy had heard such numbers tossed around ever since he'd first entered a Navy recruiter's office back in Ohio. During boot camp he'd been told how hard BUD/S was, and that he would soon find himself on board a ship and working for the regular Navy when he quit the course. The term used was "haze gray and underway" to indicate a BUD/S student who had left and gone back to the fleet. And Jeremy swore to himself that he would never have that phrase used to describe what had happened to him.

He knew that training was going to be hard. But he believed that anything worth having was at least worth working for. And the Navy made a life in the Teams so hard to get that it really had to be worth the trouble once you finally got there. What Jeremy hadn't expected was just how hard it would be to get to the actual training once he arrived at BUD/S.

The first week at the training compound was not what he'd expected. Each BUD/S class was known by a number, since the outfit's first days, just after World War II. The fact that by 1974, almost thirty years later, the class numbers had only reached 78 told Jeremy

that this training was not the most common thing in
the Navy. But he knew that going in, and wanted it all
the more, for how few had gone through it. However,
it looked like he would have to wait at least a few
weeks more before he would find out what BUD/S
training would be like, since the majority of the students who would be making up Class 78—the next
BUD/S class to begin training—had not yet arrived at
the compound by the time Jeremy got there. Every
day, more students arrived at the training compound
and were assigned to the barracks. But no real training
had started yet.

Jim Alex had explained that this was a normal situation at the compound. As soon as the proper number of
students were on hand, Class 78 would "class up" and
officially begin training. Until that day, the extra personnel, who weren't quite students yet, made up a pool
of manpower for work around the area.

His yeoman's rating had already given Jim Alex duties to perform at the training compound. He was an
extra set of hands in the Admin office, a fact that Jim
was already starting to worry about. He did his job so
well that some of the instructors and officers had said
it might be a good idea to just leave him there rather
than run him through training. It was a fear Jim con-
fided to Jeremy in the barracks during their general
bull sessions.

Jeremy assumed that Jim would get to BUD/S in
spite of the general shortage of qualified office personnel. And he rightly guessed that the instructors and
other Team personnel might be playing with his head.

Jim should enjoy his time in the office while he could, he thought. It sure beat being one of the other unclassed students in the compound area.

For Jeremy and an increasing number of other students, each day consisted of general work parties around the training center and the Amphibious base across the Strand highway. All of the students were "snuffies," or basic workers who made up the lowest ranks of the training compound. They were expected to perform all of the menial and unimportant tasks around the area. This was a longstanding tradition in all of the services, and the newest batch of soon-to-be students at BUD/S weren't going to change that tradition.

The exercise that did take place during the several weeks Jeremy was with the preclass students mostly consisted of daily physical training (PT). The exercises were intended to get the students in shape before training began, as well as to familiarize them with the exercises that would be part of their regular class PTs.

Extra staff personnel, who weren't necessarily instructors but were in the Teams, ran Jeremy and his fellow students through PT every morning on the grinder, which was the blacktopped area surrounded by the buildings that made up the training compound. Jeremy and the others soon found that the grinder had earned its name from the students who had been ground down into its surface through all the exercising they had done there over the years.

When the prestudents ran out to conduct their PT, they were white T-shirts and fatigue pants. The uniforms felt too thin at first, especially in the cold morning air that settled in from the Pacific. But the number of exercises they did soon warmed them up, with sweat soaking through their thin shirts.

Push-ups, jumping jacks, and sit-ups were exercises Jeremy and the others had been doing for years, and everyone knew how to do them. Flutter kicks were fairly new to a number of the young men lying on the ground and sweating along with him. And the flutter kick was second only to the push-up in popularity during the PT sessions. At least it seemed that way to Jeremy as he went through countless repetitions of the exercise.

Looking deceptively simple, the flutter kick was simply kicking your feet while lying flat on your back on the ground. With the feet raised six inches above the ground, first one leg and then the other would be lifted three feet off the ground and then lowered. Simple enough, but at no time during the exercise could a foot rest on the ground. This put a great deal of strain on the leg muscles and stomach. And that strain quickly translated itself into real pain.

As if doing dozens of sets of flutter kicks wasn't enough, there were some strange exercises in the PT mix at BUD/S. One was known in the Teams as "Helen Kellers." It looked like someone throwing a fit on the ground. Some of the students later figured it must have been named after Patty Duke's acting when she played Helen Keller in the movie, only the exercise wasn't an act, it was real work.

Helen Kellers required balance and control to do them correctly, and strong stomach muscles to do them for any length of time. The students would first do a half sit-up, holding their backs up off the ground at a forty-five-degree angle and their hands cupped lightly around their ears. The legs were lifted about three inches from the ground, then one knee brought up until the leg was at a ninety-degree angle to the hip. Then the elbow of the opposite side was brought over and touched to the raised knee, and the same motion was done with the opposite elbow and knee.

The twisting motion of the body, combined with the legs held off the ground and then bent at the knees, made the Helen Kellers as painful and difficult to do as any of the other exercises the new BUD/S students had to learn, if not more so than most. Chin-ups, leg lifts, and a variety of push-ups added brand new pains to the students' bodies, and new skills to their minds. It was exactly the situation desired by their future instructors.

Besides the PT, Jeremy and the rest of the newest students did various scut work around the compound. Whatever the classes that were already training didn't do, fell to the snuffies. Work around the compound included the most common job in the Navy—painting. But there was also emptying wastebaskets, cleaning the heads, and standing duty. In addition, there was always someone on watch on the Quarterdeck and elsewhere around the training compound. This tedious duty went on all day and all night. The one advantage of Jim Alex's yeoman duties was that he never had to stand watch.

However, Jim did have to attend the PT sessions every morning. Most of the time, PT was run by one of the rollback students from an earlier class. If the instructor staff wanted a man to have a second shot at training, he could be assigned to the staff at BUD/S, as Jim Alex had been. Mark Green, one of the upper classmen who had been rolled back, would be joining Class 78 after they had completed Phase One of their training. For now, to keep Mark in shape, the staff had him conducting the morning PT.

Gradually, incoming students filled up the ranks of Class 78. The vast majority who arrived were young enlisted sailors, like Jeremy. Most of them came from the fleet, having served aboard ship for at least a few years since their boot camp. The average age for the students was around twenty-two. The oldest was all of twenty-eight, while Jeremy was one of the youngest, at nineteen.

A few officers had arrived to join Class 78, but the only difference that Jeremy could see in their treatment was that they didn't have to do the same grunt work that he and the rest of the enlisted ranks did. But the young officers did have to take part in the daily PT sessions. And there were some new challenges tossed out for all of the newcomers to learn.

Officially, all of the students who would make up Class 78 were in pretraining as soon as they arrived at BUD/S. Most of them did general grunt work. But there was a higher level of physical activity than at boot camp or, in Jeremy's case, at bosun's mate school. Everyone had to have passed the basic screening test just to get to BUD/S, but there were noticeable differences in the general level of physical fitness among the students. Those who had come in from shipboard duties in the fleet seemed to benefit the most from the extra physical training the class did before BUD/S officially started.

Every morning began with a session of PT for all of the students. Officers were sweating on the grinder alongside the lowest enlisted man. At BUD/S, everyone was treated equally, officers and enlisted men. And that treatment generally meant each and every student was lower than whale shit in the instructor's eyes.

Pretraining was meant to give the students an opportunity to build themselves up and to learn how to do some of the activities and exercises they would do during BUD/S. The different exercises were conducted every day as part of their morning PT. Runs always followed a PT session, to build up stamina. From their first moments at the training compound, it was drilled into all of the students that BUD/S was going to be done on the run, all of the time. It was something they would all have to get used to.

After PT in the morning and then a run, the balance of the day was mostly filled by pulling duty around the compound. Gear and materials were also worked on, to both familiarize the students with everything they would need to use for training as well as to get some of the stuff in good repair.

Pretraining was a time to learn how the compound was laid out, run, and where to find everything. Students were given a chance to learn the ropes of BUD/S training as it would apply to them. And learning about some of the ropes was taken very literally.

The students had already met the BUD/S instructor who would be their class proctor. He would guide them through training and answer questions they might ask about what they were going through. Instructor José Sanchez was a fireplug of a man. He looked like he was built from two cubes stacked on top of one another. A deeply tanned Hispanic, Instructor Sanchez almost always had a wide smile on his dark face, which was startling in its contrast to his dark eyes and short but thick black hair.

The smile Instructor Sanchez habitually wore did not mean he was amused, but it did reflect his general good nature. The fact that he wasn't going to be one of Class 78's First Phase instructors meant he could go a little easier on the students.

As proctor, Instructor Sanchez told the students what to expect in the day-to-day running of the class and what would be expected of them. BUD/S training would be twenty-six weeks long and broken into three phases. The First Phase would be primarily physical conditioning. The class could expect to be worked harder than they ever had been in their lives, and the fifth week of First Phase would be the hardest single test most of the men would ever face: Hell Week.

Pretraining was expected to last about two weeks for most of the students. First and Second Phases would each be seven weeks long. Third Phase would last nine weeks. During First Phase, the students would be getting in shape and learning basic boat drills and other skills necessary for their later training. Once they had proven themselves during Hell Week, they would go on to learn hydrographic reconnaissance and how to measure and chart out beaches and their offshore waters.

In Second Phase they would all go underwater. This diving phase would teach them how to operate with various kinds of breathing equipment. Then they would conduct compass swims, night swims, and other exercises to learn how to operate effectively in the ocean environment, which was so much a part of everyday life in the Teams.

In Third Phase students would learn more of the skills that the SEALs used, like land navigation, combat, and weapons handling. They would also learn how to safely handle demolitions and destroy obstacles and other targets with a variety of explosives. During range time they would learn the basic weapons used in the UDTs and SEAL Teams, and would take those same weapons out on training patrols.

But all of the fancy training, diving equipment, demolitions, and weapons would come after they had proven themselves during First Phase. And the biggest single test of training would be Hell Week.

During one of his question and answer sessions with the new group of students, Instructor Sanchez answered a few questions about Hell Week. He had the opinion that it was not the most important part of training. One of the terms he used was that it was little more than a "hole" that had to be crossed on your way to the Teams. But it was a deep hole, one that had swallowed many a would-be student and caused them to go back to the fleet.

Hell Week was going to be a test of the individual student's drive and desire to go through whatever it took to join the Teams. Everyone would be physically capable of going through that one week of nonstop activity. The first month of First Phase and the weeks of pretraining would see to that. But everyone had to bring the heart and drive to get through that training, and there was nothing Instructor Sanchez or any of the other instructors could do to supply that.

But Hell Week was more than a month away, and there was no use dwelling on it. Every class went through training a little differently. Each schedule was changed a bit to match conditions, weather, and the number of warm bodies that made up the class. So what the students had heard regarding another class might not apply to them. The best thing to do was face every day as it came, and not try to anticipate what was in the future. It would get there soon enough on its own.

There was an expression common around BUD/S: "the only easy day was yesterday." That phrase didn't mean a whole lot on first examination, but Instructor Sanchez explained it in part. Every day at BUD/S would be hard. Yesterday was over, it was behind you, and now you had to face whatever was coming. That made yesterday easy, because you had survived it and it was over.

For Class 78, BUD/S was just beginning. The last few students were arriving during the first full week in February. The next Monday, February 12, Class 78 would officially class up and begin training. They were going to start with what seemed to Jeremy a huge mob of people: 112 enlisted men, five officers, and one foreign exchange officer would make up the initial complement. From what had been said earlier, less than half of that total would be standing on the grinder in July, when Class 78 graduated.

The makeup of the class was an amazing mix of people. The class leader was Lieutenant (junior grade) Reginald C. Butterworth III, and on first impression he seemed every bit as pompous as his name. A tall, slender man with brown hair, Butterworth was a graduate of the U.S. Naval Academy, Class of 1973, and he also hailed from what Jim Alex called "old New England money." A prissy, very correct young officer, Butterworth seemed out of place at BUD/S. But he too was a volunteer.

In fact, Butterworth had graduated high enough in his academy class to have picked almost any initial assignment in the Navy. What he had chosen was to attend the hardest, dirtiest, most miserable training course there was. If he had something to prove to himself or anyone else, BUD/S was a place he could do it.

The oldest student in the class was no longer the twenty-eight-year-old veteran petty officer. Instead, that honor now went to another officer, one who wasn't a member of the U.S. Navy. Lieutenant George Staverous was all of thirty-two years old, twelve of those years having been spent in the Greek navy and their Monas Ymourhin Katastpofon (Underwater Destruction Unit), the MYK or Greek SEALs.

Serving in the Greek underwater forces was something of a tradition with George's family. His father had been one of the early Greek operators who was trained in submarine techniques by a detachment from SEAL Team Two only a few years after they were commissioned. Now Staverous was back with the U.S. Teams as a military foreign exchange student to go through BUD/S training and take back the skills to his own country.

A bear of a man, Staverous was dark, burly, and looked like he constantly needed a shave. Though his English was a bit broken, his spirit was anything but, as he would always find the humor in any situation. He could be silent as death for long periods, possibly because he listened intently, then suddenly boom out with a laugh when he felt the situation warranted it. The only time he appeared to resist the instructors was when he was told to shave off the huge mustache he had when he arrived. But the next day at morning quarters, he showed up with a pale upper lip and a serious expression on his face. Staverous wasn't very tall, but he more than made up in bulk what he didn't have in height.

The biggest guy in the class was easily one of the officers, the lowest ranking one, Ensign Richard Kozuska. He was immediately christened "Zeus" by a very amused George Staverous. Kozuska had been a Naval ROTC graduate from the University of Michigan, where he made a big name for himself with the U of M Wolverines football team. A star of the gridiron, Kozuska had also excelled in wrestling and swimming, an unusual combination for so large a man. At six feet four inches tall and over 240 pounds of muscle, he gave the impression that he could do anything by depending on one person— himself.

At the other end of the scale from Kozuska was one of the smaller students of Class 78. Staverous wasn't the only foreign student in Class 78, but he was the only non-American one—Nguyen Hong Thanh was a naturalized American, having been adopted by a Navy SEAL from SEAL Team Two at Little Creek, Virginia. Nguyen's biological father had been a South Vietnamese SEAL, an LDNN or Lien Doc Nguoi Nhai (soldiers who fight under the sea).

While operating with a detachment from SEAL Team Two in 1967, Nguyen's father had been killed, and his U.S. Navy SEAL friend had taken the orphaned twelve-year-old home with him to be raised as his own. Now, the nineteen-year-old Nguyen was going to be in the same unit as his adopted father, and by proxy his biological father. A slight young man, Nguyen was short, quiet, and intense, but very friendly toward all of his classmates.

But not all of the students in Class 78 were as friendly as Nguyen. One particular individual hailed from the back country of Louisiana, and he brought a whole load of racial bigotry and baggage with him to the class. Travis Rappaport was loud, strong, and from a background that made him less than tolerant of other ethnic backgrounds. Almost immediately nicknamed "Redneck" by both the class and a number of the instructors, Rappaport made his feelings of having a "gook" in the class loudly obvious to all.

Very soon after Rappaport's announcement, Instruc-

tor Sanchez carefully explained the situation at
BUD/S. The members of Class 78 were there to learn
how to be a team and work together. Teamwork was
the bedrock that the SEALs and UDTs was built on.
And intolerance to others was very bad and even de-
structive to the effort of the instructors made to try and
instill a mentality of teamwork among the students.

Whether Redneck was actually taking Instructor
Sanchez's words to heart couldn't be seen by any of
the rest of Class 78. It was hard to see Redneck's face
while he was doing his push-ups. And Rappaport's
neck wasn't the only thing that was red at that moment.
The strain of doing his push-ups, with Instructor
Sanchez's boot in the middle of his back and shoving
down hard, had caused Rappaport's face to turn a
bright red as well.

Rappaport voiced his racial opinions toward other
classmates as well. There were several black students
who were classing up with Class 78. One of them,
from the streets of Detroit, Michigan, was Washington
Irving Sledge, six feet tall and with almost no body fat.
The muscles of the young black man's arms stood out
as he did his part in the morning PT and runs. The two
other black students also worked hard in the class, but
the "Hammer"—short for "Sledgehammer"—had a
quiet intensity about him that could almost be felt in
the air.

There were relatively few black men in the Teams
since swimming wasn't a popular sport in most of the
inner cities. And a low body fat percentage tended to

make most black men negatively buoyant. They sank, which made swimming even harder for them. But if the expression on Sledge's face meant anything, it was very possible there would be another black man in the Teams after Class 78 graduated.

Bob Miller was the smallest man in the class at five feet three inches, half an inch shorter than Nguyen Thanh. The small, lightly built Miller had brown hair, dark eyes, and constantly bitched about anything the class may have been doing at any moment. But in spite of his complaints, he usually kept quiet around the instructors, and Miller always worked hard to keep up in the runs and exercises.

Class 78 was made up of big men and small men. Physical stature didn't seem to mean very much when the students looked around the compound at the instructors and the occasional SEAL who passed by. There were almost no "bodybuilder" types among the men of the Teams that could be seen by the class, though Class 78 did have its share of big, heavily muscled, sports star types. What could be observed among all of the instructors and SEALs that the students had seen was a penetrating gaze, a purposeful look that immediately sized a person up. And when it was one of the students who was being sized up, the look also told them that they didn't matter at all at this stage in their training.

On Monday, 12 February 1974, the Soviet Mars 5 satellite went into orbit around the red planet after firing its braking rockets. On that date, a radio survey listed Barbra Streisand's "The Way We Were" as the top song in its area. And in Coronado, the 118 officers and men of Class 78 officially began the First Phase of BUD/S.

## Chapter Four

Some BUD/S traditions were followed by the students just before they officially began training. One was the head-shaving party. All of the students gathered on the weekend before Class 78 got under way and showed the camaraderie that was supposed to develop among them.

The party was something they had all been looking forward to. It meant that it was time for them to get on the road to becoming SEALs and frogmen. Several kegs of beer were on hand for the class, and 118 happy little maggots set to shaving off each other's hair.

The haircut party was usually at someone's place away from the training compound, often at a married student's house. But Class 78 was unusual since it included few married students. George Staverous was married, and had several sons who he was very proud of, something he pointed out to anyone within earshot. But Staverous's wife was back in Greece. So Instructor

Sanchez allowed the class to use his place in Imperial Beach.

The fact that they were at an instructor's home hardly dampened spirits. A large number of students filled the instructor's backyard and ranch-style home, and Sanchez's family spent the day elsewhere, his wife taking the kids for a visit to nearby friends. The entire class hadn't descended on Instructor Sanchez's house all at once, but it looked like the majority of them were there. The students realized that it would be an excellent idea if they made sure the house was spotless and in fine repair before they left that evening.

There was some friction among different members of the class. Redneck Rappaport didn't make any secret about his wondering how black students made it to BUD/S. His opinion was that since white men couldn't jump and play basketball, black men couldn't swim and shouldn't be moving in on a sport that wasn't theirs. Sledge, however, had shrugged off a lot worse than that on the hard streets of Detroit. He was there, and he was going to give training a shot, the very best one he had. And he felt that if he could show up Rappaport in the process, so much the better.

A couple of the older students tried to settle things down and quiet Redneck before a fight broke out. When Kozuska finally broke in and told Rappaport to zip it, it was hard to tell if it was the officer's rank or his size that convinced Redneck to keep his opinions to himself.

But the party did what it was supposed to do—it helped bring the class closer together. The shaved heads looked funny at first, but since everyone in the class had the same "haircut," it was obvious that either they were all together or the Shaolin monks of Kung Fu fame had moved onto a Navy base.

Another tradition was carried out on Sunday, after the shaving party was over. The lightweight helmet liners everyone had been issued needed to be cleaned off and repainted to show the class number, each student's name, and the color that indicated which phase they were in. Green helmets showed that the wearer was in First Phase, light blue was for Second Phase, and red was the final color, only used for Third Phase.

After the helmets were cleaned, the students held a painting party. This was a time when the class started to pull together. Instructors encouraged this kind of group activity as it helped build the teamwork mentality that was so important at BUD/S. All of the students had been working together for at least a week, many of them for two weeks or more, during pretraining. That gave some time for friendships and cooperation to develop between them. And it helped spread the enthusiasm for the program and boost everyone's motivation.

New sweat bands had been installed inside the helmet liners, and the straps were adjusted to the individual wearer. Then they were cleaned, painted, the number 78 stenciled on the sides of each liner, and each student's last name painted on the back of the liner. That helmet liner showed who an individual was and where he stood in training, and it would be a symbol of those who had left.

Within the first day of training, Jeremy noticed a

couple of helmet liners underneath the bell at the corner of the grinder. Class 78 had lost its first students before it had really even started. The helmets were never even broken in.

Jeremy didn't notice when the first guys had quit. During the night, as he lay in his rack, he thought he heard a quiet series of dings. Obviously, someone had rung out and quit; the mute evidence of that lay there on the ground the next morning. During the PT sessions, the sound of the bell rang out, but Jeremy and the rest of the students were so busy trying to keep up with the class, so the instructors wouldn't single them out for a particular hammering, that they never looked at the bell and who might have been leaving.

The sound of that bell, and the fact that each student had to ring it in order to leave, was considered demoralizing by some of the outsiders. They meant well, but had no real idea what went on at BUD/S. For Jeremy and a number of the others still sweating out the training, each time the bell rang helped boost their own resolve. The line of helmets was growing, but they were determined not to put their own liners on that piece of ground.

Things were tough on the class, from the start. But morale stayed high for most of the students. Every time one of them left, the rest knew that they were still hanging in. There might be a question rising up inside of an individual. He could be bluntly thinking, How in the hell can I keep this up? Then the bell would ring and he'd pull himself together, get past that momentary question, and keep on going. And with what they were going to be facing, every student needed all the help he could get.

The painting party was one sign of solidarity growing among the students, but it was hardly the only time they had to put green paint on that liner. When the paint on a helmet was chipped and damaged, it had to be repainted and repaired. The grinder had a very rough surface, and a number of the instructors found an excellent way of expressing their displeasure with an individual's performance. They bounced, kicked, and threw their helmets all over the area.

A helmet liner was one thing. It was an inanimate object that could simply be picked up, cleaned off, and repainted. But the students also felt the wrath of the instructors, and the results of that needed a lot more than a coat of paint to make it go away.

At the beginning, the large size of the class helped keep some of the attention of the instructors away from individual students. Jeremy and some of his classmates found that if they just put out hard, they didn't draw attention to themselves and could get by with the normal punishing output required by the training. But if an instructor saw even a minor error, or felt like choosing a student at random to make an example of him, they had a variety of ways to make a miserable experience that much worse.

The sugar cookie was a big favorite. Jeremy already had his first taste of that tradition when his time at BUD/S was still measured in minutes. Dipping in the surf and rolling in the sand while still wet was a popular pastime at BUD/S. More than one student had gone up to the bell and rung out while still dripping wet and trailing sand behind him. Push-ups were another big favorite. A set of twenty could be awarded at any time, for any reason. Some of the instructors seemed to think push-ups could be given as a reward. Considering some of the other things they could have a student do, maybe they were.

A variation of the sugar cookie effect was to get into the surf, roll in the sand, and then, instead of running to the water, the student would be told to crawl there, as low as possible to the ground. When the tide was out, the crawl could be hundreds of yards from the grinder to the surf. And it might not just be the student, but his swim buddy was often sent along to the surf zone with him.

From almost the first day, the instructors had pushed the importance of staying with their swim buddies, no matter what. Students had been paired off, and the pairs could be changed on a whim of an instructor. But once assigned a swim buddy, a student was supposed to know where that man was at all times. In the operating environment of the Teams, the instructors explained, your swim buddy could be the only means of surviving if you had an accident or malfunction while underwater or in combat. That made a lot of sense to the students, but it didn't matter if it did or not. The fact that the instructors told you to stick with your swim buddy was enough, and their reaction if you weren't with him when you were supposed to be was bad—very bad.

Some instructors had favorite ways of dealing with

the students. Chief Max Packard—always addressed as Chief Packard by the lowly students, officers, and enlisted alike—had the nickname "Maximum Max." None of the students knew who had coined the name, or if it had just followed the chief around from class to class. But he earned it almost every day.

Chief Packard liked to see the students do flutter kicks during PT. When there was a break in the schedule, he liked to see them do flutter kicks when they weren't doing PT. The orderly lifting and lowering of the legs of sweating students seemed to have a calming effect on the chief. But when the rhythm of the flutter kicks broke up as the students weakened, Chief Packard became much less happy.

According to the chief's logic, his enjoyment of the situation was due to the students not being able to do what he considered a reasonable amount of exercises, such as fifty sets of flutter kicks or more. His answer to that problem was simple—make them do more. That would help build the students up, break down the ones who shouldn't be there in the first place, and please Chief Packard immensely.

As the pain in their thighs, legs, and backs increased, the students thought that making Chief Packard happy was a good thing, as long as it didn't kill them. The line of helmets under the bell seemed to grow that much faster on the days when Chief Packard ran the morning PT. Which also pleased him no end.

The students' days quickly fell into a routine, not much different from the one they followed during pretraining. Now, however, they weren't doing scut work around the compound. Instead, they were literally running around the compound, constantly.

A normal day started with reveille at about 0430 in the morning. Right away, the class would get dressed and perform their field day, cleaning up their immediate areas and the barracks in general. The class would then muster up as squads just outside of the barracks and move out to the grinder for 0500 PT.

Sometimes the schedule would be changed, depending on what the situation or plan of the day was. Instead of going from the barracks to the grinder for PT, the class might be sent over to the Amphibious base for chow and further evolutions later on.

Since every part of training was intended to help create operators for the Teams, everything the students did in terms of exercises or training was referred to as an evolution. Each exercise was another step to evolving that final graduate of BUD/S, something every student intended to be.

PT was a stand-alone evolution that didn't lead to further skills, just greater strength, endurance, and the ability to do more PT. The PT itself varied, from either an hour or so of straight exercising to a short PT followed by a run. Or there was no PT exercise at all, but a period of stretching followed by a longer timed run. The class would do morning PT from 0500 to 0600 or 0630 every weekday. Then the students would be cut loose for chow. By the time the class got back from chow, it was time to clean up and go on to the plan of the day.

There were days that began with a burn-out PT,

where the exercises went on and on until the students were all so exhausted they could barely move. Other days there were long runs that went up north along the beach to the rocks in front of the Hotel del Coronado, a trip of several miles. There were also extended runs of over three or four miles, or more. Running was considered the way of building up endurance and leg strength for the long ocean swims while wearing swim fins that would come later.

Classes and other evolutions followed PT, chow, and any morning runs. The classes were rarely given in a classroom, but were active participation events involving such arcane subjects as surf passage, beach recons, hydrographic recons, knot tying, pool training, and even semaphore signaling with flags.

Afternoon chow was usually called around noon. Like all of the other student meals, it was served in the Enlisted Dining Hall across the Strand highway on the Amphibious base. Almost no one referred to the building as the dining hall; it was the chow hall to students and instructors alike.

The food at the chow hall was among the best in the Navy. It was a longstanding tradition in the Navy service that the best food was served aboard submarines. Morale on long cruises spent underwater, with little to do but work, was raised considerably by good food. The lesson learned aboard submarines was put to good use in the chow hall for men who would later also operate under the sea, but without the protection of a submarine's hull. At BUD/S the students' heavy workload was broken by the serving of good food, and morale, along with motivation, was raised.

After noon chow, less strenuous evolutions were conducted. Most of the instructors considered it a good idea to let the students' food settle a little bit before hammering them with heavy physical exercise. But the activity level quickly went back up to its usual high level.

The class was often secured before evening chow. The evening meal was served at around 1700 or 1800 hours, and the students were released from the training day shortly before then. On days when evening training was on the schedule, the class would go to the meal and then return to the training compound to prep for that evening's evolution. Lost sleep was not made up the next day, though an instructor might cut short that next morning PT and just send the class over to chow.

Lack of sleep was just another aspect of First Phase training, and it was one more little step in preparing the class for Hell Week.

When a class was secured for the day, the students were on their own. After the day's training was done and their duties completed, the students were on liberty and free to leave the compound. Coronado was a short walk up the road, and San Diego, with lower prices and a greater variety of attractions, was a short car or bus ride away.

On weekends, the students had more liberty. As during the week, they were free to come and go from the training compound. On Saturdays, some of the more serious students might remain on the compound to work out more on their own. They would try to work harder at getting into better shape, but bull sessions often broke out and ended the good intentions. Relaxation, whether on the base or off, was the general rule for a weekend.

Saturday night was usually the big night out for all of the students. They knew without question that if they got caught doing something that would get them noticed, or arrested, by the authorities, military or civilian, their chances of remaining at BUD/S would drop through the floor. As a result, rowdy times tended to be confined among themselves in private beach parties or groups going to a specific restaurant or bar.

Sunday was another day off with no restrictions on students' movements. The only rule, besides staying out of trouble, was for each student to be at morning muster outside of the barracks. The students knew they had worked too hard for too long just to get to BUD/S to risk it all by being late to morning muster.

The mornings after a weekend were harder to face, the cold haze from the Pacific reminding the students that they were in what was called a winter class. The mist and a cold film of water on everything caused them to shiver in their white T-shirts as they stood to morning muster.

The fallout by squads to the grinder and morning PT came as almost a relief to some of the students. Jeremy, having grown up in Ohio, knew how cold a winter could get. The weather and temperatures at Coronado in February were hardly what he would call a cold midwinter situation. For him, it was more like a late winter/early spring thaw. But back home he would have braved those relatively mild temperatures in a coat or jacket, not just a thin cotton T-shirt.

The exercises conducted during PT soon warmed the class up. But the rough surface of the grinder took its toll on their clothes as well as their bodies. It was a good thing that T-shirts were relatively inexpensive and easy to get. The rough surface usually ripped and wore them to the point where they couldn't pass muster within two weeks of being first worn.

Jeremy and some of his fellows learned that there was an advantage even to the cold, wet mist of a Southern California winter. The film of water acted like a lubricant to their backs and bodies as they pushed, leaned, and shoved against the tarmac of the grinder. The friction was cut down by the water, and the cold had another beneficial effect. Skin quickly became numbed by the cold breeze and wet conditions, and numbed skin didn't feel itself rub against the hard tarmac as much as warm skin would.

Before the students were able to start training hard, they all had to prove themselves over again, this time for the record. The proof they all had to supply was to complete the BUD/S screening test again. This second screening test was done with a higher set of standards than when the students had done it back in boot camp or in the fleet. And the instructors expected to see improvement on the original scores.

The test wasn't particularly hard, certainly not from the viewpoint of a BUD/S instructor. All of the members of Class 78 had been at the training compound and going through pretraining for at least a week, and many of them had been there several weeks or more. Instructors were of the opinion that the time spent in PT during pretraining should have raised everyone's scores, especially those students who had reported in from a ship, since there wasn't a lot of room aboard a Navy warship to exercise, and especially to run over distance.

At BUD/S for less than two weeks, Jeremy's screening test scores were not much better than when he'd been in boot camp. He passed the five hundred-yard swimming test in under eleven minutes, well under the twelve minute, thirty seconds maximum. His sidestroke had improved a bit, but he was still developing his kicking ability.

After only a ten-minute rest period, the test resumed, for push-ups, at least forty-two had to be completed in two minutes. Jeremy managed fifty-four but was pushing hard for those last few. The minimum for sit-ups was fifty in two minutes, and he did much better, doing seventy-five in the time limit with much less strain than the push-ups. The minimum of eight continuous chin-ups was still a struggle for Jeremy. He managed ten good repetitions before he had to stop. His score was noted, but the instructor voiced his opinion that Jeremy needed to "work on it."

The mile and a half run in boots and trousers had to be completed in under eleven minutes thirty seconds, and the instructors vocalized their opinion that anyone who had to take that much time to complete a simple run needed to be in the hospital rather than BUD/S. Jeremy made the minimum time easily enough, but running had never been his best sport, and he was worried that the nausea that swept through him after he put out everything he had on the run would be noticed by the instructors.

But the opposite occurred. As far as the instructors were concerned, his nausea was a sign that he was putting out with everything he had. Since he just didn't seem to have enough, they would build that up in him. There was a minimum physical ability expected of every student at BUD/S, and the repeat of the screening test demonstrated that minimum. But the test of attitude and desire—that a person was doing everything he was capable of—would come much later, during Hell Week. And that determination was something the instructors couldn't build up in a student—the student had to have brought it with him.

A number of the instructors had said that BUD/S training was ten percent physical and ninety percent mental. If that was true, Jeremy thought, he just might be in trouble. If the stress of training was just ten percent physical, just what could the instructors be expecting with the other ninety percent?

The students' first introduction to the obstacle course demonstrated just how daunting some of the physical demands of BUD/S training could be. It took place in the south area of the training compound, where a confusing pile of logs, ropes, and pilings made up the obstacle course. The O-course, as it was better known, was a series of over a dozen obstacles that had to be climbed, crawled, run, slithered, or handled. The place looked like the nightmare of a children's park designer. And the weekly completion of the O-course was soon to become a nightmare for a lot of the students.

The intent of the O-course was to force the students to use every muscle in their bodies at one point or another. Added pressure was put on them by the fact that they had to get through the course under a time limit. They would soon find that the time limit for completing the course would keep getting shorter during the training cycle.

Form was everything in order to get through the O-course. You couldn't just attack the obstacles and expect to get through them, though an aggressive attitude toward the course was considered a very good thing by the instructors. Some of the obstacles were dangerous if you didn't do them right, and almost all of them were painful at one point or another as you completed them.

Instructor Sanchez, as class proctor, walked them through the course and showed them several ways that each of the obstacles could be completed. Sanchez was familiar with the course, and he made each of the obstacles look easy to do. Then it was time for the students to do the course, and none of the obstacles proved easy.

Technique was everything in getting through the O-course in proper time. That first day, technique was what everyone wanted to learn just to complete the course at all. Jeremy didn't believe just how hard most of the obstacles turned out to be.

Several obstacles were familiar to all of the students

from either school sports or being in a playground as
children. The tire sequence, for one, was familiar to
anyone who had competed in high school football. It
was a double row of about a dozen tires staggered
against one another, and the student ran through the
obstacle, trying to place a foot in the center of each tire
without catching a foot on the rim, tripping, and hitting
the sand flat on his face.

The monkey bars was just a horizontal ladder high
enough off the ground that the tallest student could
hang from his hands and not touch the ground with his
feet. Completing that obstacle took hand strength and
enough coordination not to let go of one bar before
getting a good grip on the next one. Everyone in the
class had obstacles that they were good on, and everyone very quickly found the ones that they hated.

Jeremy's worst obstacle was dubbed the "Dirty
Name." It was a series of three horizontal logs that had
to be climbed over, each log much higher off the
ground than the one before it. The first log was a foot
off the ground, and the student would just stand up on
it. The second log was on tall posts that put it well over
six feet off the ground. The last log was almost taller
than it was wide, and was suspended over twelve feet
above the ground by posts at either end. Each of the
log assemblies were spaced about six feet from the
next one, and they all had to be climbed over before
you could drop to the sand and continue the course.

Jeremy hated the Dirty Name. The first log was
easy, but then you were supposed to leap up and catch
the next log against your lower stomach and lever

yourself up with your arms. He had a problem leaping high enough to avoid hitting the second log. Scrambling hard, he continually smashed into it with his stomach and had to kick and climb up from his elbows. His first time he hit the tallest log with his stomach, got the wind knocked out of him, and discovered another reason the logs were spaced so far apart: it gave the student room to fall back and land flat on his back on the soft sand without knocking his skull on the lower log behind him.

It wasn't fun. The instructors' encouragement didn't help a lot. If you failed to get through an obstacle correctly, you had to go back and do it again. The instructors shouted, "Work it out, maggot!" and, "Quickly, quickly!" and, "Hustle, hustle!" But the most popular instructor line was, "Make up your time!"

The smaller, more wiry guys could get up on the logs of the Dirty Name and almost leap through it. Instructor Sanchez, though not wiry, had made it look simple as well. Jeremy found it amusing to watch George Staverous go through the Dirty Name. He was so big and hairy, even with his skull shaved, that he looked like a bald black bear climbing over a garden fence.

Jeremy's next worst obstacle was the Weaver: a strange-looking, wide, low pyramid of squared beams rising six feet above the sand. Extended between the two pyramids were parallel four-inch iron pipes, spaced over two feet apart. The obstacle was negotiated by weaving over and under alternating pipes up one side and down the other. The Weaver took a lot of coordination to get through. The instructors found it could slow students down in getting through the course more than almost any other obstacle. Jeremy's problem with the Weaver was just getting through it without breaking an elbow. His technique needed a lot of development, since he pushed down on the pipes with his arms and banged his elbows on almost every one.

But the one obstacle that cost Class 78 the most, both in time getting over it and in students who quit because they couldn't face it, was the cargo net. It wasn't the physical difficulty that stopped a number of students, but the mental one. The rope cargo net was stretched and secured between the uprights of a log frame. The net swayed and moved as it was climbed, and it had to be climbed high, since it extended over forty feet into the air.

Students with a fear of heights had to swallow it and just climb. Once at the top of the net, the fear some students had got a lot worse, since they then had to swing their legs over the top of the net, and the pipe it was secured to, and climb down the opposite side.

Some of the students froze up at the top of the net. Their classmates tried to help get them over, but one student was so frozen, an instructor had to climb up and get him down. That young man was the first Class 78 student who was performance dropped from BUD/S because he couldn't complete an evolution. He wasn't going to be the last.

Nguyen Thanh clambered up the net and down the other side lightly and quickly. He was able to go hand over hand down the cargo net, something none of the other students were able to do.

The tower, one of the last obstacles almost stopped Nguyen, however, and several other students as well. It was a four-story structure of logs and planks that stretched forty feet above the sand of the O-course. There were three platforms on the tower, and a student had to climb up to the top platform and then back down to complete the obstacle.

Some of the students just grabbed hold of the next platform and pulled themselves up to where they could swing a leg over. Then they would lever themselves up and do it again. Other students, especially the smaller ones, went with the back-flip method. Facing out from the tower, they would jump up and grab the edge of the next platform up. Then they would swing their legs out, up, and over to get on the next platform. It was the fastest technique for the obstacle, as well as the hardest one.

On some obstacles, the taller, bigger students had an easier time. Shorter students found other obstacles easier to negotiate because they didn't have as much mass and bulk to drag through, over, or up the obstacle. The tower and cargo net were good examples of that. The variety of obstacles on the O-course made everyone work at about the same level.

It took forty-three minutes for Jeremy to complete the O-course his first time through, which was the class average on the first attempt. To graduate First Phase, he would have to shave that time down to fifteen minutes or less; preferably less, according to the instructors. To actually graduate BUD/S, the course had to be completed in ten minutes. He knew he had a long way to go.

## Chapter Five

Training moved along quickly. Class 78 was soon introduced to the single most hated and commonly used piece of equipment in the Teams. Since the training days of World War II, the rubber boat—officially known as Inflatable Boat, Small, or IBS—had carried swimmers, raiding parties, and shipwrecked sailors, soldiers, and Marines. It could carry seven men and a thousand pounds of equipment and be launched from a ship, submarine, aircraft, or land. The instructor staff at BUD/S thought it was only fitting that, after they had carried so many of them, the rubber boats be carried by the students, in order for them to best appreciate the workhorse little craft.

Little is a relative word in Navy craft. The IBS was one of the smallest boats in the Navy, but it was still twelve feet long, six feet wide, and normally weighed 289 pounds with all of its equipment on board. In case that weight wasn't enough to meet an instructor's tastes, the IBS could be made much heavier by shoveling sand into its interior, or by the even better expedient of an instructor climbing up inside one.

This was all something the students of Class 78 were going to learn soon after being shown the IBS. The rubber boats at the training compound were tough, but they had also seen a lot of abuse and hard usage over the years. The class was broken down into boat crews of six people each and the boats were issued. Then all of the crews had a day to get their boats prepped, painted, and repaired.

It was going to be the boat crews' job to keep their IBS repaired and operational throughout training. The condition of some of the boats gave the crews immediate experience in gluing repairs and patching them up. None of the rubber boats at the compound were new, but all of them were usable.

Like every other boat and ship in the Navy, each IBS had to be painted. The spray tube—an inflatable collar that ran around the top of the main tube of the IBS—had to be painted a bright yellow for safety and visibility. That yellow safety tube made the boats stand out in the dark waters around the training compound. The number of the boat crew assigned each boat also had to be painted on the bow, in Roman numerals. The balance of that day was spent painting, patching, and inflating the rubber boats that would be the students' almost constant companion during much of their First Phase training.

The paddles the boat crews would be using to drive their craft were in much the same condition as the boats: well-used and worn. In fact, they were pretty beaten up, and being made of wood, they were easily broken. There were enough of the standard canoe-type paddles with a wide, triangular-shaped top at the compound to replace any breakages.

Boat Crew IV consisted of Jeremy White, Patrick Neil, Mike Zundleman, Howard Johns, Tim Beardsley, and Jim Alex. They were all pretty big guys—"beef," as the instructors called it. As a second class gunner's mate, Patrick Neil was the highest ranking man in Boat Crew IV, which put him in the coxswain's position as their LPO (leading petty officer). Other boat crews were similarly commanded, some by the highest ranking petty officer, others by actual commissioned officers.

Boat Crew IV had not picked its own IBS. Instructor Holmes had led the crew up to the IBS rack at the rear of the compound, pointed, and said, "There's your boat." As far as Jeremy was concerned, they'd been given a wreck.

The instructor had pointed to a flat, roughly boat-shaped lump of deflated black rubber. Everyone in Boat Crew IV looked at each other for a moment, then dragged their boat from the rack and set to work on it.

The first thing they learned was that it was important to make sure the rubber boat could hold air. Not because they needed to float the damned thing right away. But manhandling a deflated rubber boat, pulling it from the rack and carrying it across the area—God help any crew that was caught dragging their boat, because the instructors would have no pity—was like wrestling with a large dead octopus. But dead octopus might have smelled a little better than that IBS did, Jim Alex said.

Finding all of the holes and patching them up was a learning experience for all of the boat crews, IV among them. There was a patching kit that was always to remain with the boat. Pockets and pouches attached to the boat hull held an air pump, the repair kits, and other minor equipment and gear. The patching process was an involved one that included scrubbing the IBS with a wire brush or sandpaper, painting on several coats of cement, letting them dry between applications, and then securing a fitted patch in place. By the time Boat IV tightly held its air, the men of its crew knew how to properly apply a patch.

The lines of the IBS had to be properly coiled and stowed. There was the towing bridle attached to both sides of the bow, the safety line that ran around the top of the main tube, and the bow and stern lines. Coiling and securing them was the first chance Jeremy had to use his bosun's mate training, something he had learned what seemed like an eternity ago rather than just a month earlier.

Each IBS had to pass a boat inspection. Besides the lines, other things were checked like the crew's paddles, which had to be properly shoved in under the seats and sticking out from the boat only a given distance.

Along with the boats, the crews were issued their kapoks. These were heavy life vests, the red canvas bodies packed with heavy kapok filler material. The kapoks were not the lightweight swim vests you might find on a pleasure boat or for use while swimming, but were the heavy vests that had been used by the Navy since before World War II. The thick neck collars and padded front and back of the vest could keep a man afloat in the roughest seas. But they were not comfortable.

The students wore the kapoks every time they used their boats in the water. And they were very soon wearing them and getting the boats wet. Crews had worked out, under the guidance of the instructors, who would sit where and do what they would do in the IBS. How each man would sit, who would steer. From the front to the back of the boat, every man would sit in a numbered position athwart the main tube, with one leg inboard and one hanging outboard with a foot trailing in the water.

The positions were numbered from one at the front to three at the back. These positions were repeated both port and starboard. At the rear of the IBS was the coxswain, who both steered the boat and ordered the crew as to how, when, and where to paddle.

Drills were conducted on land, with all the boat crews learning their positions and what they were supposed to do as part of the crew. Once the crews had some idea about how to paddle their boats, they were introduced to surf passage, which they would have to employ over and over while at BUD/S. The instructors gave an introduction on surf passage and dropped some serious hints and suggestions. But even so, there was no better way to learn surf passage than to just go ahead and do it.

A boat crew had to work as a coordinated team in

order to get through surf passage. Waves had to be watched and timed as they traveled in sets and crashed up onto the shore. The coxswains had to steer the boats hard and not let them drift to the side. The waves had to be ridden over straight and true—anything else would usually result in a boat turned sideways against the wave, broaching, and being swamped. The students were also shown how to right a flipped-over boat and get the bulk of the water out of it. Then the lesson turned to how to ride a wave back in to shore.

The heavy surf crashed on the shore as the students picked up their rubber boats and carried them down to the waves on top of their heads. The command to "Up boats" meant that every man of a crew would pick up their boat, lift it over their heads, and set it down on top of their skulls. This was the best way to carry the rubber boats around. It was far from comfortable.

But the students' comfort was the last thing on the instructors' minds. Surf passage was always an interesting day of training. And Class 78 did not disappoint the instructors. It was a good show.

The instructors had tried to pick a day for the surf passage indoctrination evolution that had decent waves. Decent meant ten- or twelve-foot plungers. Schedules would be adjusted to ignore calm, smooth water days for surf passage training. Just paddling through the water was no way to learn. And the class learned a lot that day.

The waves roared in with a whoosh, and then curled over and pounded down with a heavy crunch into the sand. Those sounds helped mask the screams and yells of the students as they were thrown from their boats. The kapoks kept them all afloat, and they were under the constant, watchful eyes of the instructors.

As the boat crews went out through the surf, if they didn't hit the waves right, the bow could turn back and the whole rubber boat bend. When the boat straightened out as the wave passed, it would snap back suddenly. That snap could throw an unwary student through the air and into the water. This was the part the instructors seemed to like best.

"Check this one out," Instructor Nick Holmes said to Senior Chief Bill Fletcher as he pointed to Boat Crew IV. "We're going to get some distance on that bow man!"

Aboard Boat IV, Patrick Neil was shouting out the stroke and trying to steer straight into the huge wave that was crashing down on them. Bent over in the front of the boat in the number one starboard position, Jeremy dug in with his paddle and tried to hear what was being called out. Suddenly, he was looking up at the sky as the IBS bent sharply in the middle. Just as suddenly, the boat snapped back, throwing Jeremy through the air.

"Wow!" Instructor Holmes laughed. "Must have gotten fifteen feet of loft on that one!"

Jeremy flew through the air and into the roiling ocean. Spitting saltwater and sand—whatever else was there, he didn't want to know—he was pulled to the surface by his kapok vest. He had managed to keep a grip on his paddle, as he was supposed to. Then the balance of Boat Crew IV were trying to paddle over to where Jeremy and Patrick Neil, who had also been tossed from the boat, were floating. Picking up their crewmates, Boat IV continued with the evolution.

It was the end of a pounding day when they finally secured from surf passage. The roller-coaster boat rides had by then become fun, as the crews learned how to go out through a wave and come in while riding one. Some of the crews hadn't learned the lessons as well as the others. They remained out in the water practicing while a few of the better crews were brought in to shore. It was one of the first demonstrations some of the students had with the BUD/S expression, "It pays to be a winner."

The camaraderie had been building among the students, and among groups of students, as the weeks progressed. At first, roommates had formed cliques to share information, help, and to bitch with each other. When the boat crews formed up, those became the groups the students tended to gravitate to during their spare time.

Since Jim Alex was in Jeremy's boat crew, Jeremy's situation was a bit easier than that of the other students. Though Jim had been rolled back before he'd gone through much of BUD/S the first time, he still had information to share on how to get through some of the evolutions.

The instructors got tougher on everyone as the weeks went by. The PTs were difficult by the time they had gone through surf passage. By the third week of training, they were doing PTs that lasted better than an hour in the morning, and swims that took up a good part of each afternoon.

Sets of exercises during PT now included fifty flutter kicks and twenty-five Helen Kellers. These were a four-count exercise, so they actually did a hundred and fifty, respectively, per set. Regular push-ups went to sets of thirty. Triceps push-ups, where the hands were close together, were done as sets of fifteen. And wide-grip push-ups, where the hands were more than shoulder width apart, were done in sets of twenty. Sit-ups were done as sets of fifty or seventy-five depending on who was running the PT.

By the third week, students were doing five sets of everything during an average morning PT. Not including the stretches and other exercises, that added up to 500 flutter kicks, 250 Helen Kellers, 250 or 375 sit-ups, 75 triceps push-ups, 100 wide grip push-ups, and 150 regular push-ups during a PT. The sets were mixed up and spaced out from one another so that the class didn't do a hundred push-ups in a row. The total amount of exercise done during a PT was now staggering. It was surprising that the T-shirts lasted more than a single PT, what with backs moving against the grinder so much.

Runs were also mentally challenging. Instructor Lubi tended to be the man who most often led the runs during First Phase. The slightly built Filipino instructor didn't seem to sweat at all, no matter how long a run was. When the students were staggering and gasping from the effort of running through the soft sand of the beach, Instructor Lubi was right there with his big smile and constant question of "What's wrong? You don't think this is hard, do you?"

The ease with which he ran, and his lack of sweating, were difficult to watch. The fact that the instructor could also do the miles' long runs while smoking a cigar seemed a bit much. Sometimes, just to mess with the students, Instructor Lubi would pace the class while singing running songs, and running backward. Not one student ever saw him trip and fall. And none of them wanted to be nearby if he did.

About fifteen people quit Class 78 and BUD/S during just the first week of training. It was simply because the harassment from the instructors never stopped. They were constantly yelling at the students and getting on an individual's case whenever he caught their attention. "Maggot" was a constant term used to describe the students by several instructors. To hear them, they considered the whole bunch to be the worst thing that ever crossed onto their grinder and they didn't like anybody in the entire class. The opinion of the instructors was that they would have an easy Hell Week: there wouldn't be any students left by then.

The instructors, in fact, were intentionally making life hard for the students. They were also watching everyone's reactions carefully. When they spotted a weakness, they quickly moved to exploit it. They picked on problems, and there were a lot of problems for them to spot.

One of the easiest problems to sit was the friction between Redneck and Hammer. The instructors didn't exploit the situation to make it worse. Instead, they looked on it as a way to help build up teamwork among the students. This was the time and place for them to weed certain individuals out of the pack. If a student couldn't cooperate with his fellow classmate, he would fall away and quit.

Instructor Lubi exploited this situation. He knew that being a darker-skinned Filipino had to rub Redneck the wrong way, so he always tried to pace near the biased student on a run. In addition, Rappaport was paired with Sledge for swims. When he didn't like the idea of swimming with a slow black, who he complained just held him back, the instructors gave him an excellent way to forget about the lack of speed in his swim buddy by making him wear a hawser collar that connected him with his black swim buddy. The three-inch hawser was about six feet long and with a loop at each end.

The idea was simple: Redneck would either slow down and help his swim buddy pick up speed, or he would keep swimming with that hawser dragging him back. Of course, because of the hawser, Sledge didn't get a lot of slack cut for his lack of swimming ability. If he wanted to get rid of that damned rope collar, he would have to become a better swimmer.

Rappaport started to learn to keep his opinions to himself and cooperate with his classmates. And Sledge gained strength and ability in swimming because of the extra strain.

The instructors were also trying to get the class to start working together more. Slower guys on runs were paired up with the faster runners. Psychological games were played on the class. When they were told that a run would be so many miles, it would actually be much longer, and completion times on the O-course were announced as longer than they actually were.

The pressure worked. Students who didn't want to keep up, rang the bell and weren't a problem any longer. The rest of the students in the class began to help each other more. One man would pull another man over the top of the cargo net when they slowed down, and students would cheer each other along on their runs and swims.

By the third week the cooperation among students was noticeable, even to themselves. About ten more students had added their helmets to the line growing underneath the bell at the corner of the grinder. The 118 students who had begun training with Class 78 were now ninety-three. And according to the instructors, a lot more would quit before First Phase was over.

The students' bodies were now capable of enduring more punishment; it was becoming a matter of mental rather than physical ability to keep going. The instructors could continue to performance drop anyone who couldn't complete an evolution, as they saw fit, and they could do it up to graduation day itself. And there was always the specter of an injury that could cause a student to be dropped, or at least rolled back to do it all over again.

Jeremy noticed shin splits starting up in his legs on the longer runs. The pain in his lower legs told him he might be in trouble, and soon. But for the moment, he could ignore the pain without a lot of trouble. And he hoped the splints would go away as he built up strength in his legs.

The running through soft sand while wearing boots had always been a problem at BUD/S. Some students actually cracked their legs—had a hairline bone fracture form about where the tops of their boots ended. They sucked up the pain and kept going as long as they could. But the fractures didn't heal while they were still being run on, and that kind of injury always ended with a student having to leave his classmates and being rolled back.

The instructors expected that support among the students would become even more pronounced now that they had been broken up into boat crews. But there were still some hard evolutions to go through, and a number of students would probably quit before the really big test of a student's mettle came along: Hell Week.

## Chapter Six

Before Hell Week, there were still several very serious evolutions the class would have to go through. One of the most dangerous evolutions of the phase, if not the course, was rock portage. The students had to conduct a surf passage out from the beach and then back in, land their boats and move inland with them. The landings wouldn't be on the nice, smooth sandy beach that was just outside of the training compound, but north of the compound, at one of Coronado's more famous landmarks.

The Hotel del Coronado was on a twenty-six-acre site that looked larger than the entire BUD/S training compound at first glance. The Hotel del, as everyone at the base called it, was a huge rambling building surrounded by a number of smaller buildings, tennis courts, and swimming pools. Built back in 1888, the red-roofed structures of the Hotel del looked out over a white sand beach and the waters of the Pacific beyond.

To protect that white beach from the actions of the

heavy surf, piles of rocks acted as breakwaters. The surf smashed down on rocks that ranged in size from roughly three-foot cubes to those the size of a refrigerator and larger. Some of the rocks were the size of small cars. They were piled up ten feet high and more in spots, the edges and corners of the black stones— most were at least worn from the actions of the water—sticking out in all directions. It was on these mounds of forbidding rocks that the students would land their rubber boats for rock portage.

The men of the Teams couldn't pick where they would be able to land their boats on a given mission. The beaches might look even worse than what the students would face near the Hotel del. But that first day of rock portage, you couldn't have convinced them that a person could even live through landing on the rocks they were looking at.

Though the situation was a serious one, and the evolution was always conducted with a heavy eye to safety, the instructors were amused by some of the students' reactions. Ensign Kozuska, the biggest guy in the class, always tried to hold the attitude that nothing could bother him. Chief Packard had seen that expression in Kozuska's eyes a number of times before.

"That boy's pucker factor is so high," Packard said to Instructor Hawke, "you couldn't drive a nail up his ass with a ten pound hammer. If he doesn't loosen up, he'll break like a glass window."

Instructor Hawke just grinned at Chief Packard's comment. Then they both went back to paying close attention to what was going on offshore.

Class 78 had received an introduction as to what was expected of them and what they needed to know to successfully conduct a rock portage. In its simplest terms, the boat crews would follow their coxswain's instructions and try to paddle their craft right into the rocks. The coxswain would steer the boat straight and try to time their approach by calling out the stroke to the paddlers. Properly done, they could catch the top of a breaking wave and ride it in to the rocks and onto them, if the wave was big enough.

The surf that day was light, according to the instructors. Only four- to six-foot waves were breaking down on the rocks. Once they landed, the bow man would immediately jump out of the boat and into rocks, settling in between them. He would have the bow rope of the IBS with him, and once he'd "taken a bite" and braced himself against the rocks, the bow man would wrap the rope around his waist and pull the boat straight, perpendicular to the rocks.

With the boat straight and stable, the rest of the crew would pile out and lift the boat up and over the rocks. Dragging it on the rocks would most likely tear it up. Then the reaction of the instructors would tear up that boat's crew. Being under or anywhere too close to the boat as the waves picked it up could get you trapped between it and the rocks. Even empty, a nearly three hundred-pound boat would do a lot of damage to a student who was between it and the sharp-edged rocks. The waves pounding down on the rocks could also pound a student down on those same rocks if he wasn't careful and managed to get himself thrown from the boat.

So now the class had all the lessons and practice from the surf passage to build on. All they had to do was add the extra problem of landing on and over the rocks. Then they would get to do it all over again—at night.

Working as a team was absolutely critical to the rock portage evolution. Just one man failing at his job could spill the entire crew, forcing them to do the evolution over, at best, and at worst injuring some or all of them. People could get trapped in the boats or the rocks. There were real hazards here, and the instructors were accepting nothing but the very best from all of the students.

The first boat to come in to the rocks, Boat Crew XIV, had Ensign Mark Beekman as the coxswain, a young hard-charger. The instructors had seen to it that Rappaport and Sledge were both on the same crew, and they were with Boat Crew XIV. As they started their run in to shore, Chief Packard was on top of the rocks, signaling when they were properly aligned in order to bring them in to the landing site. Beekman called out the stroke, and Boat XIV was in on its way.

As the rubber boat began to crest the wave as it came in, the boat crew dug their paddles in all the harder. Chief Packard was bellowing out from his position on top of the rocks, "Speed it up, you're losing the wave!"

Either Beekman didn't hear him or he forgot exactly

what he was supposed to do, As the wave passed by underneath them, the rubber boat with Boat Crew XIV aboard slipped back off the crest and started going backward, in spite of the students paddling hard. Then, as the water got shallow behind the wave and they were at the rocks, disaster happened.

Jim Ceiner, the number two starboard paddler, dug his paddle down and stuck it right between two of the rocks. Before Rappaport, sitting behind him, could even react, Ceiner's paddle snapped off, driving the young man back against Redneck and knocking him off the boat entirely.

Boat XIV turned suddenly against the resistance of Ceiner's paddle, then flipped over against the rocks. Ensign Beekman was tossed out and into the rocks as another wave surged up and in on the tangled boat and crew. Sledge saw his coxswain go over backward and into the rocks as he was tossed from the boat. The bellows of rage and concern from Chief Packard were lost among the general noise and confusion.

As Sledge landed between two rocks, he saw Rappaport go under nearby. Reaching out, Sledge clamped down on Redneck's arm, the only part of him that was still up and out of the water. The powerful muscles of the young black man heaved, and he dragged his classmate up from the water.

As Rappaport was coughing and heaving up the water he'd swallowed, the wave picked up the rubber boat that was next to them and dashed it down onto the rocks. Turning away from the incoming wave, Rappaport saw Beekman among the rocks just as the rubber boat came down on him. The rest of the crew were floundering around as the instructors were just getting to them.

Rappaport dove forward to where the boat was down in the rocks, and Sledge heard him bellow, "Beekman!" Sledge immediately followed his classmates' lead. They reached the boat within seconds and the two young men heaved up on it with more strength than they knew they had. Underneath the boat, Ensign Beekman was weakly trying to pull himself from between the rocks. The reason for the young officer's distress was obvious. Even without being corpsmen, Sledge and Rappaport both knew that a leg wasn't supposed to bend the way Beekman's right leg was turned.

Beekman had the worst injury of the incident, but he wasn't the only one. The splintered end of the paddle had dug into Ceiner's arm, cutting a large, deep gash. As Chief Packard took over Ceiner's treatment, clamping down on the gash with one huge paw, the corpsmen took Ensign Beekman up from the rocks.

The cost of the incident to Class 78 was the loss of one of their officers, since Beekman had to be dropped. The severity of the young officer's injury might be enough to keep him from ever being able to return and complete BUD/S. The gash in Ceiner's arm was bad, but he could have been rolled back to heal and try again. But the man's guilt at believing he had caused the accident, and might have cost Beekman his naval career, was too much for him. Ceiner dropped from training. Three more students dropped rather than face the rocks that had just chewed up a boat crew. For the evolution, Class 78 was down by five more students.

The rest of the crews saw what had happened. But that wasn't going to be enough to call off the evolution. Every one of the thirteen remaining boat crews had to conduct a landing and portage across the rocks. The crews set out with determination. The pucker factor was high, as everyone now knew exactly what could happen. So they worked through the landings. Besides, all the rocks could do was break them up or kill them. The rage that radiated from Chief Packard was something they didn't want to face.

The rock portage during the day was rough, but all the crews completed the evolution. Even the members of Boat Crew XIV, who were separated and spread out among the rest of the crews, did their landings and learned what to do. As part of Boat Crew V, Sledge and Rappaport completed two successful rock portages. The instructors had put them both in the same crew again, and the two very different students looked at each other in a new way.

Teamwork was continuing to grow among the students. And they would need it that evening. They all had to do rock portage again, this time at night. But the lessons of the day hadn't been forgotten. Under Chief Packard's directions, the boat crews came in without any major incidents, and relatively few minor ones. But there was still plenty of reason for Chief Packard to award push-ups and sugar cookies, just to keep the students alert and awake.

## Chapter Seven

As the time passed in training, Hell Week approached. The instructors were pushing the idea of teamwork harder and harder, emphasizing that the class had to work together to get through the coming trials. But though teamwork and cooperation with each other was emphasized, the students still had plenty of opportunities for individual effort. One of these opportunities came in the form of the drown-proofing evolution.

All of the students had spent plenty of time in the pool by the fourth week of First Phase. Swimming lengths and other exercises were common for them now. They had even practiced some of their rubber boat drills in the controlled environment of the pool before taking them out to sea. Their newest challenge, the drown-proofing evolution, was one that had to take place in the pool for safety. But even with the pool's environment, the idea of the evolution was a scary one.

The class was shown how to form a beehive in the pool, with all the students clumped together as tightly as they could. They learned how they could all remain like that in the water for as long as they needed to, helping to support and protect each other. The technique was a good one for shipwrecked seamen. But the BUD/S students were shown it to teach them more about working together, and how they could tread water in their clothes.

The instructors showed the class how to take their boots off in the water, tying them together and hanging them from their necks. Flotation devices could be made from shirts and pants, which was the next lesson for the class. As they were becoming more relaxed in the water, they were preparing for a much more challenging evolution, one they didn't expect at all.

First, everyone was put through floating for a long period, to help build their confidence. When the students could do that, which was basic drown-proofing, they took the next step, one unique to BUD/S: with their hands tied, they had to go back through the floating procedure.

Once they learned that they could float and control their breathing with their hands tied, their feet were also secured, at the ankles. This was scary for several of the students. Their panic caused them to lose their flotation and sink down into the water. Before anything serious could happen to them, the instructors, who were swimming around, dragged them back up to the surface. Sputtering and choking, they were taken to the side of the pool and out of the water.

The panicked students were given a moment or two to calm down, then were given another chance to try the evolution and get through it. In spite of their best efforts, several of the students couldn't complete the evolution. A few wouldn't even enter the water again, no matter what the instructors or their classmates said. They just rang out and quit.

Jeremy didn't find the evolution that hard. He knew that if you could relax in the water, you could do everything the instructors asked you to, even floating for fifteen minutes with legs and hands tied. Being negatively buoyant because of his muscles building up, Jeremy had to kick to keep himself at the surface. But a simple dolphin kick could be easily done, even with the ankles tied together. And that was all it took to keep him afloat.

The next step was more than a little harder. The instructors had each student submerge to the bottom of the pool and retrieve his swim mask. However, they weren't to dive down. Instead, they had to let the air out of their lungs and sink the ten feet to the bottom. Once on the bottom, they turned their heads to the sides and grabbed their masks with their teeth. Then they kicked back up to the surface.

The technique sounded easy, but it's a lot harder to hold the air out of your lungs than to hold it in. More than a few students ran out of air, or control, and had to be dragged up to the surface, kicking and sputtering. They were shaken up, but no more of them quit. A few who tried hard the second time still had to be dragged to the surface after sucking up water. Several of them were rolled back to the next class.

The instructors accepted the inability to complete an

evolution as long as they saw a good attitude and an ability to learn. Though they constantly mentioned how easy it was to quit, a good student was someone they wanted to keep around. Drown-proofing was hard, but its completion was an absolute requirement to get through First Phase.

Once the students had successfully retrieved their masks, they were told to drop them by the instructor. Then, still bound hand and foot, they had to swim to the far side of the pool. Being negatively buoyant, Jeremy had to work harder, but made it without any trouble. Having even more muscle, and almost no body fat, meant that Sledge and Carl Flack, the remaining black student, had to work very hard to swim with their hands and feet tied. Before Sledge even had a chance to complete the evolution, Flack panicked and sank toward the bottom.

The instructors pulled Flack from the pool and told him to try again. But he had taken enough. Hacking and coughing up water, Carl Flack of Kansas City rang out and quit BUD/S. That left Washington Sledge as the last remaining black student in Class 78.

Over at the side of the pool, Redneck Rappaport sat with the majority of the class, pointing out what he'd been saying all along. The instructors let him go on to see just what reaction Sledge would have to the taunts.

"Yep," Redneck said in his thick southern drawl, "black boy just ain't gonna make it. I told him he just wasn't cut out for this. None of his kind are."

Redneck's racist remarks didn't have the same edge to them as they once had. The instructors weren't worried about what the rest of the class would do. They didn't expect them to throw Redneck into the pool, and they weren't agreeing with him either. Sledge sank down to the bottom of the pool and picked up his mask. He may have had an easier time of that than the rest, since he didn't have to let much air out in order to sink. Muscular black men had a hard time floating to begin with. He picked up the mask and rose to the surface.

Once he got the signal from the instructor, Sledge dropped the mask and started off to the far side of the pool. The man was determined, but he also had to swim harder than the rest of the class in order to make it. The long period they had spent in the water was taking its toll as Sledge's efforts flagged as he came closer to the side of the pool.

The rest of the class was cheering him on. He was one of the last students still in the pool, and they were all calling out for him to make it. Then, above all the others, a thick southern voice sounded out.

"Damn boy," Redneck said clearly. "You gonna prove me right and just sink right there?"

Pushing harder, Sledge got over to the side of the pool. Several sets of students' hands grabbed him, supporting him as his hands were untied. Holding him firmest were the hands of his swim buddy, Redneck.

The last part of the evolution, an absolute requirement, was the hardest. Each student had to swim underwater all the way across the pool and back on a single breath of air. It was a distance close to seventy meters, a long way to move underwater on one breath of air. The students had to start in the water, and they couldn't push off the side of the pool at the start. But they could push off the far side for their return trip.

For all his big mouth and hot air, Rappaport had a hard time getting back across the pool. Nor was he the only one. The instructors ordered the students who had broken the surface early to get out of the water. They sat huddled together until the rest of the class completed the evolution. Then it was their time to try again.

When Rappaport went back to the edge of the pool, he looked across and saw Sledge on the end of the pool with the rest of the class. Sledge had made it across and back on his first try, while Rappaport surfaced like a blowing whale. Now it was Redneck's turn to be taunted.

"What's the matter, white boy?" Sledge called across the pool. "You gonna let a brother who can't swim beat you on this?"

The rest of the class called out encouragement as Rappaport got into the water. Though students couldn't kick off against the side of the pool on the swim, but they could have a moment to clear their lungs and get a good breath of air.

"Come on, Redneck!" Sledge called out. "You've gotta have enough room in that big mouth for a whole lotta air. Suck it in and go!"

Rappaport was on his last try. If he didn't make it there and back on a single breath of air, he would be performance dropped and have to reapply to get back to BUD/S. With the cheers of his classmates ringing out, he heard Sledge one more time.

"Come on Redneck, the rocks didn't beat you," Sledge said. "Suck it in and go. You can do it, my man."

Rappaport pulled in a deep lungful of air and started out. His heartbeat was thundering in his ears as he made the turn on the far side and started back. The side of the pool looked an impossible distance away as the pressure in his lungs built up. To relieve the demand for air, he let some of his precious air bubble out from between his lips while kicking hard on the return.

His lungs screaming louder than his own heartbeat, Rappaport closed his eyes and kicked as hard as he could. Suddenly, his hands hit a hard tiled surface. He had made it across and back. As he surged up from under the water, the stale air burst out of his lungs and he gulped in a fresh breath. Sticking down from the side of the pool was a pink, hard palm, the back of the hand almost shiny, it was so black.

As Rappaport grabbed the hand and was pulled from the pool, Sledge said, "Nice going, Redneck. You made it."

As several of the instructors looked on, they thought that there just might be some teamwork building up in Class 78.

## Chapter Eight
## 1998

Everyone in the Teams knew that the test of an individual's heart, drive, and commitment to the BUD/S training program during First Phase would be during Hell Week. That week proved that a man had the heart to push himself through training to pass the course and join the Teams. But Hell Week was far from the end of training. In fact, for a lot of men in the Teams, it wasn't even the hardest part of training.

The work the students would have to do to complete the over twenty weeks of BUD/S that came after Hell Week would get more demanding, specific, and dangerous. Still, for almost everyone who had experienced it, who had gone through those long, impossible days and were still standing at the end, Hell Week was the most memorable part of training—even though the memories of it were usually blurred.

Hell Week was the only way the Teams had found to tell if a man had what it took inside him to complete training. It forced the students to experience something very close to the stress and exhaustion of combat. If they could function under that level of stress, they would prove to themselves that they could do whatever it took to get the job done.

Master Chief White had taken on the problem of increasing the number of students who completed training at BUD/S. It was unacceptable to him to lower the standards; do that, and men would die in the field and in combat. But the Navy, and the Training Command, were always looking to save money. And one way to do that was not to waste it on training someone who would DOR—would quit during Hell Week.

There was also a big push from Command to increase the number of BUD/S graduates to fill open billets in the Teams. Filling the open jobs in any of the Special Operations forces was always difficult since men who could complete the training were always in short supply. And it was important to keep the strength of the Teams up because it took a year of training just to turn out a qualified operator—not an experienced one, just one who was fully qualified to start doing a job.

During the Vietnam War, standards had been lowered in some of the other services to fill the ranks of the Special Operations forces. After the war ended, those ranks had to be seriously trimmed to get rid of the men who just couldn't do the job in a peacetime unit. That had been a costly mistake, and one Master Chief White was not going to make.

If Hell Week was a test of a man's commitment to completing the program, motivating him to try even harder would be a good way to cut down on DORs. So

White changed the last few days of the program that led up to Hell Week. He knew that part of his job was to help motivate the men, that it was one of the reasons he had been chosen for the slot—to show the students just what a SEAL career could mean. So he improved the motivation system that Command already had in place.

Shortly before a class was scheduled to enter Hell Week, a motivation day would be set up. The entire class would be brought into a room where the captain, the CO of the Training Command, would address them first.

If it could be arranged, a guest speaker would be brought in for the students. This would usually be a man who had completed training years before, maybe a vet from Vietnam, Korea, or even a World War II frogman. These men who could tell the students about the background of the Teams they would be striving to join. How some of the evolutions they would have to complete in the following week, no matter how strange they appeared, were based on real-world experience. And how some men, their forefathers in the Teams, had died to gain that experience.

Students would be told, by the men who had "been there and done that," how tossing sand up in the air and all over themselves re-created the feeling of crossing an enemy beach while machine gun bullets kicked the sand up around you. How the incoming barrage of shells and explosions around them had to be ignored while they steadily completed their job. How they had to concentrate on the smallest detail of something as simple as tying a knot, to do it successfully while explosions rained mud and water down on them.

And the most important lesson of all: how they had to complete their mission, do their job. Because if they didn't, the thousands of men who would be coming up after them, landing on that beach or crossing that jungle, would be killed or maimed because they failed. The Teams couldn't accept anyone who might quit along the way—the cost of such failure was just too high to pay.

But each of the individual students who made up a class knew that they weren't one of those who would quit. They would keep going. They would support their buddies, their boat crews. And it would be as a Team that they would complete the ordeal they were facing.

With the students now filled with war stories, rowdied up from what they had been told they could accomplish, the guest and the other instructors would leave the room, and Master Chief White would enter to speak to them alone.

Now, as he walked across the compound to the classroom, White passed the instructors' office and the bell mounted on a post facing its door. Along the ground were a line of helmets, already a long line. There were twenty helmets lined up in a row, signifying twenty people who had already quit from a class of over a hundred. Injuries and rollbacks had accounted for more students having to fall back out of the class. The remaining students waited for him inside the classroom.

His job was to help these students make it. And part

of that job was to inspire them. It was hard, tremendously hard, for a man to have just reached this point in training. From all of the people who said they wanted to volunteer for the Teams back at boot camp or wherever, only about four percent ever even got to this point: the chance to face Hell Week and go on. So now he would motivate these individuals for their next major ordeal.

He liked being the last one to address the students for several reasons. For one thing, they tended to remember best what they heard last. Even though the stories from the guest speakers would stick in their minds, as would a lot of what the captain had told them, it was the words that came from the man they saw almost every day that would stick with them the most.

So Master Chief White wanted to set an example. It was even more important than usual that he made sure his uniform was immaculate. Boots were shined until they gleamed almost in the dark. Khakis were spotless and razor-sharp creases lined the shirt and trousers. On the collar points were the anchor and twin star insignia of a U.S. Navy master chief petty officer. But it was what was on the left breast that would draw the students' eyes.

The five rows of brightly colored ribbons indicated at least fifteen awards given to the master chief, many of the ribbons holding metal devices indicating multiple awards. And the Combat Action, Commendation, and Joint Unit Citation ribbons were not the kind of thing handed out just for showing up every day.

Below the rows of ribbons shone a gold set of Navy Parachutist Wings. And centered below the wings was the oval gold badge that declared the wearer to be a Command master chief. But above all these awards and devices, above all the ribbons—it would even be above the ribbon of a Medal of Honor if the wearer held such an honor—shone the gold eagle, trident, and anchor of the Navy Special Warfare breast insignia. That gaudy, large device alone told the world at large that the wearer was a member of a most elite fraternity. Only someone who had completed BUD/S and joined the Teams could wear the trident, the insignia of a Navy SEAL.

As Master Chief White entered the room, the class leader shouted out, "Attention on Deck! Master Chief White!" Snapping up out of their seats to the position of attention, the whole class bellowed back in unison, "HOOYAH, MASTER CHIEF WHITE."

White stood there for a moment in front of the students. He looked down at them from the small stage at the front of the lecture hall, the only room at the Training Command that could hold an entire class at once. He looked at the students while they looked at him. Then he barked, "Take your seats!"

While the class scrambled back into their seats, White had the one reaction that an instructor tried never to show the students—revulsion. My god, they stink, he thought, but just for a moment. One thing that was never talked about was the results of a group of men who exercised hard, built up a sweat, and regularly soaked themselves in the open ocean—they stank.

It was a heady combination of sweat, seaweed, and seawater that resulted in an effluvium that took over a room. The students tended not to be able to smell it themselves, but the instructors could. And up there on the stage, White was in the thick of it. And the smell was something that only got worse—much worse—as Hell Week ran its course.

But White was quickly able to concentrate on something else. The eyes of every student in that room were on him, and he wanted to look each one of them in the eyes. There were no other instructors or officers in the room now, except for those among the students. So while they studied him standing there in his uniform, he studied them.

Their eyes hungrily took in what he was wearing, as he knew it would, especially that large gold trident up on his chest. In turn his gaze tried to see something he had always wanted to discover but never had: some sign, gleam, concentration, or gaze that would tell him if that individual would make it through the next week.

Up front in the student group were the class leaders and the leading petty officer (LPO). Behind them were the ranks of students who made up the class. All were individuals, and all were striving for the same thing. But who would make it, and who wouldn't? After a few moments had passed, White began addressing the class.

"Good morning, gentlemen," he said. "How's everybody doing?"

A chorus of "Hooyahs" came up from the students in answer to his question.

"I'm going to let you all know something right now," he continued in a somber tone. "I look into the eyes of every one of you because you deserve that much for having made it this far. But they don't show me what I would like to see. I cannot tell if this program is for you, if you have what it takes to complete training and go on to the Teams. Only you can determine that. And beginning this weekend, you will have your chance to show whether or not you belong here."

White paused and looked out at his audience. The students sat quietly for a moment, digesting his words. Then he continued in a brighter tone of voice.

"But I'll bet you guys aren't thinking about that. Instead, you're all sitting here getting pumped up about what you are soon going to do. But do me a favor. This is the time for you to get pumped up, but don't get to the point where you're burning yourself out. It's time to get your heads straight, set your hearts and minds on a single goal. And that goal right now is to work up your motivation.

"We're here to talk a little bit about that motivation you're building up to help get through those few days we call Hell Week.

"I'm going to tell you gentlemen right now that Hell Week is going to be the toughest evolution, both mentally and physically, that you have ever faced in your entire life. Why can I say that? Because I've been there.

"You guys have been working up to this moment in your training, learning about teamwork and what it takes for you to work together with each other. This is the time that you have to put that all together, gentlemen. There is no room for the 'I,' the individual, in what you are going to face. He should have been weeded out of your ranks by now. If he hasn't, he will be gone soon.

"It will be as a team, as members of boat crews, that you will conduct Hell Week. But it will be as an individual that each and every one of you will have to overcome it. What you are going to have to do is give all you have and more to get the job done. Giving a hundred percent won't be enough to get you through. You're going to have to give a hundred twenty percent. And one of the big lessons you'll take away from that week is that you really do have that much to give.

"From the very first days of training, back during World War Two when Hell Week was first started, the theory was that a man was capable of putting out ten times the effort he thought he could. And during those war years, and all of the time since then, that theory has been proved over and over.

"Up to this point, what you gentlemen have proved to both the instructor staff and to me is that you have what it takes to go through Hell Week. Now, we have to put the pressure on to make sure that you can operate in a stressful situation. The week that you are about to attempt—no, belay that—that you are about to complete . . ."

There was a small growl of assent that moved through the students when the master chief corrected himself.

". . . is designed to put you under the stress of a

combat situation," White continued, ignoring the small interruption. "That's what it will take to show us that you can mentally and physically perform under real stress. You have to be able to do that, to perform under stress. Because that's all part of being in the Teams.

"We all depend on each other. No one man carries the mission forward, it is always a team effort. If you can't perform under the stress of Hell Week, then something could happen out there in a real situation. It could be my life, it could be your life, or it could be the lives of all your Teammates. But if you fail under the stress of combat, if you fold up and quit, someone will die.

"Then one of you guys would have to come home and tell those that were left behind that the rest of us aren't coming back—ever. And you just might be the lucky one who would get to do that.

"None of us will accept that situation, not in the Teams and not here. Every one of the instructors here, myself included, have operated for years in the Teams. And our Teammates out there expect us to only send the best to operate with them. Most of the instructors here will go back to the Teams after their tour is over. And those same men might have to operate right alongside you. Do you think they're not going to make sure that you have what it takes? It's their lives on the line too.

"So that's what you're gearing up for, gents.

"There are some things I want to mention about Hell Week. We've already pushed you hard physically during the last several weeks of training. And we've pushed you hard mentally a little bit. But I'm going to tell you, men, that was nothing compared to what you are going to face.

"What's going to happen to you this coming week is that we're going to push you harder than you've ever been pushed before. The instructor staff and I are going to break you down both physically and mentally. Several things are going to happen to you. First of all, your bodies are going to start giving out. When that happens, you have to mentally pick yourself up and keep going. That's when you have to reach deep down within yourself and pull something out that you may have never realized you even had. You have to talk yourself through—and each of you can do it.

"That's what you have to do as an individual, pull up what you have inside yourself and keep it together. But you won't be alone, you will be working as part of a team. And that will help you. It is as an individual that you first face Hell Week. But it is only as a part of a team that you complete it.

"What's going to happen, first of all, is that you'll become physically drained. Then your mind will start to play tricks on you. Even if you swear right now that you will never consider quitting, your mind and body may betray you. That's when being a team can keep you going."

Up on stage, White had the total and undivided attention of the students. As he spoke, he paced from side to side on the small stage, turning and facing the students directly to make a particular point. Now he stopped and pointed down to the front row of students, and the class leading petty officer who was sitting there.

"Hell, we could be sitting in the chow hall," White continued, "and me and the LPO could be sitting just across the table from one another. That's when it could sneak up on me. 'Hey, Smitty,' I could say, 'hey man, I'm done. I'm going to go out there and ring the bell.'

"That's when he looks at me and reaches down inside himself. Sometimes, when you can't do it for yourself, you find you can do it for a teammate. You find what you need to keep going. That's when he would turn to me and say, 'No, Jeremy, not now, let's stick it out for just one more evolution. One day at a time.'

"Okay, I agree and go on for that one more evolution. And the one after that, and the one after that. Sure enough, I pull through and find I can keep on going. Then it comes time for midnight rats and now it's his turn to be down.

"He turns to me and says, 'You know, Jeremy, you were right. I'm getting burnt too. It's time to ring that bell.'

"Now I turn to him and say, 'No, man, we do it one evolution at a time. And we have to do one more together.'

"So what we're doing is bouncing back and forth. We support each other and pull together. You won't be alone out there. You will be doing everything as a boat crew. Throughout the entire week, you will be functioning as a boat crew. As a crew, you will face every evolution. And as a crew, you will get through them.

"Now you guys will get irritable," White continued as he paced back and forth even faster than before. "You're going to find out that you get on each other's cases. But you'll have to bypass that, find a way to step over your feelings and pull it together. Because each one of you will have to perform. And you will all have to perform as a team.

"Let's compare this to something serious. And combat is the most serious thing there is. What I'm going to do to get you guys pumped up a bit is tell you a little story, and it's about when I first went into combat.

"A detachment of us from SEAL Team Four were assigned to the 22nd Marine Amphibious Unit. We were being deployed to Beirut, Lebanon, to support the multinational forces actions there. En route, we were going to participate in some landing exercises in Spain. It was October eighteenth when we deployed to sea. October eighteenth, 1983.

"We never did get to Spain at all, and we didn't get to Beirut when we thought we were going to. We received orders at sea and were diverted. Instead of going to the eastern Mediterranean, we were on our way to the southern Caribbean and a little island there called Grenada.

"When we approached Grenada, word came down to us that four of our Teammates had been lost at sea jumping into the waters off the island. It was a big operation, and a lot more SEALs than just our small detachment had been tagged with special missions. A team of SEALs were going to take down the island's radio station. Another group was going to go in to the airfield and help set up a forward air controller's station to guide the incoming aircraft carrying the Rangers who were going to jump in. And another group of SEALs was going to go to the Governor's Mansion itself and rescue Governor Scoon.

"As usual, almost nothing went according to plan once the first bullets were fired. Our Teammates who were sent in to take out the radio station found themselves facing more armor and troops than they were told were on the whole island of Grenada. The team who went in to the Governor's Mansion expected to be in and out in under an hour. They were on the ground fighting with just what they had heloed in with for over a full day.

"And we were there, sitting offshore with a whole bunch of Marines when we heard our Teammates were being pinned down. But the Marines couldn't go in to shore without a recon, a detailed recon of the beaches and the enemy forces around them.

"So that's what we did—our job. Our detachment took in a Seafox crewed with men from Special Boat Unit 20. We went in to the beaches over fifteen kilometers of rough waters and dark seas. We started off at 2200 hours, and were told at the last minute that they had moved up the deadline for the landings. Now the Marines were coming in at 0500 hours.

"The mission changed, or at least the timeline for it did. Nothing new, you just keep going forward with your job, and your Teammates will do the same thing right alongside you.

"So we spent hours checking the beach area around

Pearl. We arrived about 2400 hours and started closely checking the beaches, surf conditions, and reefs to see if the Marines could come in on landing craft or tracks.

"And some of us went ashore to check out the airfield itself. I was one of those SEALs who went in to that hornet's nest, gentlemen. And the pucker factor was high.

"But all you can do is trust your training and your Teammates. So that's what I did. I had a big wad of dip"—chewing tobacco—"in my mouth from the ride in. And my mouth dried up like a desert when we went in to that airport.

"Was I scared? You bet your ass I was. Anyone who tells you they weren't scared their first time in combat is wrong. Anyone who tells you they were never scared in combat is wrong. There's nothing wrong with being scared. It's nature's way of telling you that you are not in a friendly area and you had better keep your head screwed on straight otherwise someone there may just take it off.

"But you know what else was there? The excitement was there. I had trained for years to do just what I was doing that day. My heart was beating and I felt more alive and in control than any other time in my life before then.

"And you train to control that kind of feeling when you go into a hot op. And you train to be able to do your job. And you train to be able to do your Teammate's job in case something happens. You train to do the mission, and you train to face down your fear.

"But my fears for myself weren't anything hard to

face that day. The fear that I could possibly let my Teammates down, that was a hard one. But the fact that there was an enemy out there didn't raise the hackles on my neck very high. I did some stupid stuff at the very beginning. Slammed into the beach so hard I almost knocked myself out. And my swim buddy did damned near the exact same thing. So we just looked at each other for a second, grinned, and got our shit together and got on with the job.

"We didn't really spot any major forces around the airport. There were militia forces and some antiaircraft gun emplacements. But nothing that couldn't be handled by what we had waiting to come in. But the beaches and the offshore waters and surf were too rough for the amphibious tracks to come over and land. Landing craft would have been swamped and wrecked in minutes. So we signaled back to the Marines, and they came in on a heliborne assault.

"For hours, I never even noticed that damned dip I had in my mouth. When I finally did notice it, I had been so scared that my mouth had dried up and that tobacco had turned into a rock inside my cheek. I finally had to dig it out with my finger and get water later when I could. But the big thing was that we had done our mission.

"And you know who was depending on our mission? Our Teammates in the Governor's Mansion, that's who. We had received reports that our Teammates were running low on ammunition and had suffered heavy casualties at the hands of Grenadan and Cuban troops. So the Marines loaded up and headed out after the landing to relieve our Teammates. The reports we had heard about the situation at the Governor's Mansion had been greatly exaggerated. But our Teammates had been pinned down, and the Marines we had helped bring in was what caused the enemy forces around the mansion to pull out.

"We did our job, completed our missions no matter how hard and fast they changed. And our ability to do that, every SEAL's ability to get the job done, starts right here at BUD/S. And your first real mission, the first big job you have to get done, is to complete Hell Week.

"Gents, we were up for over twenty-four hours straight gearing up for that recon op. We went in, did the mission, and remained on standby to supply what was needed to get our Teammates out. But add on to that operational time the days before then, just getting ready. The planning and gearing up for the op took days. No one slept. At most, everyone just caught a catnap now and then for the better part of a week. And our brothers in the other Teams? They did the same thing.

"But all of us, when it came time to go in, had to be sharp and alert. If we hadn't seen the reefs and shoals off that beach, Marines might have come in, broken up, and drowned without ever having even reached the shore.

"What I'm doing up here, gents, is to tell you that this is what it's all about. It's life and death, and you don't get any more serious than that. This week, I want you to consider your vest as your gear, your paddle is going to be your weapon, and your IBS is going to be how you get there and get out.

"You will be in as close to a simulated combat environment as we can do without just shooting at you. Your gear and your IBS is going to be your bread and butter all week. If you have a hole in that IBS, it's going to drain you, gents. So as soon as you get the chance, you're going to want to patch that boat up.

"You're also going to want to take care of each other. You're going to help each other get your gear on and off in a timely manner. Pressure is going to be put on you. And as the week goes on, your mind is going to play games with you.

"Your head isn't going to want to be there. Your body isn't going to want to keep doing the things that you're going to have to do. At some point—probably at chow while you're sitting there resting for a moment in a warm room, hot food in front of you—that's when your head is going to put a little guy up on your shoulder. And that little bastard is going to whisper into your ear.

"He's going to say: 'Hey, fuck this! I'm tired. Fuck this. You don't need this shit.' And you know what? You're going to start believing him.

"But before he talks you into getting up and ringing that bell, I want you to get that other little guy up on your shoulder. That's going to be the good guy, and you listen to him. He's going to tell you not to worry about it. The only easy day in the Teams was yesterday. And that's only because it's over. And that day you'll be in the middle of, that one will be over soon enough too.

"One evolution at a time, gentleman. That's how you get through, by doing things one evolution at a time. And when you're in that chow hall, when that bad little guy gets up on your shoulder, I want you to pick up your fork and stab the little bastard before he talks you into doing anything you may regret the rest of your life.

"Once he's gone, gents, you're going to be okay. You're going to learn the big rule of training. Now listen to what I have to tell you, because it is the honest truth. If you can survive and keep going, by Wednesday, you're going to be so dingy you'll be seeing things on the water. Hell, I saw my chief walking across the water during my Hell Week. And no matter what a chief might want you to believe, we can't actually walk on water."

There was a small chuckle that ran through the students at White's humorous remark. But it didn't break the unwavering attention each student held for every word that he was saying. Some of the intent young men were leaning forward, their own slight aches and pains forgotten in their concentration. Others just sat with serious looks on their faces. But none looked away, and not a single student failed to listen.

"Gentlemen, by that point you will be seeing things that you'll say you'd never seen before. But guess what? We can't hurt you by then. I don't care what the instructors do, they cannot hurt you. You will have learned the great truth about Hell Week, that it's all mind over matter. If you don't mind, it won't matter.

"You will survive as long as you keep stabbing that

bad little guy every time he gets up on your shoulder. The worst thing that might happen to you guys is you may be given a catnap. That's going to be the worst thing that you could do because if you then fall into a deep sleep—and you will almost instantly—oh my God, it's going to be hard to get started again.

"But remember one of the big things about training. It pays to be a winner. When you're going out there as a boat crew and doing your evolutions, you put this thing called teamwork together and it's going to pay-off, gentlemen. Because if you come in first, your crew may be the one to get a little rest. But you're going to have to earn that little bit of rest. Just like you have to earn the right to even face Hell Week. There is no given, you have to earn every bit of the right to join the Teams.

"There are some evolutions out there that you gentlemen may have heard of. Well, I want you to put any thought of what you may have heard right out of your heads. Do not worry about the next evolution. You worry about what's going on right then.

"You take each evolution only as it comes to you. Don't anticipate, just do. Take each step, each day, each hour, each minute, as it comes to you. If you don't, if you try to look ahead, it's going to cost you. You think about it, you worry about it, and your resolve to get past it weakens.

"For some of you—hell, for all of you—I'm going to guarantee that at some point it's going to enter your mind. Just as it has entered the minds of every man who has ever gone through this course of training. And what's going to enter your mind is that thought of ringing the bell. Just ding ding ding and you can be clean, warm, and dry again. You think about it at some point, everyone has. But you pull yourself past that point.

"When a bunch of us were getting ready for Panama, we spent a lot of time offshore practicing in our boats. If we had a bell out there, probably half of the guys would have rung out. That's how cold it was—we froze while doing our workups for the op.

"We had been out there on the open water for four hours. Can you imagine being out in a fiberglass boat with a wind chill factor of about twenty degrees? And that was off the coast of Florida in the middle of the night, believe it or not. By the time we got back, our feet were so frozen we had to thaw them out.

"And we had to do that practice evolution three times within a twelve hour period. It seemed that nobody thought about us out there freezing for all of that time. If we had a bell out there, you would have heard it ringing.

"And you want to talk about buddies? We hugged each other hard. And that's another thing you're going to be doing this week. That's why we call it 'buds,' gentlemen. You're going to be hugging each other to try and help yourselves, and your buds, to get warm. And I'm going to give you a hint on getting through the cold: take turns being in the middle. Rotate around so that each man spends some time in the center of a big group hug. That way you all get a chance to be warm for at least a moment or two.

"When I went through Hell Week, during escape

and evasion we teamed up with another pair of trainees. My partner and I would take turns, I would lay down on the ground and my partner would lay down on top of me. In about fifteen minutes, my arms got so numb that they woke me up. Kind of a built-in alarm clock. Then we would switch places and crawl forward. We watched out for the other pair, and they watched out for us. Then my partner laid down and had a chance to get a little rest. With our little automatic wake-up alarm, we just had to make sure that we got back into camp before morning.

"I've just given you guys some hints on how to get through. Now I'm going to give you a warning—don't get caught. Along with that warning is some good news and some bad news.

"The good news is that I am your Command master chief. I will be out there pulling for each and every one of you, motivating you as much as I can. The bad news is that I'm also going to be out there on one of the shifts as an instructor. And when I'm on a shift—I'm going to be your worst fucking nightmare.

"I will no longer be the master chief when I am on a shift. That won't be my job. And my job isn't going to be to get you to quit. My job will be to make it miserable enough for you, to force you to stick to the standards, and show without a doubt that you have what it takes to go on to the Teams.

"What I'm looking at, gents, is that someday, someday, I might be out in the field with you. I might be operating right there alongside you while we lay in a gutter with bullets and frags flying overhead. We might be side by side in the middle of a war. And I will know that you have what it takes. And I will know that because you will have passed the test right here.

"That's what the whole staff here is looking for—that you have what it takes. There is no way we have ever found to test for it. No examination that will prove you have it or you don't. The only way to show that you have the drive is to go through what you have to do.

"From that point on, gents, it becomes more of a learning curve. We teach, and you have to meet the standards. But we're not going to worry about that now. Because that's in the future, that's down the road, another evolution. What are we concentrating on right now?

"I asked you a question, gentlemen," White snapped out in a command voice. "What are we concentrating on right now?"

"HELL WEEK!" the class shouted back in ragged unison.

"That's right," White continued in a conversational tone, "Hell Week. We are concentrating on just getting through the next week.

"Teamwork, that's what it will take. I can't stress that point enough. You will have to each work as part of a team to get through the next week. Some of you will probably decide that the program just isn't for you. And the next day, you're going to get your senses back and realize that you could have made it. At that point, you're going to come and knock on my office door. Gentlemen, that will be too late. You will not return to training. You will be on your way back to the regular Navy.

"And you will have a good long time to think about your decision while you are out there, haze gray and under way aboard a Navy ship. Then you just may decide to try and come back again. And guess what, gentlemen, you'll be just a little bit stronger and a little bit wiser the next time. But the only time to really make it through is while you are here right now.

"What I will guarantee you is that I am here to try and motivate you to make it through with this class. We have what in here, about seventy students? I tell you what, I'd like to see each and every one of you standing there Saturday, sore, tired, beat, and stinking—and also proud. I will not tell you when we are securing you, but I would very much like to see seventy students standing there on the grinder when you are secured from Hell Week.

"Now, I'll make a little bet with you. If all seventy of you get through this little week's evolution, I owe you over one thousand push-ups. As a class, I will tell you that I will give the class fifteen push-ups for each man who is standing there that last day if you all make it. And I am the Command master chief—I keep my word.

"What I cannot do is stress enough about the fact that this is what you have been gearing up for. This is what you have been working for. This will be the hardest evolution that you will see here at the center as far as SEAL training goes. I'm going to wish you gentlemen the best. And I will be there to motivate you.

But remember, I also have to watch out for my own ass. So I'm going to make sure that you have what it takes.

"When I leave here, you will have some time to talk among yourselves about what's coming up. All I can say now is get a good rest, we'll see you out in the playing field."

With that, White turned and walked off the stage and out the door he'd entered. Echoing behind him, the walls of the classroom rang with the shouted "HOOYAH!" bellowing from each student's throat.

As he was walking back to his office, Master Chief White passed the Group commander, Rear Admiral Farmer. As the admiral returned White's crisp salute, he said, "Students a bit loud today, Master Chief?"

"Motivation day, Admiral," was all White had to say in return.

"Of course," Admiral Farmer said, nodding in complete understanding. Shining high up on the admiral's chest was a gold trident, a match for the one on White's chest and on the chest of everyone in the active Navy who had gone through Hell Week themselves.

## Chapter Nine
## 10 March 1974

It was the end of the fourth week of training, and the students could feel a change, an anticipation that had come over both the class and the instructors. The instructors hadn't lightened up on dishing out push-ups or punishments for infractions—even those that only they could see. And they still got right up into a student's face and chewed on him when he tried to follow their shouted directions. Their opinions of the abilities of the students in the class hadn't changed. What had changed was the subject matter they talked about to the class as a whole. Teamwork was what they pushed over and over now.

And every night in the barracks, the subject of discussion was the upcoming week. Hell Week was a frightening thought. Everyone said it was the hardest thing you could do. Six days straight without any sleep, with constant running, exercising, and nearly impossible evolutions—tasks that had to be done.

There were a couple of rollbacks from earlier

classes who told everything that they could about what to expect during Hell Week. But the information wasn't really useful. Some of the students on the second deck of the barracks, who had completed their First Phase of training and were in the Second Phase and working on diving, came down to the main lounge and talked about what they had experienced.

Jim Alex had rolled back from that class when he bashed his head during rock portage. But that was before his class had gone through Hell Week. Jeremy, Frank Ball, Jim Alex, and the others in their barracks room could only lay in their racks at night and talk about what was coming. It was like seeing the headlights of an oncoming truck and being frozen in the road. You knew it was coming, you knew it was going to hit you, and you knew that it was going to hurt. And there wasn't a damned thing you could do to avoid it.

So that Saturday, it was a fairly subdued group of students that made up Class 78. The word had been put out earlier in the week for everyone in the class to be in the first deck lounge at 1400 hours Saturday. Instructor José Sanchez was going to address them about what would happen the following week.

Everyone gradually gathered in the lounge after noon chow. There was some small talk, mostly about getting enough chairs in the room so everyone could get a seat. It was crowded by the time Instructor Sanchez showed up.

When Reginald Butterworth saw Instructor Sanchez approaching, he called out, "Instructor Sanchez!"

The rest of the class bellowed, "Hooyah, Instructor

Sanchez," just as they had been taught to do over the last month.

Sanchez grinned widely at the class. His short black hair and dark eyes looked out from a face that sat on top of a body that resembled a cinder block standing on end and wrapped in a blue and gold T-shirt. He was their class proctor and looked out for the well-being of the men. They hadn't seen a whole lot of him during their first weeks of training, but now he was here and he wanted to talk to them all.

"Gentlemen, gentlemen," Sanchez said in a soft voice. "I know you are hoping I'm going to tell you a bit about what you should expect next week. Well, I'm going to disappoint you. I'm not going to tell you what to expect to face during your Hell Week. That wouldn't really do anyone any good. But what I will tell you is how to get through it."

The room was packed full of students, but the sound level had dropped to little more than breathing. The only voice was that of the instructor, and each of the students strained to hear every word.

"This is going to be the toughest week of your whole training," Sanchez continued, a very serious look on his face. "It will make or break you as far as this course goes. More students quit during the next week than do for the entire course—it's that hard."

As Sanchez paused to let his words sink in, every student in the room seemed to stop breathing for a moment. Their class proctor said he was going to tell them how to get through the following week, and what was he saying? That it was going to be the hardest thing they were going to face. And most people never did complete it! They quit along the way.

As if reading everyone's mind, Sanchez continued, in a louder voice, "But I will tell you this, gentlemen. I made it through and so did each one of your instructors and every last man in the Teams from the commanding officer to the newest seaman. It can be done!

"And here's your incentive to do it. It's the same thoughts that pulled most of the men in the Teams today through their training. When you get through Hell Week, you will have the chance to become a member of the most elite military fraternity in the United States. That is a brotherhood that will stay with you for the rest of your lives. There is no greater feeling than knowing that the man operating next to you in the Teams is willing to lay his life down for you. And you will come to realize that you will be willing to do the same thing for him.

"And that is not just words, gentlemen. It's only been a couple of years since the Teams have been pulled out of Vietnam. We lost forty-nine of our brothers during that war. But for each one lost, a couple of hundred of the enemy had to go first.

"Just about every one of your instructors has a number of combat tours in Vietnam under his belt. You may think that they are just going to harass you until you can't stand it next week. But it isn't anything personal, gentlemen. Or maybe it's the most personal thing there is.

"Those instructors are going to make sure you have

what it takes to be a SEAL or UDT operator. And the reason they want to be absolutely sure that you can do the job—that you can face anything and keep going— is that they may have to operate right alongside you later in the Teams.

"None of us are professional instructors. This is a duty billet for us, and every man I know who has the job is looking forward to going back to the Teams after his tour here is over. Being here is a chance to give something back to the community that has given us so much over the years. And what we are going to give back is to make sure that only the very best people graduate and go on to the Teams.

"You are going to face the hardest single week of your entire lives starting tomorrow. And you are going to wonder just what it is the instructors are trying to do to you. Well, you don't have to wonder about it at all. You just have to do it.

"What's going to happen to you next week is that you are going to be exposed to pain, cold, noise, hardship, and confusion. The whole week is designed to take you to the very edge of exhaustion, and past it. We are going to re-create a combat environment and put you right in the middle of it. All of you are going to learn just where that grinder earned its name—because it will grind down each and every one of you.

"Those of you who learn that the body has to do what the mind tells it are going to be the ones who are standing on that grinder next weekend. What you have to do is learn to put your body in gear and your brain in neutral. It's simply a case of mind over matter, gentlemen. If you don't mind, well, then what happens to you doesn't matter.

"You have heard a lot of the stories about Hell Week, about the pain, cold, and exhaustion. Well, what can I say? They're true. You are going to go for over five days without sleep, without rest, and you will be constantly on the go. And do you know what you are going to have learned by the end of that week? That you can do it, you can do anything that you set your mind for.

"Do any of you know what happened just six months ago in Washington? Do you?"

A few hands tentatively went up in the air, but very few. The students had been learning that volunteering for things wasn't the best way to get through BUD/S. But Instructor Sanchez seemed to be sincerely asking a question. And he pointed to the class leader, Lieutenant Butterworth, who was one of the few with his hand up.

"Yes, Mr. Butterworth," Sanchez said with his wide grin showing again. "Do you know?"

Standing up, Butterworth said, "I believe what the instructor may be asking about is the awarding last October of the Congressional Medal of Honor to Navy SEAL Michael Thornton for extracting his wounded officer out from under enemy fire in Vietnam the year before."

"Excellent, Mr. Butterworth," Sanchez said, his smile even wider now. "You win a gold star for the day."

Butterworth sat down immediately while a slight chuckle went through the class.

"And let me tell you what Mike Thornton did that caused him to be awarded that distinctive honor," Sanchez continued. "It was a little more than extracting his wounded officer while under enemy fire. He went back toward the enemy when he was told that Lieutenant Tom Norris was hit. In fact, he was told that Norris had been killed. And even if he wasn't already dead, the lieutenant was lying right in a spot where incoming Navy gunfire support was due to land any minute.

"Did that even slow Thornton down? Not for one minute did it. He went back and scooped up Norris's body even while the NVA troops were advancing on his position. He threw back grenades that landed with their fuses burning right at his feet. He cut it a little close with one of those grenades because it went off and peppered his back with fragments.

"Then he ran, carrying Norris under one arm, and firing back at the NVA with his other arm. When the naval gunfire landed behind him, the blast of the five-inch shells blew him off his feet. And he just got up, picked up his lieutenant, and kept going.

"When he finally got to the water, Thornton realized that Norris couldn't swim a stroke. So he inflated his life vest and swam out to sea pushing Norris in front of him. And one of the LDNNs—they were South Vietnamese SEALs—who was with him had been badly wounded and couldn't swim either. So Thornton tossed that man up on his back and carried him out to sea as well.

"Thornton swam for hours, pushing Norris in front of him and towing his LDNN behind him. When they were finally picked up by another Teammate who was in the same junk that had dropped them off the night before, Thornton was just about spent.

"But he never quit. He never quit! When they finally got to that boat, Thornton was so done in that he couldn't pull himself on board. But he had saved two other men's lives besides his own, as well as leading his other LDNNs out to sea and to safety.

"So next week, when you think you're tired, when you think that you can't take another step, swim another yard, or crawl another foot, you remember Mike Thornton. He didn't quit, and men are alive today because of that fact. And he went through exactly the same training on this very beach, in these same buildings, that you gentlemen are going to.

"But there's something else that will get you through Hell Week besides your own will. Remember, you are doing all of this to try and become a member of the Teams. The Teams, gentlemen. That means you are never alone, you always have a Teammate there to help you out. Just like Thornton had to go back and help Norris, next week your Teammates in this room are going to be there to help you out.

"It's when you are absolutely fried, you don't think you can go on and you tell your buddy that you think it's time to quit, that's when your Teammate will help you. He'll pull you up that last inch, tell you that you can make it. And maybe just give you that little extra push that you need just then. And later on, you'll be there to do the same thing for him.

"You can make it, if you have the heart and drive to do so. You each have the physical ability to get through Hell Week and more. If you didn't, you couldn't have made it this far. But things are going to be a lot more than just physical next week. Now you're going to have to prove to each one of us that you won't quit when the going gets hard. No matter what, you won't quit.

"And you want to know something really good? After next week, after you've been secured from Hell Week, each one of you is going to know that there is nothing, nothing, for the rest of your lives that you can't do if you set your mind to it. That's what next week is going to give to you."

There wasn't much to say after that. Instructor Sanchez told the students that they were off the rest of the weekend and that Hell Week would begin on Monday. The lounge was gradually emptied of a mostly subdued but determined group of young men.

The rest of that day was spent by various groups of students kicking back and trying to take it easy. A couple of the rollback students talked about what they had seen. One of them tried to describe what it had been like to listen to the Breakout, the start of Hell Week, for Class 77. But there wasn't a whole lot of detail he could add.

Breakout had come up in the middle of the night, and it had been loud and confusing. There were explosions all over the place, machine gun fire, and a bunch of shouting instructors ordering around a mass of confused students. Within about an hour, they had been marched on down the beach, and that was about it.

What was known for sure was that Hell Week was going to physically and mentally break down each student. They all knew that a lack of sleep was going to be a problem for most of them. But even though a person's body was going to say it couldn't go on anymore, all of the instructors had told them they had to mentally tell themselves that it didn't matter. No matter how tired they would become, they could survive the situation.

Jeremy decided to try and take it easy and not anticipate what was coming. He had made the decision a long time ago that he wasn't going to quit, wouldn't ring that bell, no matter what. The instructors would have to kill him before he would do that. Hell Week was going to be tough, there wasn't much question of that, but it was what he had been waiting for. If he could just get through what was coming, through this great big evolution, then the worst of training would have come and gone.

That wasn't quite true, but Jeremy had no way of knowing it yet. What he did know was that all of the advice from everyone who had actually gone through Hell Week seemed to center on trying to make it one evolution at a time. All anticipation would do is drain you of energy. It didn't do any good to worry about what was coming. Just take it as it came.

Yeah, right, he thought. Easy advice to hear. But really hard advice to follow.

Just hanging around the barracks and the base area quickly wore thin. A number of students had their own vehicles at the base and planned on heading in to San Diego for a good part of the evening. Jeremy and a bunch of his fellows joined in on the little road trip. In San Diego there was a restaurant called the Spaghetti Factory where they could all load up on pasta, all they could eat, at a price even students could afford. Some of the real jocks in the group talked about "carbohydrate loading" and how that could build up a reserve of energy for the week ahead. Jeremy didn't think that any reserve they built up would last until Sunday night, but he did like the food.

But none of the students seemed to like the food at the restaurant as much as Bob Miller. For a little guy, Miller was packing it away almost as quickly as he could fill his plate. Four full platters of pasta and clam sauce disappeared into his bottomless pit of a stomach. And he couldn't have weighed 120 pounds soaking wet. The students knew this, as they had all been soaking wet quite a number of times since training had begun.

So between eating themselves, and watching in awe as Miller packed it away, that Saturday evening flowed on. After finally leaving the restaurant, they weren't sure Miller would be welcome back again for the all-you-can-eat menu. Some of the guys headed off to various bars and night spots around the area. Others piled in the vehicles and headed for what they thought were the livelier night spots downtown. For Jeremy and a fair number of the other students, a return to the barracks and a waiting rack held the most appeal.

Sunday was even more relaxed for most of the students, though everyone in the compound could feel the anticipation building. Jeremy, Jim Alex, and a few others went out for a light jog. Just hanging around the base waiting was building up too much tension for most of them anyway. That afternoon, the theater at the NAB was showing *The Godfather*, so Jeremy, Bob Miller, and Jim Alex joined with a group of the BUD/S students who were heading over to the film.

The day was running down. There wasn't anything else to do but wait in the barracks then and deal with what came when it came. There was relatively little talking as the evening wore on. Each of the students were lost in their own thoughts as they gradually settled in to their racks.

"Hey, Jeremy," Miller called out, breaking the quiet.

"Yeah," White called back, "what do you want?"

"Do me a favor."

"If it means getting you any more food, forget it," Jeremy said. "I don't think I can carry that much."

"No, I mean really," Miller said with sincerity in his voice. "Next week, if I start to fold and try to ring the bell . . ."

"Yes?" Jeremy said, his voice all seriousness now.

"I want you to cut my hand off," Miller said.

"Man," Jim Alex piped in, "that's going to pretty much wipe out your social life, isn't it?"

The laughter that sounded in the room after that was the last sound heard for a while. In spite of their excitement and anticipation, most of the students slowly slipped into sleep.

## Chapter Ten
### 1998, Sunday Night

Things were a whole lot different for Jeremy White, being on the instructors' side of training. As a student he just had to complete the course, which seemed like quite a lot at the time. Now, as the Command master chief, he was learning all of the complicated mechanizations that went into running the schoolhouse.

Hell Week was the big hurdle that every student saw as the watershed event of BUD/S. Master Chief White had to not only make sure that it remained as tough as possible—to uphold the quality of the graduating students—he also had to keep it as safe as possible. And along the way, higher command would like it if he could increase the number of students who actually made it through the week.

White had a lot of help from his experienced instructor staff on keeping Hell Week tough as well as safe. When restrictions were added to certain exercises, cold exposures, or events that had to be changed—usually for good reason—the instructors would always rise to the task. The staff was determined to make sure that the students had to work and earn the passage of every evolution. They excelled at creating new obstacles for the students to overcome when an old one was eliminated or made too easy.

As for increasing the number of graduating students, it was an ongoing problem. White was using his motivational speeches and the constant example he set for the students as his method of cutting down on the quitters. For the time being, that would have to be enough, as far as he was concerned. Cutting back on difficulty was a nonstarter for him. Quality far outweighed quantity in the greater scheme of things for Master Chief Jeremy White.

The safety factor was another thing entirely. What the SEALs did in their everyday operations and training was dangerous—there was no question of that. The ocean was an unforgiving environment. The slightest mistake on the part of anyone who dared to operate in the depths and the sea could snatch their life away.

But at BUD/S the danger had to be contained, controlled, and prevented whenever possible. Things might look almost deadly to the students, so dangerous that they couldn't see how to even complete an evolution. If a man was afraid of explosions racking the area around him, it was a lot better to weed that person out at BUD/S than in the field during a hot combat operation. But in fact the explosives the students were exposed to were controlled shots in very limited circumstances. White considered it a good thing that the class as a whole was usually so dingy by the time they reached that evolution that they couldn't see how careful the instructors were.

And it was his instructor staff, White knew, who would be crucial in creating another class full of future SEALs. Hell Week ran twenty-four hours a day for six days. That broke a day down into three shifts of eight hours each. For some shifts, the evolutions were particularly hard and dangerous. Evolutions such as the rock portage needed extra eyes and experience on hand to keep solid control of the situation. For those shifts, White had to add extra instructors. Other times, when the students were doing "easier" tasks, such as just paddling over long distances, the shift could have fewer instructors.

White had to keep ahead of the paperwork when it came to balancing the assignment of his instructors and their experience to the job at hand. There would always be four instructors on duty, with a corpsman available immediately on site at all times. But some of the shifts could be broken in half, creating a four-hour assignment instead of eight, which permitted White to conserve his instructor staff.

The students would have been astonished to know how hard the instructors worked during Hell Week. While undergoing evolutions, they could only see their own misery. But the instructors had to constantly move, keeping all of the students under control and in relative safety. At the beginning of Hell Week there were a lot of students to watch all at once. As the week continued, and students decided that the program wasn't for them and rang out, those numbers dropped.

Up to seventy percent of a class might drop out during Hell Week, and normally about forty percent quit during the first few days. But there had been a few classes in the past where no one rang out during the entire week. It was rare, but it could happen.

White had all of his instructors lined up and assigned to their shifts. The ratio of instructors to students wasn't high, but it was well within acceptable levels. And there were a number of instructors on standby for each of the shifts, in case his motivation speech took hold and there were fewer drops than usual. More students meant they would need more instructors on shift, which was not a problem White would mind dealing with.

With the paperwork done, White was ready to go out and join the instructors for Breakout. The beginning of Hell Week was an intentional and carefully choreographed scene of apparent madness and obvious confusion for the students. Simply put, for the next half hour or so the students would not be able to do anything right.

Mixed orders would be given by the instructors, most of which would make little or no sense. And the orders wouldn't be spoken, they would be shouted, screamed at the students, as the instructors made themselves heard over the blasting of machine guns firing blanks and the detonations of artillery and hand grenade simulators.

Just outside, Instructor Rawlings—a tall, wide, black man with a big grin, deep voice, and almost glowing bald head—knocked on the door to Master Chief White's office.

"Come in," White called out.

Pushing the door open, Rawlings held out one of the two cups of coffee he held in one big hand. "Something hot before the party starts, Master Chief?"

"Thanks, Rawlings," White said as he accepted the proffered cup. "Everything set?"

"All on schedule, Master Chief," Rawlings said, and took a sip from his own steaming cup. "Ah," he said with obvious relish, his deep voice booming. "There's just something fine about a nice cold Sunday evening, a hot cup of coffee, and the anticipation of scaring the crap out of a whole slew of students."

"Now, you're sure I don't have to force you to be part of this first shift?" White said, sarcasm dripping from his voice. "I'd hate to see you not enjoy your work."

In answer, Rawlings's eyes closed to slits, his face tilted up, and a wide, closed-mouth grin spread from ear to ear. Rawlings considered himself to be an angel among his lesser mortals. That his chest and shoulder muscles were so big that he looked like he was wearing football padding underneath his T-shirt took something away from the angelic image. He would have been a huge, black, dangerous-as-hell angel.

"So, Master Chief," he said, "just how many students do you think are asleep right now?"

As White zipped up his blue windbreaker he replied, "In five minutes, will it really matter?"

"Not really," Rawlings said, his smile shining across his face.

As the two instructors left the office, they entered the surreal world of the drastically changed grinder area. Most of the bright lighting had been cut back considerably. Instead, a weird glow was supplied by lines strung up around the compound. Dangling from the lines were dozens of green and orange chemlite chemical light sticks.

To further suffuse the glow of the light sticks and add to the unearthly and confusing appearance of the grinder, two fog machines were spreading their output across the area. The ground-hugging fog lifted and swirled about wherever an instructor walked through it. And the area was full of instructors.

This would be the time that the maximum number of students were being pushed through the smallest area. A large shift of instructors was needed to control the flood of stampeding humanity that would soon come boiling out of the barracks.

At the two southern corners of the compound, the fog machines poured out their chemical smoke. "Damn," Master Chief White said as he and Instructor Rawlings walked past the machines, "that smoke tastes like badly done cotton candy."

"It does have kind of a fruity sweet smell and taste, doesn't it?" Rawlings answered.

"I thought there would be more of it," White observed.

"There will be," Rawlings said. "There was trouble with one of the machines, and they only got it up and running a few minutes ago. But don't worry, the smoke will build up fast."

"Colored smoke grenades would be even faster," White said.

"Yeah," Rawlings responded. "They were used during my Breakout too. But with all of the buildings around here now, it's just too hard to clean up after using them."

Two metal drums were standing near the fog machines, each one surrounded by a layer of sandbags. A safe distance from the drums were wooden cases of M116A1 hand grenade simulators and the larger M115A2 artillery simulators. Inside the cardboard bodies of the simulators was enough flash powder composition to make a thundering explosion and brilliant flash of light. In fact, the hand grenade simulators had been used to make the flash-crash stun grenades the Teams had first used back in the early 1980s. The artillery simulators made the same shattering noise and light, but with them, the explosion followed a two- to four-second earsplitting whistle, like the sound an artillery shell made coming in.

Instructors stood by the drums, ready to toss the simulators in to create a lot of battle noise and flash effects. Around the compound, several instructors had M60 machine guns at the ready, blank adaptors on the muzzles. They had already loaded the belts of ammunition, and that together with the spare ammo standing by would add a nice touch of machine-gun fire to the scene the students would have to deal with.

Other instructors had fire hoses ready to wash down

the students and introduce them to a level of cold they would have to encounter all week. And just in case the hoses couldn't get a student wet enough, several rubber boats were standing by, filled with water. The students who were told to cross the boats would have to do so by ducking under the water and moving from one end to the other, underneath the inflated rubber seats in the boats.

Inside the barracks, several instructors held M80 firecrackers and had trash cans at their feet. At the nod from the master chief, the signal was passed among the instructors. Firecrackers were lit and tossed into the cans. Whistles were blown and orders screamed for the students to wake up and fall out on the grinder wearing a bewildering array of uniform parts. The machine guns opened fire, simulators screamed and detonated, and the shouts of "Breakout!" were bellowed all over the compound. Bullhorns were used liberally by the instructors to increase the already high volume of their shouts and orders.

"Oh, I'll bet the people in the condos are not pleased," Master Chief White said to no one in particular as a grin appeared momentarily on his face. The grin vanished immediately, since it would not do for the master chief to be smiling during Breakout. Then he too joined in the shouting and ordering of the milling students as their Hell Week began.

The students had no way of knowing it, but within a few minutes of Hell Week beginning, every item of uniform clothing they were issued would be soaking wet, and it would remain that way for the balance of the week. Sand would soon be added to those uniforms by the simple expedient of having the students roll, crawl, and otherwise move through the beach. Many of the instructors still bore scars on their bodies where the sand, wet abrasive uniforms, and gear of their Hell Week wore through their skins. Many of these students would soon be developing their own crop of sores and abrasions.

Just about all of the students had fallen asleep by 1800 or 1900 hours. Their sleep was suddenly shattered by the sound of explosions and machine-gun fire. Noise roared through the hallways as weapons were fired and detonations took place inside the barracks. To the sound of M60 machine guns and M80 firecrackers, room doors banged open as instructors shouted orders.

"Fall out! Fall out!" they bellowed. "Everyone get the hell out of your racks!"

It was one minute past midnight. Hell Week had officially begun. The first obstacle the students had to overcome was surviving Breakout.

The instructor who knocked open the door to the room where Jeremy and his fellow students were sleeping had the added volume from shouting his orders through a bullhorn. "Get up and fall out, you maggots!" he bellowed. "Uniform of the day is a boot on your right foot, a sock on your left foot. T-shirts, soft cover, and swim shorts. Have your left swim fin in your right hand and your left hand empty. You have twenty seconds, maggots! Fall out!"

The room was a melee of colliding students and emptying wall lockers. Gear was snatched up, tossed out, and piled onto the floor as the students tried to make sense of the strange "uniform" they were ordered to wear.

"Was that a boot on your left or right foot?" a voice called out over the din echoing through the room.

"Who the hell knows, just get moving," another voice shouted back angrily.

Piling out of the barracks, the rushing students found themselves in a weird kind of hell.

Green and red smoke was drifting across the grinder, generated by M18 colored smoke grenades burning at the sides of the compound, though none of the students noticed that fact. One of the instructors was blasting away with an M60 machine gun, right over some of the students' heads, the flame of the muzzle blast appearing in the dim light. Several students ducked out of the way of what they thought were bullets being fired over their heads, and not very high over their heads at that.

Thundering explosions and flashes of light sounded out across the grinder. And the instructors were everywhere at once, shouting orders and spraying out streams of cold water from hoses.

Instructor Hawke stopped the mob of students that Jeremy found himself part of.

"What the hell kind of uniform is that, you maggots?" Hawke shouted.

Before any one of the students could say a word, Hawke cut them off.

"Too late, you miserable bunch of garbage," he growled. "On your bellies and knock out twenty."

As the students hit the ground and started doing push-ups, Hawke sprayed a stream of ice cold water out across them.

"Faster, faster, you worthless maggots!" he shouted as he played the water from the hose, soaking all of them.

When the group of students finished, they shouted in unison, "Hooyah, Instructor Hawke!"

"That was a pathetic display," Hawke screamed. "I can't stand to look at the sight of such miserable humanity. You aren't even maggots. At least they eat garbage and do the world some good. Get out of my sight, you worthless piles of shit! I want you all to go hit that surf and become a sugar cookie. MOVE!"

Jeremy and his fellows jumped to their feet and ran to the surf a few hundred yards away. Other students were either passing them, going back to the grinder, well-soaked and covered with sand, or they too were headed for the surf zone and the beach sand.

The very cold ocean water caused a few students to gasp, but they didn't slow down. There were even instructors by the surf zone, making sure the students followed the directions to become well-coated sugar cookies.

Back at the grinder, other instructors were bending over the students who were scattered all over the compound, screaming out incomprehensible orders. The students were writhing on the ground, performing a variety of exercises according to any instructor's whim. Others were up and running back and forth from the barracks to the grinder.

"Uniform jackets and soft caps," an instructor would shout at them.

"Right foot bare, left foot swim fin," another would bellow.

"Run! Run!" all of them seemed to shout. "You're not moving, maggot!" rang out across the grinder.

No matter what the students did, it was wrong. They couldn't get the orders straight and move fast enough to satisfy any of the instructors. And each error cost them some kind of punishment. Jeremy was told to swim under the seats of a water-filled IBS at the side of the grinder. His infraction: he had the one sock he was supposed to wear on the wrong foot.

The shock of the ice cold water shocked his system as he dove into the boat and scrambled along its bottom. If he had been able to notice, he might have seen the ice cubes floating in the water, placed their by caring instructors who didn't want their charges getting overheated. But at least the icy water washed the sand out of his eyes and face.

While some of the instructors got up close and personal with some of the trainees on the ground, shouting at them from a distance that seemed an inch or less, Chief Packard lifted a bullhorn to his lips and issued a new set of orders.

"All right, you maggots, listen up!" he said. "You

people are not putting out! So it looks like you may need a little encouragement."

Hearing the instructor's catch phrase, "You people aren't putting out," meant they were going to get hammered with some kind of exercise. Chief Max Packard had not earn the nickname Maximum Max for his preference for short exercise periods. And his orders continued to ring out around the dazed students.

"You will fall into the barracks and change uniforms," Chief Packard announced. "I will see each one of you back here wearing fatigue pants, T-shirts, one swim fin, one boot, and your face mask. You have twenty five seconds, maggots! MOVE!"

Still trying to puzzle out the bewildering uniforms, the students scrambled up from the ground and ran into the barracks. The open doorway immediately became a choke point for the students who were running in and the rushing students who were trying to get out. Fatigue uniforms, boots, and swimming gear were quickly scattered around all of the rooms. It became a matter of trying to just grab up what you could, rather than to try and sort out your own gear and clothes.

In seconds Jeremy and a bunch of his fellow students had tried to match their uniforms to the orders they had been given.

"Was that boot on the right or left foot?" a voice shouted up from the confusion.

"Who the fuck knows?" another answered. "Just move!"

The conversation was punctuated by a burst of machine-gun fire nearby and several loud explosions.

Though none of the students could hear it, there was another sound in the air: that of a brass ship bell being rung nearby. Hell Week was already beginning to rack up its casualties from among the students of Class 78.

Rushing outside, most of the students had on some semblance of the bizarre uniform ordered by Maximum Max. At least all of them were wearing the swimmer's face masks. But they were far too slow in leaving the building and getting back to the grinder. When they arrived, a disappointed-looking Chief Packard was standing there with a stopwatch in hand.

"People, people," Chief Packard said softly through his bullhorn while shaking his head. "I give you a simple order, and plenty of time to carry it out. And what do you do? You ignore me. What am I to do?"

The fact that Chief Packard was speaking in a soft voice sent chills through some of the students standing rigidly at attention. They were almost certain that the instructors weren't allowed to just outright kill them. But the explosions, shouting, smoke, and gunfire were having its desired effect. A number of the students were badly shaken, and Hell Week wasn't ten minutes old.

"Drop!" Chief Packard shouted.

Every one of the students hit the ground flat, almost diving forward. With their palms flat down on the ground and their legs stretched out behind them, the students lay there waiting. They didn't have to wait long.

"On your backs!" Chief Packard shouted.

The students flipped over immediately.

"Flutter kicks, gentlemen," Chief Packard said. "Start knocking them out."

There was no cadence being called, so each student just started by lifting his heels six inches off the ground. With each count, they lifted one leg and then the other in a kicking motion. The students started sounding out, "One-two-three-ONE, one-two-three-TWO . . ."

As they lay on the ground doing flutter kicks, the hoses never stopped spraying ice cold water across them. Several instructors stood by to give some individual students "private" instruction. One of these students was Ensign "Zeus" Kozuska.

"Come now, Mr. Kozuska, you must set an example for these men if you intend to lead them," Instructor Lubi said in an easy tone to the big man lying on the ground.

Instructor Lubi, the fairly slight Filipino instructor, could run the class into the ground, as he had proven over and over, without ever seeming to break a sweat. And he almost always spoke in a reasonable tone, as he was now. But he would have seemed a lot more reasonable at that moment, as he cajoled Zeus, if he hadn't been standing on the man's stomach with both feet and looking down at him while he did his flutter kicks.

Zeus just grimaced and continued his flutter kicks as Instructor Lubi stood on him.

"Oh, I am sorry, Mr. Kozuska," Lubi said apologetically. "I have not been allowing you to properly lead your men. Allow me to correct that."

And Instructor Lubi stepped off Ensign Kozuska's stomach. Immediately, Instructor Nick Holmes took up where Lubi left off and stood on Kozuska's stomach. The ensign's flutter kicks faltered for a moment, then continued at a noticeably different pace. Instructor Holmes was almost twice the size of Instructor Lubi, and he too was making life momentarily very difficult for student officer Richard Kozuska.

The torturous exercise in the straining conditions seemed to go on forever. But the instructors only let it continue for a few minutes. They didn't want the students to lose their momentum, or confusion.

"On your feet!" Chief Packard suddenly bellowed. And once again the students were sent back into the barracks for another change of "uniform." They were given a very generous twenty seconds to complete their change and return to the grinder.

In spite of the fact that the students actually shaved several seconds over their turnover time in leaving and returning to the grinder, they were far too late to satisfy the instructor staff. This time push-ups were the chosen exercise. For those students too slow in dropping to the ground and assuming the position, the ice water in the IBS awaited them.

As a new entertainment, several of the students had their face masks filled with water by the instructors. Then they had to continue doing push-ups. Jeremy didn't have to concern himself with a mask full of water on his face. His only special attention involved a large instructor placing a foot in the middle of his back during the push-ups.

Another set of shouted orders was followed by another mad scramble to reach the barracks, change, and return. This continued while the M60s fired, smoke floated through the area, and the echo of simulators exploding was not allowed to die away.

On one of their returns from the barracks, Chief Packard had a new item for them to learn.

"Drop!" he shouted.

Each of the students immediately hit the ground and lay ready for what would come next.

"Recover!" Chief Packard ordered.

All of the students immediately scrambled to their feet and stood at attention. Slower students were given added reasons for speeding up from the ever attentive instructors circling the area like a school of sharks.

"Drop!"

"Recover!"

"Drop!"

"Recover!"

It went on like this for several moments. A couple of students decided that the program apparently wasn't for them. They stood and slowly walked to the waiting bell in the northeast corner of the compound. Three sideways tugs of the rope, red helmet liners dropping, and they were done.

For the most part, the rest of the students didn't even notice their ex-classmates final moments at BUD/S. All of those on the grinder were desperately trying to move fast enough to satisfy Maximum Max.

Their attempts seemed to make an impression of Chief Packard.

"On your feet!" he bellowed. That order usually signaled the end of an exercise. But the Hell Week evolution that was Breakout was far from over. There was a new skill the students now had to learn.

"It is time for whistle drills, maggots!" Chief Packard said in a very loud but clear voice. "You will follow my directions to the letter. What you are about to learn may just save your worthless lives one day."

"At the sound of one whistle blast," Chief Packard continued, "you will immediately drop flat on the ground, facing away from the sound of the whistle. You will cross your legs at the ankles, cover the backs of your heads with your hands, and keep your mouths open.

"This is the position you would take if there was an artillery round coming in to your position," Chief Packard explained. "Your hands will keep your head from bouncing off the ground, your open mouth will keep your ears from blowing out, and crossing your legs will help save what you so jokingly call a set of balls.

*TWEEET* . . . the whistle Chief Packard had been holding shrilly sounded.

Most of the students hit the ground in something like the proper position. The ones who didn't quickly received correction from the circling instructors. As the students lay on the cold, wet grinder, Chief Packard continued his instructions.

"When you hear two blasts of the whistle," Packard said, "you will immediately start crawling toward the sound of the whistle. At the sound of three whistle blasts, you will immediately recover."

Three distinct, loud whistle blasts sounded out. The students tried to quickly scramble to their feet in spite of their awkward starting positions.

"Too slow, maggots!" Chief Packard growled. "Far too slow."

One whistle blast sounded—they dropped to the ground and assumed the blast position.

Three whistle blasts sounded—up to their feet they scrambled.

One blast—down.

Three blasts—up.

One blast.

Three blasts.

One blast.

Then two blasts. Some of the confused students just froze in place on the ground, forgetting what they were supposed to do. The quicker ones followed the example set by their fellow students. The slower ones received immediate correction from an instructor. The IBS had its waters disturbed as the students continued.

Three blasts.

One blast, then quickly two more as the students reached the ground.

Three blasts.

This went on for an eternity, or five minutes by the clock, depending on whether you were a student in the class or an instructor. Finally, three blasts sounded and echoed away.

The students stood gasping for air. But the pressure from the instructors didn't let up for a moment. While they had been conducting whistle drills, the smoke from the burning colored smoke grenades had begun to dissipate. The acrid burning gunpowder smell from the grenades was still in the air, but they could see that the smoke was mostly gone.

The M60s had finally stopped firing, and there had only been the occasional artillery simulator detonating to punctuate their whistle drills.

"Gentlemen," Chief Packard said. When he was polite, the students knew there was something to worry about. "You have three minutes to fall out to the barracks and return. You will be wearing a full fatigue uniform, boots, and soft cover," by which he meant a cap. "You will fall out back on the grinder and form up into boat crews," he continued. "Now move, maggots!" he shouted as he pulled out his stopwatch.

There was a dash for the barracks again as the students tried to put together a complete uniform from the soggy mess each of their rooms had turned into. As Jeremy struggled to locate a full set of his boots, he didn't notice that there were now only four students in the room. Out on the grinder, Henry Ward and Ed Franks had added their helmets to the line growing next to the bell.

As the students started out of the barracks and headed for the grinder, one loud shrill blast of a whistle sounded out. The students hit the ground, covered their heads, and crossed their ankles. Even the slower students who had been momentarily confused quickly followed the example set by the others.

"Shit!" Jeremy cursed as he sat on his rack trying to lace up his boots. Bob Miller was the only other person in the room with him now, only he was pulling on his fatigue jacket as the whistle sounded.

"Better safe than sorry," Miller said, hitting the deck and assuming the blast position. Jeremy abandoned securing his boots and hit the deck only moments behind Miller. Two loud whistle blasts sounded out. Jeremy and Miller crawled out of the room on their elbows, and found themselves in a winding line of students crawling toward the grinder.

Moving like a badly arthritic snake with a spine broken in dozens of places, the students of Class 78 gradually made their way to the grinder. When Jeremy and Miller were only halfway to the grinder from the barracks, three loud whistle blasts sounded out. Scrambling to their feet, most of the students made a dash for the grinder. Those few who weren't certain which way to go were quickly moved along in the mob.

"Move it, maggots!" sounded out from more than one instructor's throat.

"Fall in, boat crews!" another shouted.

The students ran about, falling into the crews that had been formed only a few weeks before. Collisions took place as students banged into one another. But none of them, not one student, made the horrible mistake of bumping into an instructor. The hell that would rain down on a lowly maggot who actually touched one of the instructor's godlike persons would be too terrible to even imagine.

The boat crews were now confusing. Even more so for the coxswains of the crews. They were the officers and leading petty officers responsible for maintaining an accounting for each man in their crew—and there were a lot of students missing.

As the coxswains tried to make sense of the situation, Jeremy joined up with his boat crew. The class had gone from twelve full boat crews of six men each to less than ten full crews. In fact, some of the crews standing about had only a few men in them, and some didn't even have coxswains.

The answer to the missing-men question lay in the line of helmets extending away from the bell in the corner of the grinder. Though knocked a bit out of line, twenty-two new helmets lay on the ground. The class had fallen from seventy-two students to only fifty within the first hour of Hell Week. This was a fact not unnoticed by the instructors.

"Fall in, you maggots!" Chief Packard shouted through his megaphone. "You have taken up far too much of my time. Drop and give me twenty! Coxswains report!"

While the entire class dropped and started pumping out the push-ups ordered by Chief Packard, other instructors walked about the mob, bending over to question coxswains about their crews. The fact that most of the coxswains couldn't account for their men did not seem to please the instructors. As the students completed their twenty push-ups, Chief Packard did not recover them but left them in the front leaning rest position while he approached the class leader.

"Mr. Butterworth, recover!" Chief Packard shouted.

As Lieutenant Butterworth quickly snapped to his feet, Chief Packard growled at the rest of the class.

"The rest of you maggots can just remain in that position while I have a little conversation with your class leader here.

"Mr. Butterworth," Chief Packard said. "You seem to be missing a large number of men."

"Hooyah, Chief Packard," Butterworth said, there being no other answer he could give.

"You seem to be unable to retain your men, Mr. Butterworth," Chief Packard said in a deceptively soft tone. "Your leadership just may manage to make the instructors and me very happy."

Butterworth didn't say a word and just stared straight ahead.

"You do understand, do you not, Mr. Butterworth, that at the present rate, all of the class will have quit before breakfast is even served. My instructors and I will have an easy week of it once you and the rest of your class are gone. So why don't you save us all a little time, Mr. Butterworth. Lead your men over to the bell and ring out first."

"NO, Chief Packard," Butterworth said very firmly. "I will not."

"Oh you won't?" Packard said softly. "YOU WON'T?" he shouted at Butterworth, leaning in to within an inch of the young officer's face.

"You are a waste of my time, maggot!" Packard

shouted, intentionally spraying spittle with each t-sound. "Let's see if you can even manage to lead the rest of this rotting pile of corpses to their boats!"

"Hooyah, Chief Packard," Butterworth said as he remained ramrod straight. Turning to the rest of the class, he shouted, "Class 78, fall out on your boats!"

Boat crews were smaller, but they all had an IBS assigned to them. As the staggering group of students moved to the boat rack, they didn't notice the change in the situation. In fact, the change was fairly slight, the guns and explosions gone for the moment. They had completed their first evolution of Hell Week. Class 78 had gone through Breakout.

## Chapter Twelve

The sudden dam burst of students quitting during Breakout had changed the boat crews drastically. Once the students had gathered around the IBS rack in the crews, the instructors could see just how many crews were too short of men to be able to function. Some shouting and shuffling the students about, liberally sprinkled with push-ups and sugar cookies when the instructors were dissatisfied with a student's response, led to the assembly of eight boat crews, most with a full complement.

Boat Crew IV had only lost one man during Breakout. But Bob Miller's pre–Hell Week crew, Boat Crew IX, had almost completely disappeared. So Miller was assigned to Boat Crew IV in place of Howard Johns, who was already packing his gear and leaving the compound. Among the mostly beefy guys of Boat Crew IV, Miller looked even smaller than his slight stature rated.

Jeremy had been lucky about one thing so far during Breakout: he and his swim buddy Jim Alex happened to be assigned to the same barracks room. So when they were run in and out of the barracks to try and satisfy the instructors' maddening orders, they at least had to go to the same room. Most of the other students had their swim buddies in different rooms, and it had been very easy to lose track of each other during the mass confusion of Breakout.

And when you were separated from your swim buddy, the instructors pounced. Punishments were given out liberally, along with sprays from the water hose and trips to the surf zone or the water-filled IBSes. Boat crews had been badly separated, but now they were finally back together and moving out. The trouble was, they were moving toward that cold Pacific Ocean.

Now the crews had to move their boats and start their next evolution. Things had only slowed down in comparison to Breakout. The instructors were still shouting for everyone to speed up and get things moving. And no matter what the students did, it still couldn't be good enough for the instructors.

Shuffling boat crews around to fill in empty slots didn't change the basic ways the crews functioned. Each of the students knew what to do and how to do it. They just didn't know how to do things well enough to satisfy the instructors.

When they were ordered to "Up boat," of course the crews didn't pick up the boats fast enough, or get them on their heads straight enough. And they certainly didn't move quickly enough. So the instructors told all the boat crews to switch to the extended arm carry. This meant that instead of the heavy boat grinding down on top of their heads, crunching their necks into their shoulders in the process, they got to lift the weight up. Of course, the only way to lift the boat up was to push it into the air with your arms. So now each man had his share of the almost three-hundred-pound rubber boat bearing down on his uplifted arms.

The extended arm carry made sure that each man carried his share of the boat. The shorter members of a boat crew had to push up just as hard as the taller students did. And it put a hellacious amount of stress on each man's arms. The students wore out much faster using the extended arm carry, which was the instructors' objective.

But the instructors had a plan to make the extended arm carry much easier for the students—at least the ones who survived Hell Week: they would build up the muscles in the students' upper bodies and arms. The best way to accomplish this feat was through the liberal use of push-ups. As the students got down to the beach sand and away from the blacktop surface of the grinder, the instructors introduced them to a new fun way to build up their muscles through exercise—boat push-ups.

The students didn't have to push up on the boat. Instead, they rested their feet across the rubber tube sides of the boats. "Put your feet on the tubes and your paddles across the backs of your hands," Chief Packard shouted. "That paddle had better not touch the sand, maggots, or you will all start again from the beginning!"

Individual instructors scurried about to make certain that each student did the exercise to the best of his ability, which wouldn't be good enough in any case. Ensign Kozuska, who was strong enough to juggle anvils, by the look of him, was singled out by Chief Packard as he circled the struggling students.

"Maggot Kozuska!" Packard's voice rang out from his bullhorn. "You have allowed your paddle to touch my beach! Class, begin again, courtesy of Maggot Kozuska."

In spite of the fact that Zeus had not done anything wrong, the class began their struggle with the new push-ups again. This would not be the only time an instructor would put the blame for a class's punishment on a student he'd singled out. It was just the first time it had happened that morning. The instructors didn't consider war to be a fair game, so there was no reason that the training for war should be fair either.

There were enough instructors around to have one for every boat crew. And they watched the students' struggles carefully. There was nothing else for them to do but watch every individual, and dish out whatever abuse they felt that individual needed at the moment.

Bending over, the instructors would come up to a student and look him directly in the eye, from a distance of about an inch away. Then the lectures would start.

Each student was a maggot, according to the instructors. No, they were lower than that, they would have to work up to be a pussy. The instructor selected an individual and they told him in no uncertain terms that he wasn't going to make it. None of them were going to make it. But the student the instructor was talking to would drag the rest of his boat crew down with him. He just couldn't handle it. So why didn't he just ring the fucking bell and save all of the heartache he was causing for the rest of the boat crew?

Anything wrong with a student's uniform or gear was reason for an instructor to pounce and cause the rest of the boat crew to suffer additional punishment. This had the effect of causing each of the members in a boat crew to watch out for the rest of the crew. That simple act of self-preservation was a start to creating a better team. The students would learn to take care of each other, even more so than themselves.

Finally, the new push-ups were completed to the satisfaction of the instructors. Or they just became bored and wanted to move on to something new. It was the latter impression that they wanted to give Class 78.

"Hell Week is simply a case of mind over matter, you maggots," one of the instructors shouted over his bullhorn. "We don't mind and you don't matter. Now—UP BOATS!"

Boat crews dropped their feet from the side tube of the boat and scrambled to their positions. With men on either side of what was quickly becoming a hated chunk of equipment, the heavy IBS was heaved up and again placed on top of the heads of the trainees. A conditioning run was called for, and the agony of the boat on top of their heads was increased by the students now having to run with it.

No description could ever capture what the weight of a rubber boat grinding down on your head actually felt like. At least, none of the students were able to really describe it later, though the memory would stay with them for the rest of their lives.

Even in the bigger boat crews, each individual had fifty pounds riding on the top of his head. And the students' arms couldn't relieve any of the pressure since they were too busy just hanging on to the damned boat to keep it in place. But the weight bore down. You felt it first as just a hard pressure on the top of your head, and then as the pressure quickly built, it seemed to drive the back of your jaws together, and you quickly found yourself gritting your teeth at the weight.

Then there was the run that bounced that weight on the top of your head. In spite of the noise of the instructors shouting, you could "hear" the grinding sound of the bones in your neck every time your head moved with that weight on top of it. The sound was startling, and at least the noise the instructors were making could be used to block it out.

Everything had to be blocked out: the pain, the noise, the stress—everything. The only thing that mattered was to keep going, place one foot in front of the other, and just get through the evolution.

And this was just the first night.

As the run went on, the pain increased and so did the strain. Now each movement of a student's legs told him that his ankles did not like what he was doing to them. Each impact of the rubber boat on the top of his head, or the side, front, or back, as the run caused the IBS to jounce around, each and every movement of it, could be felt not just in the neck, but all the way down the student's spine.

And the sand dragged against the student's legs and feet. But the instructors trotted along beside the struggling mass of students, seemingly oblivious to their pain. Only they weren't ignoring it, but reminding the students at every opportunity that relief was just a bell ring away. And the bell was following the students along.

In the back of a navy-gray pickup truck, the instructors had placed another ship's bell, identical to the one standing vigil next to the line of helmets on the grinder. This bell also shone like a gold icon, and it was carefully braced and supported by a wooden framework.

Finally, the grueling "conditioning" run reached its conclusion. The command to "Down boats" caused as much pain as it did relief. It was hard just to lift up the boats enough for each of the crew members to slip their heads out from underneath that black rubber torture device. While they desperately struggled to maintain control of their boat and try to lower it in some kind of unison, their bodies let them know just what they thought of the evolution.

The body can speak to its owner in a variety of ways, but the only body language the students heard was pain. Necks ached from the release of pressure, as did shoulders. Knees and ankles added their measure of pain to the overall misery. But the students had to ignore anything their bodies said. That was the real start of the mental discipline of Hell Week.

Now another part of the discipline, dealing with a new challenge, was in front of the students. The instructors had ended the conditioning run with the boats. But they stopped right in front of the obstacle course.

The evolution in front of them was to run the O-course, something they had already done a number of times. Only this time they would run the course as boat crews—and they would be taking their boats with them.

The first time the students of Class 78 were introduced to the O-course, an instructor had shown them how they were to negotiate each obstacle. This time they had to face the course in a whole new way. They weren't told how to get the boat through the course, only that they had to do it.

Some of the obstacles were obvious. The boat crew had to pull, drag, lift, and push their IBS over what was in front of them. A simple enough task, until they tried to do it. Manhandling that three-hundred-pound deadweight of an IBS was a struggle. At one point a couple of students might be trying to pull the boat over an obstacle while the rest of their crew tried to push it. Balancing with the ungainly load was almost impossible. But almost didn't mean they couldn't do what was asked of them. It just meant that it was very very hard.

Some of the boat crews found the high wall the hardest obstacle. They had to push the boat up until it reached the top of the wall. Then some of the members of the crew held the boat up while their crewmates clambered up the wall of the climbing ropes and tried to pull the boat over the top. Once they got the boat to the top of the wall, they had to lower it back down. Simply dropping the IBS was forbidden by the instructors, on pain of further punishment. And then they would have to do the obstacle over again anyway.

The barb-wire crawl forced the students to shove the boat along under the wires. A few members of the boat crew could get in front of the IBS and try to pull it along, while also attempting to dig away the sand that the boat pushed up in front of it. And their biggest worry on that obstacle was getting the boat under the wire and pushed along without letting any of the barbs dig into the rubber and tear the boat. More than one student bled and left a little of himself behind in the way of skin and blood while trying to get the IBS through the barb-wire crawl.

None of the obstacles were easy. Some were a little less hard than others. And all along the course, the instructors were there to voice encouragement and suggestions. But almost all of the suggestions involved just giving up and ringing out.

"Volunteer in and volunteer out, gentlemen," an instructor said softly through his bullhorn. "Things aren't going to get easier. This is the easy part. You can't hack it, so just ring the bell. Why make it harder on yourself and your boat crew? Just quit. Quit. Quit . . ."

But no one stopped. This time, the psychological warfare of the instructors wasn't working as it had during Breakout. The students struggled, the students tried, and the students moved on.

But two of the daunting obstacles to be overcome

were the cargo net and the tower. The cargo net stretched up, fully supported along the edges for all of its length. Some of the students had trouble with the height of the net before. Climbing to the top, swinging over, and climbing back down had pushed against their fear of heights before. Now they had to do the same thing in the dark, while taking a three-hundred-pound boat along with them.

But they tried. Boat crew members climbed up on the net and pulled on the towing bridle, a length of rope that extended out from the bow of the IBS. Others climbed with their legs and one arm while pulling the boat along with their other hand. And still more climbed up from underneath, pushing the boat up with their hands, head, or shoulders. Whatever worked, whatever they could do to try and get that damned boat up the net, each man did.

And sometimes it didn't work. More than one IBS came crashing down, to impact in the sand. And the instructors immediately forced the losing boat crew to do push-ups, sugar cookies, or flutter kicks. Then they had to start again.

With tremendous effort, Boat Crew II had gotten their IBS up to the top of the cargo net faster than any of the other crews had. Ensign Kozuska was pushing, pulling, and dragging at the boat more than any other member of his crew. The seasoned instructors watched the spectacle and some just shook their heads. Instead of leading his men, Kozuska was trying to accomplish everything himself. That much effort would burn him out long before Hell Week was over.

At the top of the cargo net, Boat Crew II had their IBS teetering on the top, ready to go over. As some of the crew scrabbled over the top of the net to help lower the boat, Kozuska tried to hold it steady. But when one man brushed against the IBS in his haste to get over the net, it proved too much for the precariously balanced boat. It tilted over and began to slide. It was on its way to the ground, all three hundred pounds of it. And Boat Crew II would have to do the whole obstacle again.

But Kozuska wasn't going to accept that. With his legs secured to the rope at the top of the net, he hooked his arm through the heavy hawser that stretched across the top of the obstacle. Grabbing at the bow of the slipping IBS, Kozuska got a grip around the bow tube with his right arm.

Gritting his teeth and screaming with the effort, he stopped the IBS from completing its fall. For a moment the big man was hanging over the top of the net and holding up the entire weight of the boat himself. It should have torn his arm off, or he might have injured himself so badly he would be unable to complete the course, let alone not be crippled for life. But he hung on for the moments that were needed for his boat crew to grab at the boat and support it. Then Boat Crew II continued with the evolution.

Reaching the bottom of the cargo net, the men of Boat Crew II stood for a moment, breathing hard. Immediately, Chief Packard dropped them into the front leaning rest position, their feet up on the tube of the IBS they had just struggled so hard with.

"Kozuska, you maggot!" Chief Packard said to the

ensign while not six inches from his face. "This is a team effort. You do no one any good by getting yourself or any of your men killed in training. Try to do Hell Week all by yourself and you will fail, maggot! At best, all you'll manage to do is take some of this worthless shit you call a boat crew out with you."

"Hooyah, Chief Packard," was all Kozuska could say as he lay there panting.

"Recover and move out, you worthless turd!" Packard continued.

As Boat Crew II moved on through the obstacle course, Chief Packard watched them go. Instructor Lubi walked up to him as the crews continued.

"So, what do you think, Chief?" Lubi asked.

"I think he has the making of a good operator, Henry," Packard said in a low tone. "But if he doesn't learn to let his men carry their share of the load and become a leader, he'll never make it. He needs to have a team, and not be a muscle-headed mule at the front of a pack."

For Boat Crew IV, the tower stood in front of them and the end of the obstacle course. Now they had to lift their IBS up more than three stories into the air. Neil had several members of the boat crew get up on the lowest platform and try to pull up on the side of the IBS while the rest of the crew pushed up from underneath.

Each platform of the tower was about seven feet above the one below it. And there were four platforms altogether. Getting the IBS up onto the first platform was easy. The men underneath the boat could stand on the ground and push for all they were worth. On the rest of the platforms, they had to lean out over the ground to push up as hard as they had to.

Jeremy was one of the bottom men on the third platform, pushing up on the IBS. With the boat on its side rather than going bow first, the crew effectively had a shorter distance to lift it. And they could each get a good area to shove on. The men who had pulled up on the IBS to get it on the platform they were on now would push on the boat to get it up to the next and last platform.

But training was dangerous. And it paid to keep your wits about you when you were leaning out over an open drop of over twenty feet—even if the ground was mostly soft sand.

Working so hard to get the boat up that last little bit, Jeremy forgot the rules of self-preservation. He leaned out too far and overbalanced himself. When the guys on the top platform finally managed to pull the IBS up, Jeremy found himself starting to fall.

The curse that was just coming up on Jeremy's lips stopped when his fall did. A hand had grabbed the back of his shirt and swung him hard to the side. Slamming up against one of the four telephone-pole-like logs that made up the corners of the tower, Jeremy hung on for dear life. With his arm wrapped around the same pole, Bob Miller let go of Jeremy's shirt when he could see his crewmate was secured.

"You about done learning how to fly?" Miller asked. "This isn't the Air Force."

"Thanks," Jeremy said weakly.

"Pay me back later," Miller said with a grin. "But let's get moving, that instructor is starting to eye us."

So Boat Crew IV climbed up the rest of the tower and crossed over to lower the boat down the opposite side of the structure. The strain was still tremendous. They were still working against gravity, which tried now to snatch the boat away from them and drop it to the ground. When they finally reached the ground, Jeremy had pushed so hard that his body rebelled. Leaning over, he vomited into the sand.

Wiping his mouth, he felt ashamed of himself for showing such weakness. But his wasn't the only stomach that decided to show its feelings. A number of trainees were soaking the sands with the contents of their now almost empty stomachs. It was all just a part of the wonderful world of Hell Week, according to the more sympathetic instructors.

As the students finally gathered up in ragged boat crews as directed by the instructors, a few of them wondered what might be next. The answer to that question was not long in coming.

Shouting through his bullhorn, Chief Packard again addressed the class and let them know just what they were in for. "It's time for surf appreciation, maggots," Chief Packard bellowed. "Line up and lock arms."

All of Class 78 lined up facing the surf. Each student looped his arms through those of the man standing next to him. This was one of the things they knew and had faced before—the cold waters of the Pacific. The California current offshore normally kept the water cold, even in the heat of summer. But in March the water felt frigid every time they had been ordered into the surf to make a sugar cookie. Only this time, the students knew they wouldn't be coming out of that water for a while.

Realizing they were in for the ride of their lives, they hooked arms together and drew close to one another. In part, their closeness would help conserve what little body heat they could between each other. But the linking arms also indicated that the students were drawing tighter together as a group. It was them against the instructors and the ordeal known as Hell Week.

So, tightly linked together, the students obeyed the order and marched into the surf zone. Inside that line of students, Travis "Redneck" Rappaport was marching alongside Washington Sledge. Both men had linked arms with one another, and both men stayed close to each other. The prejudices they had been brought up on since childhood were forgotten against a much greater enemy—the cold, uncaring water. It didn't matter what color you were, your age, intellect, or background. The sea took on all comers, as it had for millennia.

Strength only mattered so much. Endurance and the ability to withstand the cold when your body told you "Enough!" was much more important. So for one of the few times in his life, Richard Kozuska faced a problem that he couldn't wrestle down or knock out of his way. His great strength meant very little against the cold. Just a few men down in the line from Kozuska was Bob Miller, the smallest man in the class. He gritted his teeth and went into the water with the others. Size didn't matter here; the cold surf would pound down on them all.

The water was breathtakingly cold. Which was exactly what they expected. When the order sounded out from Chief Packard's bullhorn for them to sit down in the surf, the students immersed themselves in the water. The pounding surf landed directly on their heads while the cold sucked at their bodies. The orange cords that secured their covers to their uniforms were the only thing that kept their hats from floating away for some of the students in that line. And their time in the cold water continued.

The temperature of the water was less than sixty degrees Fahrenheit. The students didn't know that, and it wouldn't have mattered if they did. It was dark, cold, and wet. The only light that shone over their situation came from the occasional pop flare that an instructor launched up from the beach. By the wavering light of the magnesium flare dangling from its parachute, the students could see the beach and each other. And they could also see the cold foaming surf as it crashed down over them.

Instructor Hawke now was on the bullhorn, talking to the students while they sat in the water. "Why put yourself through this, gentlemen?" he said in a reasonable tone. "The ocean doesn't want you. This kind of thing is unnatural for a person. Soon you're going to start shivering."

That choice bit of information came a little late. The

students were all shivering now, harder than they ever had in their lives.

"The cold will dig at you," Hawke continued. "It will sap you, drain you, maybe even kill you. Why fight it? Come on up here and ring the bell. We have hot cocoa in the truck here. Just quit and you're warm again."

"Hooyah, we love this shit!" shouted one trainee. "It's not cold, come in and join us!"

The instructors were astonished at that response. It wasn't that they didn't expect the class to have some fight in it. Hell Week was only a few hours old and the students hadn't faced any real hardship yet. But the student who had yelled was Butterworth! And he was setting an example for his classmates. Maybe the ring-knocker had what it took after all. But the week was still young yet.

"I want you to look to your left," Chief Packard called out in his electronically magnified voice. "Now look to your right. Say good-bye to each other now, maggots. Some of you people won't be here when the sun comes up in the morning."

"This isn't for everyone," Instructor Hawke called out. "But this is what every day in the Teams is like, gentlemen. Is that what you're suffering for?"

A shivering cry of "Hooyah!" came up from the line in the surf. Over ten minutes had passed, each one feeling like an eternity to the shivering, aching students. Only Kozuska and a few others were getting any benefit from the cold. Though he was hiding it, Kozuska felt as though he had torn his shoulder up when the

IBS had almost gotten away from him on the cargo net. The cold water was numbing the pain and acting in the same therapeutic manner as an ice pack would have during his college football days. For several other students, the cold was also numbing pain in sore knees, ankles, and other joints.

But the relief of some pain by the cold was more than offset by the overwhelming shivering that threatened to shake each student apart. The teeth of some of them were chattering so badly that they couldn't join in on the hooyah cheer with their brother sufferers in the surf.

But before the cold could start causing hypothermia in some of the students, Chief Packard called them back in to the beach. It was a staggering line that managed to finally get to its feet in the surf. More than one student fell back and was only held up by the arms he had linked to the men on either side of him. Helping each other, the students walked back out of the water.

"All right, you maggots," Chief Packard's voice sounded out over the noise of the surf. "Break down into boat crews. You ladies have ten minutes to warm each other up—I suggest you don't waste it."

Boat crews gathered in tight knots to huddle. Now they learned the other meaning of BUD/S—that you would be closer buddies than you had ever been before, literally. A smart boat crew leader would direct a man into the middle of the group while the others hugged and huddled around him. Each man could spend a minute or more in the center of the group, gaining heat from the other men, before he was rotated out and another took the center position.

And everyone wouldn't just hug face in. The smart ones would turn their backs to warm up and wring out those parts of their bodies a little bit. But how they did it didn't matter. What did matter was that the warm-up exercise once again helped instill the importance of teamwork.

And the teamwork aspect of BUD/S was growing for some of the students. As Instructor Sanchez looked on, he could see with some satisfaction that two of the people hugging the tightest were Rappaport and Sledge. The prejudices of Redneck and Hammer were breaking down in the face of a much greater threat— the simple survival of the next six days.

To survive the coming event, the trainees had to have their equipment in order. Though the students had no idea what was coming, the instructors had every moment of Hell Week scheduled out. And the next major evolution would be the single most dangerous one the students would face: rock portage.

## Chapter Thirteen

Crossing the shoreline with a rubber boat was something the UDTs and SEALs would be doing on a regular basis in the Teams. And the shoreline was rarely a sandy beach with a nice, flat gradient. Instead, it was most often rocky and dangerous, a spot no sane man would even want to be near when the surf was running. And that, of course, was the reason the Teams landed in such spots.

The class had done rock portage before. Now they would have to do it again, only this time at night, with the added stress of Hell Week bearing down on them. The only real break the instructors were giving the students, though most of them would never realize it, was that they were conducting the evolution early in the week. With the students still relatively fresh, they had the greatest chance of passing the evolution with the least number of injuries.

And injuries could happen easily during rock portage. Normally at this point in every class, a number of students would be rolled back due to injuries. These injuries could range from a relatively mild concussion, such as the one sustained by Jim Alex, which caused him to be rolled back to Class 78, to broken bones and even worse. The whole class now knew this lesson very well after their first introduction to rock portage the week before.

The instructors would keep a sharp eye on each boat crew during rock portage. On top of the jagged black rocks in front of the Hotel del Coronado, Chief Packard himself would signal when a boat crew was to come in to the rocks and cross them. The students would hang out in the water, just beyond the surf zone. When Chief Packard gave them the signal, they would have to head in through the surf and over the rocks.

The students could be afraid, and most already were—it was a scary situation. They remembered that several of their companions had been badly injured when they did rock portage the first time, and that was in daylight. Being afraid didn't matter; completing the evolution, that's what mattered. Fear was fine; doing what had to be done in spite of any fear was the lesson the students would take away from this evolution.

As Chief Packard looked over the wet and sandy bunch of students in front of him, he noticed that Boat Crew IV was still in one piece. The mostly big, beefy students that made up that crew caused their one smaller member to look completely out of place. But Packard knew that it wasn't the muscle that got you through Hell Week, it was the heart. And with their muscles, the big guys had a lot more weight to drag around. He wondered for a moment just how many of them would be left by Wednesday night.

Some of the big ones in Boat Crew IV were stoic, quiet types. Miller appeared to be considerably different not only in size, but in temperament as well. He'd bitched and whined about what they had to do all the way through the obstacle course. The chief decided it was time to settle the lad down a bit.

"Don't like it here, do you, maggot!" Chief Packard bellowed as he approached Boat Crew IV, standing by their IBS. "Boat Crew IV, drop and start knocking them out."

Immediately, the six students hit the sand and started doing push-ups. Chief Packard walked over to where Miller was pushing at the ground and leaned over so his face was only inches away from where Miller's head was moving up and down.

"If you don't like what you're doing here, maggot," Chief Packard said in what sounded like dangerously soft tones, "you can always just ring the bell. Go ahead, quit. Why drag the rest of your friends here down with you? After all, they have to pay the price for that big mouth of yours. Why punish them? Just quit, it's easy."

Miller's straining face hardened considerably as he continued to do the push-ups ordered by Chief Packard. The chief's words were hitting home. But they didn't weaken his resolve, they strengthened it. Miller would not be chased out of training by anyone—they would have to carry him out before he quit.

Straightening up, a seemingly enraged Chief Packard bellowed, "Come on, you maggot, quit!"

"Not a chance, Chief Packard," Miller called up from the ground.

"Maggot, you are lower than whale shit; dumber too," Packard shouted. "And do you know where whale shit is, maggot? It's on the bottom of the ocean. And that's where you're going to be soon."

Lifting the bullhorn to his lips, Chief Packard addressed the whole class, now that they'd all finished the obstacle course. "It's time for a little more surf appreciation, gentlemen," he said.

The students had learned that whenever Chief Packard called them "gentlemen," they were going to get pounded.

"Into the surf zone!" Packard continued. "Run, you maggots! I want some nice fresh sugar cookies tonight."

The class turned and ran into the water. They rolled into the freezing surf, got up and ran back to the beach to roll in the sand. But before any of them could get back to the shore, they heard a loud blast from a whistle blown through Chief Packard's bullhorn.

The students stood there, confused, wondering what had happened. Then Butterworth remembered whistle drills and immediately dove into the shallow water with his hands closing over his head. The other students followed his example and dove flat. The ones in deeper water had a little trouble actually hitting the bottom and not being swept away by a wave, but they did their best.

Two loud whistle blasts sounded out. Even those students out in the deeper water could hear the command to crawl in toward the signal. But they were doing more of a swim than a crawl. Still, the squirming mass of humanity that was Class 78 groped their way in to shore.

Three loud blasts and the students were able to get to their feet. They hadn't taken two steps before there was one loud blast and they immediately dropped flat again. Two blasts, time to crawl forward.

Some of the instructors were now keeping a sharp eye out for the stragglers in the class. In spite of their brusque attitude toward the students, they didn't want to lose anyone in training.

Gradually, through a series of whistle blasts, Class 78 made it all the way back to shore. A loud blast caused them to drop, and two more blasts started them forward to where Chief Packard now stood by their rubber boats. As the students crawled forward, they plowed into the sand with their heads and shoulders, knowing they had to keep their heads down as low as possible. Inching forward on their elbows and pushing back with their feet, they left plowed trails behind them in the beach.

"Son of a bitch," Instructor Hawke exclaimed to Instructor Lubi, standing next to him. "Henry, I know where I've seen this before."

"You mean besides here?" Lubi asked.

"Yeah, those trails in the sand these guys make," Hawke continued. "I saw trails just like those on TV. It was on some special about sea turtles."

Putting on a very bad imitation of a French accent, Hawke said. "And now, after years in the sea, the mother sea turtle returned to the sands of her birth to lay her eggs. She pushes herself forward through the sands with her flippers. . . ."

"Okay, enough," Lubi said with laughter in his voice. "One of these students hears you and they might start to try and lay eggs—and that's something I don't want to see."

By now, the objects of the instructor's amusement had crawled up to within a few yards of Chief Packard. With three blasts of his whistle, the chief brought the class to its feet. Covered with sand, the students looked like something washed up by an ocean storm. Round white eyes peered out of tan faces covered with a heavy layer of grit. Lips and noses could still be made out in the faces, but that was about all.

"You think you all look pretty bad?" Chief Packard shouted out at the class in front of him.

"Hooyah, Chief Packard," the class shouted back in ragged unison.

"Well, the Navy doesn't care what you look like, maggots," Chief Packard continued. "But it does care what this valuable equipment you've been assigned looks like. Boat crews, line up on your boats. Boat inspection, maggots."

Again the class scrambled to complete the instructor's commands. Boat crews gathered up and stood in front of their boats. The students knew they couldn't possibly pass the inspection, and they were right. Instructors examined the boats and tossed paddles out onto the sand. Lines were uncoiled and tossed. Even sand was considered enough reason to drop a boat crew for push-ups.

But what the students didn't notice was that the instructors were also checking the tightness of the tubes, making sure that all of the inflated compartments of an IBS held air and were tautly filled. That there were no holes in the hull or bottom of the boat, and that the bow ropes weren't frayed. The students were hammered for infractions, both real and made up. But for the upcoming rock portage evolution, the instructors wanted to be sure that their gear was in the best condition possible.

"Since you can't appreciate the fine equipment your Navy has seen fit to loan you," Chief Packard called out over his bullhorn when the inspection was over, "perhaps I can find something you will appreciate. Link arms! Surf appreciation, gentlemen!"

The students again linked their arms together and turned to march into the sea. The icy water climbed up their feet, legs, and bodies as the went into the surf. Waves crashed down on them, causing more than one student to gasp from the cold. "Welcome to sunny California," Miller said as he spat out seawater.

"Take your seats!" Chief Packard bellowed out over the water.

The line of students obediently sat down in the cold surf. Now, only their heads and shoulders were above the surface, and those only intermittently as the waves crashed over them. For some of them, the cold set them to shivering again almost immediately. Muscles warmed from the exercise of only moments ago knotted up. At the same time that pain bloomed through the students' bodies, the cold numbed painful joints and other hurts.

After an eternity of torture passed—actually only six minutes—the students were ordered back to their feet and in toward shore. Before they could reach the beach, however, another order sounded out, "Drop!"

In less than a foot of water, the class dropped to the push-up position. "Start knocking them out," Chief Packard ordered.

With the waves now crashing over them completely, the students of Class 78 started doing push-ups in the shallows. Every time they lowered their bodies, the water would cover their heads. For some students, the water didn't uncover their heads when they came back up. Spluttering and gasping, they lifted their faces above the foam and drew in some air, then went back to their exercise. After twenty push-ups were performed, a ragged "Hooyah, Chief Packard!" sounded out from the class.

"Recover!" Chief Packard ordered. "Link arms!"

This was intentionally the kind of situation that caused men to waver in their commitment to the program. It wasn't just being cold that sapped the strength and will from everyone. Sometimes, now that they were back on their feet, it was the threat of more cold that made men quail.

As the students prepared to march back into the water, one of their number pulled away and continued forward back up to the shore. Those on either side of him tried to hang on, and others cried out, "No! Don't!"

But he had made his decision. As the young man walked up to the back of the pickup truck where the bell hung on its wooden framework, Instructor Hawke shouted out over his bullhorn, "It looks like we have a winner!"

Three quick clangs of the bell and Class 78 was down by one more student.

"I tell you what," Instructor Hawke called out to the line still shaking in the surf. "Two more people quit and we'll secure from the evolution. Come on now, you too can be warm and dry, just ring that bell."

In spite of the protests by his classmates, one more student pulled away from the line and went up to the truck.

"And another winner!" Hawke cried out gleefully.

But no matter how much he cajoled and tempted the class, he couldn't get another student to quit. Finally, Instructor Hawke turned to the two miserable students standing next to the truck, now blanket-wrapped but still shivering.

"Get back to the barracks and pack your shit, you pukes," Hawke said. His opinion of quitters was obvious in his voice.

"So we have a class full of people too stupid to know when to quit," Chief Packard bellowed. "Get these maggots out of my sight."

As Packard looked on in apparent disgust, the instructors ordered the students out of the water and up onto the beach. Forming the class up into two lines, Instructor Lubi took the lead and started the students on a run down the beach. Staggering along, but thankful they didn't have their boats with them this time, the class followed.

"That should warm them up," Chief Packard said as several of the other instructors gathered around him. "Start setting up for rock portage."

The students didn't know it, but they were being directed through a carefully orchestrated series of events. Their time in the icy water was calculated from the experience of the senior instructors. Before hypothermia could set in, they were drawn back out of the water. Now they were being run to loosen them up before they had to get ready for rock portage.

What the students did know was that they were on another run down the beach, with Instructor Lubi leading the class. The soft sand never felt worse than it did when the students were running through it with soaking wet boots. It clamped down on their feet and made each step an additional effort.

Instructor Lubi demonstrated his normal nonchalance about leading the class on a run. With a lit cigar clamped between his teeth, Lubi jogged along at what appeared an even, easy pace. But appearances were deceiving. The students who were keeping up with Instructor Lubi's pace would say that it was enough to plow you into the ground in very short order.

Though it seemed like the run went on much farther than it actually did, the students soon found themselves back in front of the training compound, next to their rubber boats lined up along the beach.

Next to the boats, the balance of the shift's instructors were standing about, smoking cigars and laughing.

Jeremy saw this as the class ran up to the compound. He wondered if the instructors were hammering them for some slight they had been forced to endure back during their training. And now they were laughing about it?

Whatever the reason, what the students were being forced to do was what they had to accomplish to continue training. They didn't have to like what was being done to them—no one but a masochist could—but they did have to do everything they were told.

"One evolution at a time," Jeremy told himself quietly. "Just do it one evolution at a time."

Now they were ordered to put on their kapok life vests, and the class had three minutes to accomplish the task. Those bulky, heavy vests were leftovers from World War II, and they felt like it when they were strapped on. The heavy vest weighed several pounds dry. But all of the students knew they wouldn't be allowed to stay dry long.

Vests had to be properly secured or the instructors would rain down punishments. The three minutes would normally have been long enough for well-rested and warm individuals. But the class was tired, sore, and more than a little stiff from the cold water, sand abrasion, and exercise. The upper tape on the waist of the vest had to be tied tightly to keep the vest from moving in the water. The chest strap had to be adjusted and the snap hook slipped through its corresponding ring. The thick, roll collar of the vest was secured by two collar tapes. And the leg straps had to be adjusted according to the situation.

The students hadn't been told whether to adjust the leg straps for running or use in the water. For use in the water, they were put underneath the legs and secured. For any other use, such as running, the straps were wrapped around the waist and tied. Best guess, they were going to run some more, so the students wrapped the leg straps around their waists.

Wrong guess.

A punishment of boat push-ups was awarded to the students for having their leg straps improperly adjusted when they returned to their boats. And an additional set of push-ups was ordered for getting back to the boats late. Then they were given the briefing for what would be the real punishment for the entire evening: Chief Packard gave them a safety briefing for rock portage.

The students knew the procedures, and they knew where they had to go. The signals that would be given to the boat crews by the instructor on shore were gone over again. The students would be doing this rock portage in the dark. And there was another aspect of the evolution that they could hear building up behind them.

The tide was up, and so was the surf. The sound of the big eight- to ten-foot waves could easily be heard over the instructor. And the sound of those big waves hitting the beach had really earned them the name crunchers tonight. Called the big kahunas by some surfers, the power of the waves was evident in the sound that they made. And the white foam of the curls almost seemed to glow in the limited lights of the compound.

The briefing over, the students were ordered to correctly place their leg straps for use in the water. Each student checked his partner, and then the boat crews checked each other. The instructors would punish even a small infraction. A major safety violation before a difficult evolution, and a student would rather the earth opened and swallowed him up than face an irate instructor.

Push-ups and a liberal awarding of sugar cookies, including one for the class as a whole, and the students were ready to face surf passage and rock portage. Passing through the surf went surprisingly well, with only a few boats bending and tossing their contents out into the water. The instructors had turned the headlights of the trucks out to illuminate the water, and this helped to an extent. The spilled boat crews grabbed their upset craft and turned them over. Clambering aboard, they continued on the outbound part of the evolution.

The trip out through the surf zone had been rough, but the trip in would be much worse. Having reached the relatively calm waters past the surf zone, the boat crews turned their rubber crafts north and started to paddle. About a mile north of the training compound, the Hotel del Coronado sat with all of its old world charm and majesty. In front of the hotel, along the beach, lay the rough, pointed, and edged black rocks of the breakwater.

The instructors had set up chem lights to guide the students toward their landing sites. And the boat crews would be coming in to land one at a time. With the flash of a white light in the hands of Chief Packard on the rocks, the coxswain of the boat crew would be ordering the crew in. From their earlier experience at rock portage, the students had learned that only one person gives the orders in the boat—the coxswain. Everyone else paddles as ordered, and they paddle hard.

When they came in on the chief's signal, the bowline man would have to jump at the right moment and try to secure the surging rubber boat to the rocks. The only way to do it would be for the man in the rocks to "take a bite"—snuggle down between the rocks, brace himself, and wrap the boat's bowline around his body. If he tried to muscle the boat into place, the student would quickly find that the hundreds of pounds of rubber boat and boat crew were a lot more than he could handle. At the least, he would be yanked off the rocks and into the water. At worst, he could get tossed down on the rocks as the boat landed on him and ground him into the sharp, unyielding edges.

Jeremy White was again the bowline man for Boat Crew IV as the crew waited outside the surf zone and watched for their signal. The flashlight in Chief Packard's hand flashed, and they were on their way in. "Let's do it, guys!" Neil shouted from the stern of the boat. "Stroke . . . stroke . . ."

"As a team now!" White called back, near the front of the IBS.

"Hooyah!" the crew shouted back.

Then it was just the sea, waves, and rocks they had to get by. Each stroke of the paddles brought them closer to the rocks. Neil was trying to time the landing of the boat to correspond with the landing of one of the waves. If they could grab a wave on the crest, they could almost ride it in on top of the rocks.

"Stroke, stroke, stroke," Neil called from the back of the boat. It looked like there was a good wave building up, and Neil wanted a piece of it. As the water rose, so did the rubber boat on top of it. Now everything started moving with the rushing motion of a dark nightmare.

The IBS lifted and moved forward with the speed of an express train. With Neil still calling out the count, the paddlers dug in and helped keep the boat near the crest of the wave. The wave broke, and the bow of the boat was suddenly against the rocks.

"Bowline out!" Neil shouted, and Jeremy leaped out at the rocks. Ignoring the pain of landing on the sharp edges, he struggled to get down into the rocks and turned around to face the boat.

"Get a bite!" Chief Packard shouted. "Get a bite, damn it!"

As the boat slipped back in on the ebbing wave, Jeremy jumped, fell, and pushed himself between two of the rocks. The line quickly wrapped around his waist and he braced his feet and arms against the rocks. The boat stopped its outward movement, but that was all.

Pushing with their paddles according to Neil's shouted directions, the paddlers of Boat Crew IV started swinging the IBS over to her port side. As another wave came in, the stern line was tossed to Jeremy. Letting go of the bowline with one hand, he snatched up the slack and quickly wrapped it around his waist.

The wave lifted the boat higher, and Jeremy could swear that it was going to come crashing down on him with its port side. He didn't hear the clatter of paddles being tossed behind him by his crewmates. But he did hear them shouting to each other as they went over the side of the boat and clambered onto the rocks. The incoming swell of water rose up and covered the rocks where Jeremy lay braced among them. His legs and arms didn't move as they helped him hold the boat in place, even as the cold waters closed over his head.

The boat was suddenly stopped and lifted by five pairs of hands as the students grabbed it where they could. Boat Crew IV pulled and heaved their rubber boat up and onto the rocks before another wave could lift it up and carry it away. Without any time to give thanks for his rescue, Jeremy clambered higher up onto the rocks, unwinding the bowline behind him. When he crested the rocks, he again braced his legs and leaned back on the line, pulling the boat straighter and bow first onto the rocks.

The rest of Boat Crew IV pulled and pushed at their rubber albatross, climbing up onto the rocks and away from the waves. Once on the crest of the rock pile, they lifted the IBS up by its sides and climbed down the other side. It was an almost flawless execution of a rock portage. They had done well, and knew it. And their reward as they clambered down the shore side of the rocks was to stir up the millions of gnats that had taken up residence there.

The waves had been hard, the rocks dangerous, but the gnats just plain sucked. Going through the swarm, the men of Boat Crew IV reached Chief Packard. Hands on his hips, the big SEAL chief glowered down at them.

"You got it right—once," he said in a loud voice. "Now go out there and do it again!"

As he turned his back to climb back up onto the rocks, the students of Boat Crew IV couldn't see the smile that crossed Packard's craggy face. He was interested in the best quality product to be coming out of BUD/S, not numbers of graduates. And the students of Boat Crew IV did show promise, if they could keep it together for the rest of the week.

In spite of having to do the evolution again, Jeremy and the others were feeling good about themselves. They had done something very hard, and had done it well. That accomplishment drew them together even tighter than before. Their team was building.

For other crews, it was worse. As Boat Crew V came in to the rocks, their paddling was ragged and inefficient. The stroke that Ed Lynch was calling out from his position as coxswain wasn't getting the boat up on top of the cresting wave fast enough. And he had picked a wave that was far too big to easily ride out. Shouting from the shore, Chief Packard could see the disaster coming in at him. It was like watching a train wreck take place, without being able to stop it.

As the wave came down on the rocks, the bowline man never even had a chance to get into the rocks before the boat landed on them. The wave pushed at the rubber boat and it broached, turning side on to the sea.

The shouted curses and directions from Chief

Packard were lost among the noises of the crashing waves and shouting students. As the boat turned sideways and lifted up, it tilted one side down toward the rocks, which were going by fast. The students had been riding the tubes of the IBS as they would a log, straddling the tube with one leg on inboard and the other out over the water. With the water lifting the boat and pushing it up against the rocks, most of the students managed to get their legs out of the way before they were trapped between the rocks and the boat. All the students on the port side of the boat but one.

Sledge leaned out and tried to push down with his paddle against the rocks to keep the boat straight and moving ahead. But the power of the water and weight of the rushing boat were far too much for him as it turned his paddle away and pressed it against his leg. In an instant the opposite side of the boat rose and the wave crested even more. Sledge was snatched off the top of the tube as his leg was trapped, and before he could even scream, he was pulled over the side as the IBS began to flip over.

Just moments before, Rappaport had been cursing at that stupid black in front of him who couldn't even paddle a rubber boat. Then the whole world started to tilt and twist to the side. As he watched, he saw Sledge get snatched over the side of the boat. Without a moment's thought for himself and the possible consequences of his actions, Rappaport grabbed at Sledge's leg as it went over the side.

The rubber boat tilted, turned, and dumped its contents across the rocks as the wave broke over them.

The members of the boat crew who had been riding on the starboard side of the boat were lifted up and tossed out onto the rocks. They suffered little more than a bad knocking around.

Bob Keener, the bowline man for Boat Crew V, was hurt the worst when he was tossed down into the rocks and the boat knocked into him. Slamming down on an edge, Keener heard his rib crack as the impact drove a cry of pain out of him. Ed Lynch fell over the back of the boat as it rolled under him and landed in the water to the side. And no one noticed that Rappaport and Sledge were nowhere to be seen for the moment.

Chief Packard was right in among the rocks as the students were tossed about. Quickly assessing the situation, he sent one of the other instructors for the corpsman nearby. "Lift this boat!" Packard shouted. "Lift this goddamn boat!"

The students who could, quickly forgot about their own pain and moved to the chief's side. The inverted IBS was lifted, and Rappaport and Sledge could be seen down in the rocks underneath it. As Chief Packard shone his flashlight down on the pair, the beam played across the back of Rappaport's kapok vest. The water-soaked face of the young man turned up and looked at the beam. Cradled in Rappaport's arms was Sledge's head and shoulders. Rappaport had taken the impact of the IBS coming down on the two of them where Sledge had fallen between two of the rocks.

Outside of Keener's cracked rib, Boat Crew V had probably come through the disastrous landing in better shape than they deserved. And Chief Packard made sure they knew that in no uncertain terms. In spite of the crew being shaken, they were turned back out to sea to do the landing again. Packard knew that if he let up for even a moment, the thought of what they had just done could cause the entire crew to quit. And right now it looked like the Redneck and Hammer might finally be getting it together and learning what teamwork could really mean.

Gathering up their IBS and making sure it was intact, Boat Crew V moved back out toward the surf zone. They were beaten up, but still game. And they were also short one man. The corpsman had pulled Keener away and worked on him. The man's life wasn't in any danger, but his chances of graduating with BUD/S Class 78 were over.

Now on their second landing attempt, Boat Crew II, with Richard Kozuska as the coxswain, was lining up on the green chem light marking out the landing spot on the rocks. At Chief Packard's signal, Kozuska started calling out the stroke. His immense strength had always served Kozuska well, and he still assumed that it would work for others as well. As a result, the stroke he called for rock portage had gotten too fast for the conditions. The students caught up to the wave Kozuska had aimed for, and they were now barreling in toward the rocks. But they had pushed too hard up on the wave and were in danger of sliding down over the crest and the wave crashing down on top of them.

Trying desperately to steer with his paddle and keep the boat straight, Kozuska didn't shout out any orders that the rest of the boat crew could hear. So the men

just kept paddling, breaking rhythm badly with one another. As he could see the rocks coming up, Kozuska
shouted, "Bowline away!"

Not realizing that he wasn't in a position where he
could stop the boat's forward motion, Rodney Shea
jumped forward from his position at the bow and
quickly scrambled over the rocks. But as the wave
broke, he didn't have the time to even get into position
among the rocks, let alone to get properly braced. As
the IBS moved forward and passed him, Shea was
jerked off his feet and down among the rocks, the line
snatched from his hands.

Kozuska jumped over the side from his position in
the stern of the IBS. He had a moment's time to get
down into the rocks and try to grab up the line before
the wave broke and dumped the IBS down onto the
rocks. That impact would spill the rest of the boat crew
out over the sides.

Now Kozuska was trying to hang on to the backslid-
ing rubber boat as the rest of his crew slammed down
among the rocks anyway. The IBS lifted, and came
down on the rocks right next to Matthew Dillon, trap-
ping his hand between the tube of the boat and the hard
rocks below.

The rest of Boat Crew II scrambled over the rocks to
try and grab hold of their escaping boat—all but Keith
Sanger, who lay against the rock he had crashed down
on. When he was tossed from the boat and hit the
rocks, he'd landed square on his right knee. It didn't
look like he would be going anywhere for a while.

Eventually Boat Crew II gained control of their

boat, as the wave receded and left it up on the rocks. They had to hurry to get the boat up and off the rocks before the next wave came in, but when Kozuska had to face the wrath of Chief Packard, he probably would rather have been back out on the rocks.

Chief Packard ordered the crew to drop their boat and immediately drop themselves and do boat push-ups until further notice. Then he began to rail against Kozuska and his poor style of leadership.

"You lead, Ensign!" Packard shouted at the student. "You don't try and do it all yourself, and you never leave your men without direction. Just what the hell are you trying to do, get through this course all by yourself? There isn't room for that kind of thinking here, and there sure as hell isn't any room for it in the Teams. Is there anything you can say that will stop me from giving you a performance drop right now?"

Ensign Kozuska couldn't say anything at that moment. Instead of having one of his men go out and grab up the loose bowline, he'd tried to do it himself. He had fucked up, and he knew it. But the chief ignored his silence and continued chewing out the young officer. Meanwhile, Kozuska and his boat crew were trying to do the push-ups the chief had ordered.

Finally, Packard just left them there in the front leaning rest position and walked off. They remained with their feet still up on the tube of the IBS and all of their weight held up by their arms.

Shortly before the men collapsed entirely, Chief Packard came back and recovered them. Then he told them that Dillon had badly smashed his hand and would be rolled back at least one if not two classes before he could try BUD/S again. But Keith Sanger was in much worse shape. His knee had been so badly smashed that he couldn't complete BUD/S—probably ever. In fact, it looked like it might be a near thing if he could even stay in the Navy.

Ordering the remainder of Boat Crew II out of his sight, Chief Packard turned them over to Instructor Hawke. Over the next twenty minutes of exercise and exposure to the cold water and sand that Instructor Hawke ran the crew through, two more men got up and rang the bell. That ended their time in BUD/S. Now only Kozuska, Shea, and Tim Nelson remained from what had originally been a full boat crew of seven.

With the injuries and dropouts, Class 78 lost ten people over the course of rock portage. There were other incidents, but none as bad as the two that had almost killed one student and crippled another.

## Chapter Fourteen
## Monday

All the boat crews eventually finished the rock portage evolution. Everyone had done at least one successful landing, but the instructors were anything but happy with the class. It was their opinion that it was far too early in Hell Week for everyone to be as dingy as the students' performances indicated. The problem had to be with the basic intelligence of all of the students, they concluded, which could be adjusted by the proper application of exercise.

The boat crews were lined up and ordered to "Up boats." This was a struggle for Boat Crew II, since only three people were left in the crew. Other crews had only four or five people. Of the eight boat crews in Class 78 that went into Hell Week, there were now only enough students to make six crews. But the instructors still had eight rubber boats to get back to the training compound, and they weren't going to carry them. So they set an impromptu boat crew race back to the compound. The distance was a little over a mile, mostly through soft sand.

"Remember, maggots," Chief Packard said. "It pays to be a winner."

The students had been hearing that expression throughout training, though there hadn't been any example yet on just how it paid to be a winner. But the competition was on and the race began.

As races went, a crippled squirrel could have beaten the best time, which went to Boat Crew IV. The bouncing of the boat on their heads slowed all of the students as they desperately tried to move ahead at a shuffling run through the shifting sand. More than one student slipped and started to fall, only to be grabbed up by one of his fellow crewmates before he could hit the ground. Necks aching, the heavy kapok life vests at least helped give their necks some support when they carried the boats.

The kapok vests had a thick collar, intended to help hold a man's head up above the water when he was floating. This same collar helped brace a student's neck as the weight of the IBS bore down on them. The support helped prevent any major injury to the students' necks but did little to reduce the pain from the weight that bore down on them.

Arms and shoulders already sore from exercise and paddling grew more painful from the strain of carrying the rubber boats. But that was one of the lessons of BUD/S: you could work through the pain. A man could keep going, could do anything that was physically possible, as long as his mind kept telling his body what to do.

Another BUD/S lesson became apparent to the instructors watching the students struggle on the run. They were coming together as a team. In spite of the very poor showing from some of the boat crews during the rock portage, they'd begun to cooperate on a gut level during the run. But one crew was still having trouble with its leadership.

Ensign Kozuska and the two other students who made up Boat Crew II were falling farther behind the pack. Instead of working with his men and slowing down the pace to make up for their much heavier individual loads, Kozuska was still bulling ahead. It was as if the man expected to still finish ahead of at least one of the other crews.

The instructors had seen students before who couldn't accept coming in far back in the pack or in last place. These were school or college sports stars who weren't used to failure. They had to win at all costs. But with Kozuska being an officer, his drive could cost his men. There's leadership, and there's just pushing too hard. Kozuska, the instructors knew, was going to have to learn the difference.

Chief Packard barely had to walk quickly to keep up with Boat Crew II. They were staggering along, with Tim Nelson and Rodney Shea trying hard to hold up the back end of the IBS while Kozuska moved ahead at the front of the boat. They were more than well past the halfway point between the Hotel del Coronado and the training compound when Shea slipped and fell, dropping the boat to the beach and knocking his two crewmates to the ground.

Chief Packard took immediate advantage of the situation to try and teach a lesson to the young ensign.

"You losers are far too warm to satisfy me tonight," Packard growled through his bullhorn at Shea and Nelson. "Hit the surf!"

The two men got up and ran to the surf only a few hundred feet away. When Kozuska turned to go with them, Chief Packard reached out a hand to stop him.

"Oh no, Ensign Kozuska, not you," Chief Packard said quietly. "If you think you can do this whole course without the help of your men, here's your chance. You finish this race Kozuska, or you ring that bell right now."

Richard Kozuska was a big man. In fact, he was the largest individual in Class 78. During his years in college and even back in high school, he had never backed down from a challenge. Naval ROTC had just been a way for him to do a bit more while he'd been a star on the football field and in wrestling during his college days. He had volunteered for BUD/S to beat the challenge it offered.

Kozuska had been used to stopping the opposing line in its tracks on his football teams. His strength had never failed him before, and he wasn't going to let it flag now. Without a word, the young man bent down and pulled up on the bow of his IBS. Pulling and then pushing, Kozuska stood the boat up on its stern and then stepped underneath it.

Even though he was a big man, grabbing the sides of the six-foot-wide craft was too much for his long arms. But by leaning over and letting the boat tilt, he was just able to reach both sides of the towing bridle attached to either side of the bow. The bridle was secured to two heavy D-rings on either side of the bow, and was more than strong enough to support the weight of the boat.

Pulling the bridle up to his shoulder and grabbing hold with his hands, Kozuska hunched his back up underneath the IBS and took a step forward. The rear skeg tube under the stern of the IBS dragged forward in the sand and Kozuska took another step. Then he took another, and another, and another.

Kozuska was less than a quarter of a mile from the instructors at the training compound beach. It was just something like 420 yards, 1,320 feet, or about 650 steps. As Kozuska started out, Boat Crew IV was just reaching the end of the race. They had come in first, and finally learned just what the expression, "It pays to be a winner" meant. They had the unbelievable luxury of a few minutes rest while the rest of the boat crews came in. And as they looked back up the beach, they saw the unfolding drama of Kozuska dragging his boat.

Kozuska was coming on, slowly and unsteadily, but he was still moving forward with each step. As the rest of the boat crews came in to the compound area, they lowered their boats, sometimes with a groan, at the instructor's command. Then they turned to see one of their own struggling.

Even the instructors were impressed with the herculean effort they were witnessing. Men in the Teams always worked for a total team effort, but that didn't mean a single man wasn't called on to put out a maximum individual effort. And that was what they were all seeing—an absolutely maximum effort.

Instructor Hawke came trotting up along the beach, bringing with him the two wet and sandy remaining members of Boat Crew II. For a moment they all watched Kozuska struggle. He staggered and almost fell, but the ensign righted himself and continued his singular race.

Quietly at first, a small chant was rising from the students, started by either Nelson or Shea, no one could tell which one. But as it slowly grew in volume, the single name could be heard. "Zeus," the students were chanting. "Zeus . . . Zeus . . . Zeus! . . . ZEUS!"

The struggling young officer picked up his bowed head at the sound as he started to make it out. Hearing that single word, a nickname he actually hadn't liked until that moment, his face set a bit harder and a determined look came in his eyes. With each step, as he moved that much closer the muscles in his legs bulged. But his step was steady.

Finally, he was nearest of the rest of the students, and they cheered him. For a moment it seemed that the students had won over the instructors, but that moment was short-lived.

"If you have that much energy now," Chief Packard's voice boomed out, "maybe we'll have to cool you off a little. Time for surf appreciation, maggots!"

Tim Nelson and Rod Shea had run up to Kozuska, standing under the IBS, and tried to lift the boat off his back. They actually had to pry Kozuska's fingers open to get him to let go of the ropes of the towing bridle. Then all three students linked arms with the others to march into the cold water.

"You," Chief Packard said softly to himself as he watched Kozuska enter the water with the line, "are an idiot."

Instructor Hawke came up to Chief Packard and turned to watch the students.

"Well," he said in a quiet tone. "That was fairly impressive."

"He's got heart," Chief Packard said. "But even a dumb mule can have heart. What he has to do is learn a lot more about what it means to be a leader and how to depend on his men. All he's going to do is bull his way through things himself until that lesson sets home."

Then the two instructors went back to ensuring that the students of Class 78 had a proper appreciation of the power, and temperature, of the Pacific Ocean.

This time, the students only had to spend about five minutes in the less than sixty degree water. Not too long, just enough to let the shivering start up again. The life vests kept them from going under the water easily, but the heavy waves of the surf still pounded down on their heads.

Calling the class in to the beach, Chief Packard sent them out on another two-mile conditioning run. But this time they left their boats arranged behind them in front of the training compound. As the students ran down along the soft sand of the Silver Strand, Kozuska found himself falling back in the line.

It wasn't something the ensign was used to doing on a run. And then Shea and Nelson were on one side, behind him. Neither of the two smaller students had a lot to spare for Kozuska, but what they had, he was welcome to lean on.

Returning to the training compound from the run, the students were quickly rearranged and their boat crews reduced in number and filled out. There were now only six boat crews, two with seven men, the rest with six. That number was down by half from just the evening before. The leftover boats were put back in the racks near the grinder. Then the students were ordered to pick up their boats and move out to the NAB across the street.

The instructors didn't lighten up for a minute. If anything, they seemed a little harder on the class. But the students thought that could just have been their imagination as they walked around the compound and out toward the Amphibious base.

It was about a mile and a quarter walk from the students' barracks to the mess hall on the Amphibious base. But that was following the shortest route, which was not how the instructors intended getting there.

"Bow to stern, maggots," Chief Packard shouted through his bullhorn. "Bow to stern."

Now the students not only had to carry the heavy rubber boats on their heads, but close up ranks so that the bow of one crew's boat met up with the stern of the next crew's boat. Every bump, slip, and misstep was magnified and transmitted down through the line. The result of this was that the boats farther back in line were bumped harder and harder, first, as the boat in front of them moved forward, then again as they caught up and bumped into it.

The front and back motion combined with the weight of the boats on the students' necks to make the trip an agonizing torture. Nothing any of the students could do would lessen the pain they felt in their necks, shoulders, and heads. The only thing that could be said about the ordeal was that the students' upper bodies hurt so much they didn't notice their legs hurting as much.

The first night of Hell Week was coming to a close. As they marched toward the mess hall, located west of the training compound, the mountains to the west of San Diego were becoming brighter as the sun came up beyond them.

The instructors ran up and down the line, keeping the crews in line and in contact with each other. Now, the students were running on the concrete roadbeds, first on the highway separating the training compound from the Amphibious base, and then along the roads of the Amphibious base itself. The Vietnam-era jungle boots the students had been issued were more than well-worn, which at least let them drain out the water better than other boots. But they were also a rough boot to run in. And the instructors kept speeding up the undulating line of rubber boats and suffering students.

As one crew up forward slowed down from the strain, the instructors would pull it out of line and let the boats behind it close up the space. Then the crew would be put back in, at the end of the line, where the trouble of holding the boats bow to stern was at its worst.

Jeremy was noticing the pain in his legs, rather than the pressure on the top of his head. In particular, a sharp pain was building on the inside of both his lower legs. Shin splits were starting, and he didn't expect them to go away. By the sounds of the groans and near screams from some of the students in the boat line, Jeremy knew he was not the only one hurting. But the instructors had one more ordeal in mind before the students would be allowed to relax.

Getting to the mess hall, the instructors had the students line up as boat crews, side by side with each other. But instead of hearing the words "Down boats," the students heard a horribly different set of words.

"Extended arm carry, up boats!"

Now the students had to push the boats up over their heads. And there was no order to bring them down. They had to stand there, desperately trying to hold the heavy rubber craft up above their heads. First one man in a crew faltered, and his weakness quickly spread through the rest of the boat crew. And the boat would come crashing down on their heads, usually to continue down to the ground.

When a crew dropped its boat, an instructor was right there to drop the crew down to do boat push-ups with their feet up on the side of their IBS. Gradually, another crew, and then another, would drop its boat and follow it down to the ground. But by now the students were so exhausted that they couldn't do anything that looked like a push-up. Mostly, they just ducked their heads and stuck their elbows out in a jerky, rhythmic motion.

With a scream of frustration, rage, and pain from one of its members, the last boat crew caved in and collapsed to the ground. After they added their miserable efforts to conduct boat push-ups to the class total, the men were brought to the position of attention and allowed to file into the mess hall for their first meal of Hell Week. Their first night was officially over, but Hell Week still had a very long way to go.

## Chapter Fifteen
## First Meal

By this time the students knew that the mess hall on the Amphibious base served some of the best food in the Navy. And during Hell Week, the cooks put out a little harder to see to it that the students had the best that was available. The quantity and quality of the food were more than just a luxury, it was close to being a necessity, especially during Hell Week. Class 78 would receive four meals a day—the normal breakfast, lunch, and dinner, and a special midnight meal known as "midrats." And still, every one of the students was expected to lose five pounds and up during the week.

The students would spend the next week burning calories at a prodigious rate. The engines that were their bodies would be running just about at full blast for the entire week. Their muscles were burning fuel during the physical activity, but calories were also consumed when the students were shivering with cold. Each student's personal furnace would burn everything it could strip out of the body's system to try and keep the body warm.

There were no fat students. Those very few who had shown up at BUD/S with what the instructors called a "doughnut gut" had long since either had it stripped off or had quit. Thinner students were having trouble with the cold. With a smaller percentage of body fat to begin with, the cold could get to them even faster. Nguyen Thanh, the one Asian student in the class, was already having a lot of trouble with the cold. His slim, slight form had been developed by nature over the centuries to survive and even thrive in the hot, wet environment of Southeast Asia, where anything below seventy degrees was considered cold. And he was suffering the most among all of the students.

But Thanh was just gutting it out, as all of the students had to. Their bodies had started the week in as good a shape as could be expected. And the exercise program they had been driven through by their relentless instructors was intended to get them in shape to survive the over 126 hours of Hell Week. Keeping their heads together during that time was each student's personal ordeal.

For the moment, the students had the chow hall to help support them. They ate more at that sitting than most of them ever had at a single meal before in their lives. Plates were piled high with food: pancakes, eggs, toast, milk, cereal, coffee, potatoes, bacon, sausage, and more. Everything the cooks put out in the line was scooped up and consumed. By now most of the students had figured out that food meant fuel. Eating was the one thing that they could do to help keep themselves warm.

But the warm atmosphere of the mess hall also played against the students. As they sat there eating, some of them began to chew more slowly. Even while sitting there with a mouthful of food, exhaustion would start to sneak up on them and they could fall asleep in mid-bite. But since this was still early during Hell Week, they could shake it off and come back to some kind of alert state.

Ensign Kozuska still had pain in his hands from gripping the towing bridle of his IBS so tightly. His fingers were so stiff that he had a hard time holding his fork and trying to eat. Putting the fork down, he picked up a cup of strong, black, Navy coffee. And that was almost his undoing.

The warmth from the hot cup he held in his hands was unbelievably good just to hold. He sat there luxuriating in the heat for a moment as it soaked into his hands. He closed his eyes then, and that was his mistake. The situation he was in, his surroundings, even the odd mix of good food smells and the stench rising from his classmates, faded away. Without realizing it, the big man started to slip into sleep.

A quick elbow helped knock Kozuska awake before the sharp-eyed instructors picked him out of the crowd. Rod Shea, on his right, had noticed his boat crew leader slipping away and elbowed him.

To the students sitting at the tables, it seemed like they were outnumbered by the instructors, who were prowling around. It wasn't true, but the ratio of students to instructors had changed drastically in the last seven hours.

And the instructors let themselves be known to the students constantly. "Eat up," they said. "Eat hearty, stuff it away. Because you're going to need it. None of you will probably even survive the next evolution. You were lucky just to get this far."

To remind the students just what their situation was, the instructors had made several of them bring the portable bell into the mess hall. Standing at the front of the room, the brass bell shone in the bright lights. It promised an end to the pain, cold, and suffering of Hell Week. All a man had to do was walk up to it and pull the cord three times. Three rings of the bell and everything was over. He could go back to a normal life in the Navy, on board a ship, at a shore station, anyplace but to the Teams.

It was that last thought, to make it on to the Teams, that sustained most of the students. But some didn't have the willpower of the others. That was the purpose of Hell Week—to weed out those individuals who didn't have the drive to go what seemed an almost superhuman distance. It wasn't that they were bad sailors. Some of the men who quit BUD/S would go on to rewarding careers in the Navy. But for the rest of their lives there would always be that nagging thought in the back of their heads. They would wonder if they could have made it.

For Jeremy White and a number of others in the class, however, there was no question of whether they would make it. Their minds had been set and the goal was in front of them, no matter how far away it appeared at that moment. They would make it; the instructors would have to carry them out feet first before they would quit. Nothing the instructors could say or that the instructions required would change their minds.

Nothing?

As the students sat and stuffed themselves as quickly as they could, the instructors circulated with an eye to helping them build up the calories they would need for that morning, distributing dessert to the students. Though it was an unusual dish to be served at breakfast, the instructors had a great deal of pull with the staff of the mess hall. Besides, the students' bodies were so confused right now, they didn't know that this was really breakfast anyway: nice bowls of vanilla ice cream. Thick, rich, frozen ice cream.

And there was a second treat for the students. The instructors who weren't passing out ice cream had Popsicles. Nice handy treats on a stick of fruit flavoring, sugar, and frozen water. And every student had damned well finish every bite of their desserts.

Bob Miller remained a chow hound. He consumed everything put in front of him, and more. Even his tired classmates marveled at how the little guy could eat. It was a wonder he didn't start a fire in the paper napkins by striking sparks with his knife and fork. Jeremy didn't want to reach past Miller for anything for fear of either getting stabbed, or worse still, bitten by accident.

But the food, warmth, and seductive, almost relaxed atmosphere of the mess hall did the work the instructors expected it to. During the meal, two students got up and walked to the bell. The program wasn't for them; they didn't want to hack it anymore. So in spite of the protests of their classmates, the yells of "Don't," "No," and "Come back," right in front of everyone they rang the bell and quit.

At the tables, all of the students bowed their heads. Some just continued eating. An instructor led the quitters away, and that was it. They were gone and soon forgotten. Everything that didn't immediately affect the students' survival of Hell Week was unimportant.

But the instructors had accomplished their intention by putting the bell in the mess hall. It wasn't just to cause more students to ring out. The bell was a motivation to the rest of the students in the class, to those who wouldn't ring out, who knew they were not going to ring that bell. Each brass tone that sounded out from that bell set their resolution not to quit a little deeper. The instructors were not allowed to kill them, and that was the only way they would leave.

But there were still over 119 hours of Hell Week to go, and there were only thirty-six students left in Class 78. Just one evolution at a time—that was the only way to make it. Just one evolution at a time. Jeremy White sat at his table and said that to himself almost as a kind of prayer. If he had allowed himself to think about the week that stretched in front of him, what he had to face and overcome, it could have shattered his resolve.

So he confined himself to thinking about another

swallow of coffee, another bite of food. More fuel for the fire.

With the meal break over, the tired boat crews were ordered out of the mess hall as quickly as possible. This was a new torture, to get up and keep moving after sitting even for the short time they had been given for the meal. Joints had stiffened and muscles tightened. It was an effort just to stand up. But each student did move, stiffly and slowly at first. Encouragement from the instructors, as only they could give it, helped them along.

"Move, you maggots!" Chief Packard shouted, his voice echoing through the mess hall. "This is Hell Week, not a Sunday morning at the Day/Night Grill!"

The sound of Chief Packard's voice was enough to get the blood moving quicker in some of the students. They moved to the side of the mess hall and back to their boats, where they donned their vests, rigged for travel. To remind the last crew to get ready that it paid to be a winner, they were ordered to drop and knock out twenty push-ups. Then, to keep the rest of the class from feeling left out, they were all dropped for push-ups.

As a final touch to their meal, the students were told to stand by their boats, and the dreaded order to "Up boats" rang out. Now, a set of twenty boat push-ups would remind everyone where they still were; not the kind of push-up where they lay on the ground with their feet up on the boats, but where instead they were pushing the boat up over their heads.

To lift the boat up, the students had to force their

stiff arms to shove at the rubber in unison. Boats wobbled and tilted, but none fell. Mixed crews of tall and short men had the most trouble. Either the shortest men had to push up higher than they could reach, or their crewmates had to lift and hold the boats with bent arms. Either way, the exercise was agonizing.

Men in the crews struggled and groaned. And the instructors were once again ready to add their version of encouragement to the situation. At Boat Crew IV, Bob Miller was singled out by Instructor Hawke. With his face only inches from that of the struggling student, Hawke pointed out carefully just how Miller was letting down his crew.

"You little puke," Hawke shouted. "How the hell can you stand there and force your crewmates to carry your share of the boat? They're all working like hell to lift the boat, and you're just faking it!"

In fact, Miller was working as hard as all the other men in his crew to complete the exercise. But he was the shortest, and that was what Hawke was working on. It didn't matter that the situation wasn't fair to Miller. The instructors' philosophy was that life wasn't fair to begin with. And combat was the least fair environment of all. So picking on a situation that was completely out of the students' control was another way of pointing out this fact of life. Besides, if the student didn't like it, there was always the bell waiting close at hand.

The brass bell in its wooden frame had been carried out by the last group of students in the mess hall and placed back on the pickup truck. This had caused those students to make their boat crews the last ones to be manned, and therefore the first ones punished, which was just another fact of Hell Week life. You didn't have to like it, but you had to do it.

Their arms aching from the horrible boat push-ups, the students were ordered to lower the boats and line up for a bow to stern march. With their necks grinding in their ears from the weight of the boats, the class was moved out toward the waters of San Diego Bay on the east side of the Amphibious base.

The march was led by Instructor Lubi, who set a brisk pace. To keep up with him, the boat crew at the front of the procession broke into a shuffling run. This moved them ahead of the rest of the pack, breaking up the formation, and seemed to enrage the instructors. They moved alongside the group, shouting, "Bow to stern," the command to tighten up the line. This made the situation worse for the boat crew at the rear of the line, which had to run faster to catch up with the front crews. Boats bounced against one another and ground down on the students' heads.

To change the pace, Instructor Lubi would slow, and even stop on occasion, causing the entire line of boats to crash together. Then he would start out at a brisk walk again, repeating the cycle of running, bumps, and crashes among the boat crews. Bringing up the rear of the procession was Chief Packard in the gray Navy pickup truck, the hated bell secured in the rear.

Finally, the students reached the eastern side of the Amphibious base and the shore of San Diego Bay. The order to "Down boats" came as they were standing on the concrete of a helicopter landing pad. Now they would be conducting boat crew drills in the waters of the bay and in nearby Turner Field.

A shift change took place among the instructors, with a new group of the blue-shirted demons ready to accept their charges. To make sure that the class didn't think that anything significant had changed, the new instructors immediately sent them into the bay.

The wet students would be competing with each other as boat crews. Their teamwork within the crews was improving, and competition would help enforce a team effort. Each crew was only as good as its worst member, but rewards would be given to the whole crew. And punishment would be meted out the same way.

The morning went on and new evolutions came and went. One of the advantages of working in the bay was that the enclosed water was a few degrees warmer than the open ocean at the training compound. The disadvantage was that it meant the instructors could leave the students in the water longer without fear of hypothermia.

Caterpillar races were conducted in the bay. They were an excellent means to keep the students warm and busy. After running around Turner Field, the student would have to retie the leg straps of his kapok from around his waist to under his legs. Then the crews would get into the water and sit down, each crew member facing the back of the man in front of him. Now the students would have to wrap their legs around the man to their front and pull each other in snugly. This long, bizarre-looking assembly of humanity was then a long, watergoing caterpillar.

No one could actually swim in the caterpillar position. But the kapok vests gave the boat crew all the buoyancy it needed. They couldn't kick, but could paddle with their hands to get a caterpillar moving through the water, slowly and in a backward direction.

This was how the boat crews had to move themselves out into the bay waters and then run parallel to the shoreline for as much as a quarter mile. Then they would move back toward shore and land, only now they had to crawl over rocks and up a much sharper embankment to get back to where they would continue the races on foot.

These and other evolutions taxed the students and entertained the instructors. Slow crews were awarded punishments, while the fastest crew was permitted to rest for a moment while the other crews came in and finished. But what was considered resting depended on the whim of the instructor. The front leaning rest kept the boat crews in one place while the slower ones caught up. To keep the students from getting too sleepy, or just stiffening up in the cold morning air, the instructors found the liberal use of push-ups and other exercises an excellent preventative.

But the students endured, and boat crews became even tighter among themselves. The instructors could see the building of this teamwork. Faster students were helping the slower ones in their crews along. Stronger students could paddle harder during a caterpillar race, helping their crewmates as a whole. Even Kozuska seemed to be learning that he had to work with the men of his boat crew if they were to survive the week.

Long courses were run in the bay, the boats paddled by their crews as quickly as they could. The coxswains called out the stroke, and the crews riding the tubes dug their paddles in deeply. Races could consist of running with the IBS, entering the water, and then continuing the course paddling in the bay. Entering and exiting the water also required rerigging the leg straps to the kapoks. Any error, any mistake or cut corner, and the instructors were ready to award physical punishment in what seemed like ever increasing doses.

So the students made sure that they checked each other out when they rigged their leg straps or used their rubber boats. The bosun's mate training that Jeremy White had attended helped his boat crew, since he'd been taught the proper handling of ropes and rigging. He made sure that lines were properly stowed in Boat Crew IV's IBS for the constant examinations and inspections conducted by the instructors.

Sometimes Boat Crew IV came in first, sometimes it didn't. But like all of the crews, they were learning how to cooperate better with each other. Rappaport and Sledge in Boat Crew V, for instance, had drawn tighter together since rock portage the night before. There was no extra energy to be wasted on prejudices, which particularly didn't make sense in their present situation. And the stresses and strains of Hell Week were quickly stripping off the misconceptions and hates that some of the students had been conditioned to since childhood.

Hell Week would strip everyone who went through it, knock them down mentally and physically. Only those who had the heart to rebuild themselves would complete it.

That Monday morning, the California sun shone down on a group of young men struggling harder than they ever had in their lives. And those lives would never be the same.

## Chapter Sixteen

Everywhere the students went, the rubber boats were going with them. The only reason the boats weren't on their heads was that they were paddling them in the water. And if they weren't paddling the boats or carrying them around, they were conducting some other exercises. The movement was nonstop, their output constant. And the level of that output was applied to its maximum by the instructors. The only break the students received was when the instructors lined them up and moved them back across the Amphibious base to the mess hall for the midday meal.

The pain from carrying the boats hadn't lessened, and it couldn't be avoided, so it was just endured. Hell Week had turned into a long course of pain. Changes in the evolutions they were doing merely changed the kind of pain the students felt. The amount of abuse they were forcing their bodies to endure had placed them in constant pain, the only difference being its level of intensity. Joints, muscles, hands, and feet hurt.

Actually, just about everything hurt. And with that pain, they were learning that anything could be endured and conquered.

The midday meal on Monday was great chow again. But to the students, it was just something their bodies could burn. Volume and warmth replaced flavor as the reason for choosing anything from the steam tables in the mess hall. Selection actually would take more time than the students wanted to give it, so they just piled their trays with everything.

Meat, potatoes, coffee, milk, juice, hot cocoa, bread, cereal, pancakes, grits, almost everything that was offered was consumed. Salads and cold or refrigerated items were about the only dishes that were noticeably unpopular. Thousands of calories would be expended in doing work, so thousands of calories were consumed.

But exhaustion still could not be avoided. No talking was the rule in the mess hall during Hell Week, but none of the students wanted to talk anyway. A few had picked up a "thousand yard" stare while they sat and ate. All they could do was chew and swallow. And for some the chewing slowed down almost to a standstill as they were about to fall asleep right at their seats.

But the bell was always there to remind them how easy it could be to quit and be warm, clean, and rested again. And if the bell wasn't enough the instructors were moving about, constantly cajoling the class, telling the students they could just quit and it would be over. But no one rang out that morning. The meal passed and the class was put up on its feet and out the door.

A head break was given, as they were intermittently,

to allow the students to at least try to empty their bladders and bowels in a sanitary manner. One of the things that added so much to the stench of the students during Hell Week was the tendency to urinate in their pants while in the water or the surf zone. Any warmth gained that way was quickly lost, but even the sea couldn't wash out all of the traces.

Even during their head break, the students were harassed by the instructors. Part of the verbal abuse was to make sure that none of them fell asleep while sitting on the toilet. It had happened more than once, and the instructors would startle the transgressor very badly when they saw the need.

After the break, it was "Up boats" and across the street to the training compound. The tortures of "bow to stern" added to the students' misery as they carried the much hated IBS. Necks ground down into shoulders, pain radiated out from the back and shoulders to cover the whole body. So much pain and abuse had been heaped on the students' bodies by now that they had a hard time separating one pain from another. It was all blending into one big, agonizing blur.

The instructors moved the Navy pickup truck to block traffic while the students crossed the Silver Strand Highway between the Amphibious base and the training compound. It was likely that some of the students secretly wished that they hadn't—that if the civilian vehicles that were stopped on the road would speed up and hit them, their pain would be over without them having to quit.

But one of the reasons the instructors kept an eye on

the students was to protect them from themselves. In spite of the verbal abuse, the constant threats and the temptations to try to get the students to quit, the instructors also were concerned about the safety and general well-being of their charges. It was one thing to try to get a student to quit—to see if he had the mental toughness to keep going in a hard situation. But if an instructor allowed a student to be injured or even killed due to inattention or bad judgment, his career at BUD/S, in the Teams, and probably in the Navy, would be over almost instantly. In the Teams, the job was hard, and dangerous, so unnecessary risks were controlled as much as humanly possible.

Now the students were back at their training compound, just in time for a quick dip in the Pacific as a postmeal wakeup. Though the sun was up and it was early afternoon, the water had not warmed at all. To some of the students, it felt much colder than they remembered it being just the night before.

Wet and sandy was how the instructors liked seeing their charges. Constantly, the students were reminded that every day in the Teams involved being wet, cold, and sandy—so they had better get used to the feeling.

In and out of the water, and rolling about in the sand. For something new, Senior Chief Fletcher called for the students to form a volcano. This formation is unique to the Teams and to BUD/S training. All of the class gathers in a big circle on the beach, their backs to the center. At the command, the students pick up handfuls of sand and toss it into the air over themselves and their classmates all around them. While they do this, the students are required to show the proper enthusiasm for their situation by shouting out, "I'm a volcano! I'm a volcano!"

If they hadn't been so tired, and so intimidated by their instructors, some of them might have seen just how ridiculous they looked. But the idea behind their actions was anything but funny. It was based on something deadly serious.

Gunfire, demolitions, and shells exploding would toss up a lot more sand during wartime than the students were putting up with their hands. Their actions would teach them that they could still see and function even though the sand had filled every crevice of their bodies. Eyes, ears, and noses were quickly filled and clogged with the gritty, dirty beach sand. But they could still hear, and still see, at least after a fashion.

When a single shrill whistle blasted the students reacted quickly. They dove forward, crossed their legs at the ankles, and covered their ears and the tops of their heads with their hands. The reaction to whistle drills would become instinctive and for years to come remain with most of the students who completed the course. Which was exactly what the instructors wanted.

Two blasts, and the students were crawling through the sand to follow Senior Chief Fletcher as he led them up the beach. Recover, drop, recover, drop, crawl, then recover, drop, crawl, all over again. The whistle sounded, and the students responded. Pavlov would have loved it.

Now the class was brought up to its feet near the piles of telephone poles close to the obstacle course.

The poles were the same as those used in building most of the obstacles. Now was a time for a new Hell Week torture variation: log PT.

About half of the seven boat crews that were left had a full complement of six men, and the rest had five men each. The last crew consolidation had been conducted by the instructors at the Amphibious base. The class had done the log exercises before, but not with crews as small as some of theirs had become. And the instructors were making no effort to consolidate the crews to make the evolution any easier.

Instead of the rubber boats, the boat crews now had fourteen-foot lengths of eight-inch-thick telephone poles to deal with. With the weight of the poles being around three hundred pounds, the average weight a single student had to manage was the same as when they carried the IBS. But the logs seemed a lot heavier.

The students had to all line up next to their new nemesis, bend over, and pick up the damned logs. These exercises required total cooperation within the crews. Not only could a man be seriously injured if one of the logs was dropped on an arm or leg, but the exercises themselves were impossible to do without coordination among the students on the same log.

So they all bent over, trying to keep their backs straight, and lifted the logs while rising to a standing position. The entire crew had to face the log to properly pick it up, then they all turned forward on command from the instructor and lifted the log to their shoulders. Only by following the commands together could they hope to get through this evolution. The first time they had done log PT, it was hard. Now, with each member of the class experiencing a whole new level of fatigue, it was agony.

If enough hands slipped at the same time, that log would come crashing down on anyone underneath it. And everyone was underneath the poles at one time or another. The two-arm push-up had the students pushing the log up and over their heads, holding it there as long as the instructor felt was proper.

Groans sounded out from the class merely from lifting the logs from the ground to their shoulders. The groaning seemed to enrage Senior Chief Fletcher.

"What's the matter, ladies?" he yelled through his bullhorn. "You can't take a little weight? This is just the first day of Hell Week, we've got you for six more days. If you're all such a weak, miserable bunch, get the fuck out now! There's the bell, just ring it and go."

As it had since the beginning of Hell Week, the bell followed them around. It was now hanging in its wooden frame within sight of the students. To some, it offered an end to what they were facing; to others, it was just another challenge to be overcome.

Jeremy White gritted his teeth and held the log up. He had begun losing track of time, so Senior Chief Fletcher's comment about having them all for another six days didn't hold a lot of meaning for him. What mattered now was the pain in his arms and legs, and the weight of the log bearing down on him.

Boat Crew IV was luckier than some of the other crews. They at least had a full complement of six to spread out the weight of the log. As the shortest member of the crew, Bob Miller had to work like hell to hold up his share of the log, but he was doing it. The arguments about everyone holding up their share of the log had ended. Arguments would have wasted energy, and right now the students had all that they could do just to continue with the evolution.

Up would go the log, then it would have to stay there, held up solely by the strength of the students' arms. Then, finally, the instructor would yell out the command that would permit the students to lower the log down to their opposite shoulder. Then once again up, hold, and down.

Students were shaking on the first command to raise the logs over their heads, and after a number of repetitions of the exercise, the logs were anything but steady as they stayed in the air. Then Patrick Neil at the head of Boat Crew IV, slipped as the log was coming down.

It seemed that the entire boat crew collapsed in slow motion. Neil fell back against Jeremy before hitting the ground, then Jeremy fell back and to the side. As each student at the front of the line went down, the weight being held up by the students behind them grew that much greater. Finally, the whole of Boat Crew IV had hit the ground, pushing the log away from them as they went down.

Now, the importance of the different boat crews being at least ten feet apart during log PT showed itself. In spite of their going down and the log getting away from them, no one in Boat Crew IV was injured. And the log didn't hit the boat crews on either side. That could have caused a chain reaction that would have brought down the entire class, and probably resulted in a number of injuries. The only injury was to Boat Crew IV's pride, but Senior Chief Fletcher had a way of dealing with that.

The instructors could see that no one was hurt in the exercise mishap, so most of them went back to giving their attention to the boat crews that were still standing. Senior Chief Fletcher was immediately shouting at Boat Crew IV and letting them know just how unhappy he was with their performance.

Demonstrating a command of invective that would have peeled the paint off a destroyer, Fletcher was close to convincing the crew to immediately quit. But if they didn't want to quit, burying themselves under the beach sand with the rotting fish might be a much better place for them than in his Navy. The crew couldn't move fast enough to recover from the ground and get their log back in the air to satisfy Senior Chief Fletcher. And since the senior chief wasn't happy, no one would be.

Since Boat Crew IV hadn't been able to handle a simple log, the instructor somehow concluded that the weight must have been too light for them. So the crew was awarded Old Misery, the thicker, longer log that weighed over a hundred pounds more than the regular logs.

The punishment wasn't fair, but they had become used to the idea that nothing was fair at BUD/S, especially not during Hell Week. So Neil and his crew struggled with Old Misery, getting it up and into position as quickly as they could. At least it didn't look like they would have to start log PT all over again. Then Senior Chief Fletcher ordered the overhead toss exercise.

If the two-arm push-up was hard and dangerous, the overhead toss was agonizing and almost lethal. Now, instead of lifting the log up and holding it over their heads, the students had to toss the log up in the air over their heads. Then they had to catch it and lower it down to the opposite shoulder from where they had started. Then the movement was repeated to get the log back on the starting shoulder.

Teeth ground together as the boat crews fought to complete the exercise. Everyone had to put out their maximum effort in order to keep control of the logs. The students' knees were screaming with pain, as they had to squat each time they caught the log and brought it down to their shoulders. With Boat Crew IV struggling with Old Misery, the screaming wasn't just silently coming up from their knees. A couple of crew members were making their share of noise as they desperately tried to get the log into the air and back down safely. Jeremy couldn't tell if he was one of those making noise, but he pushed and worked just as hard as everyone else to control that massive chunk of wood. Finally, after an eternity of repetitions, Senior Chief Fletcher ordered the class to "Down logs."

All of the boat crews felt a moment's relief as they were allowed to lower the now hated logs. But that relief was short-lived, since they were now ordered to continue log PT, only this time while sitting on the ground.

There was something almost diabolical in having to

do sit-ups while holding a telephone pole across your chest. As a student leaned back on the down part of the exercise, he felt for a moment that the log was going to roll over onto his face. Then came the panic as he heaved up against the log, to sit up and lift it, only the log didn't move. It took a concerted effort by the entire boat crew to lift the log and complete the exercise. And in that moment before the log started to go up, the pressure on a student's chest was almost suffocating.

To increase the misery of the students as they continued their log sit-ups, several instructors walked up and down the line of struggling boat crews with rubber boat paddles. And they used these paddles to liberally toss beach sand down the backs of the students.

But the sand and the struggle wasn't enough for Senior Chief Fletcher. As he carefully explained over his bullhorn, he didn't want the students to overheat, so they would all now lower their logs and stand up.

Obviously, this meant a trip to the surf zone and the cold Pacific waters. Some of the students dreaded the exposure to the cold. Most of the rest managed to just face it stoically. But the orders that came next bothered them all.

They had to pick up their logs and start a race around the obstacle course.

With the logs on their shoulders, the boat crews began a shuffling run. Around the course they went, and down the beach, straight toward the surf zone, at the direction of Senior Chief Fletcher. They knew that the heat they built up during the exertion with the logs would make the water feel even colder.

And the water was very cold as the students lined up along the edge of the surf zone. At the command, they walked into the waves, carrying their logs with them. Within a few moments the earlier log sit-ups on the beach were just a pleasant memory. Pleasant in comparison to doing the same exercise while sitting in the surf zone.

Now, each time a boat crew sat back with their logs, the waves could crash over a student's face. This was a real test of willpower and trust among the members of a boat crew. Sitting up still took a moment to get the log moving. But in that moment, the student was not only feeling the weight against his chest, it felt like the log was holding his head underwater.

It took concentration to both hear the orders of the instructors and not panic in the water. The sea was the natural environment for a SEAL or UDT man. And the instructors wanted the students to know that thoroughly. There was no place in the sea for someone who would panic at a difficult situation in the water. And there absolutely wasn't a place in the Teams for someone who couldn't accept a little difficulty with the water.

As the cold started to seep into the students as they lay there struggling against the weight of the logs, the instructors reminded them that all they had to do was quit. The pain, the cold, the discomfort—it would all be over with the ringing of a bell. In fact, the instructors said they would end the evolution immediately if just one student quit. All that had to happen was for one student to get up and come out of the water to ring the bell, and this agonizing exercise would end. If things were so bad for them, how could they force that same suffering on their friends?

It didn't work. No student quit and left his share of the log to be picked up by his crewmates. Senior Chief Fletcher told them that he was convinced that this was the dumbest class he had ever been forced to watch drown. So to keep their stinking carcasses from polluting his ocean, the class could get up and return to shore.

The logs would be put back where the students had found them; all they had to do was follow Instructor Burns. But nothing was said about the path Instructor Burns would take getting back to the obstacle course where the logs belonged. It was a zigzag route that the instructor laid out, and the students had to follow along. Their arms curled over the log on their shoulders, each boat crew member had his head almost pushed into his shoulder from the force of the log pressing against his neck.

But there were no breaks, no time-outs. The evolutions were coming fast and hard, though the students couldn't see the reasoning behind it. Most of the veteran instructors knew that if they let the students have the time to think, many of them would think too much about what they were doing, and especially how much they hurt. That kind of introspection could cause a man to up and quit the program, even though he had everything he needed inside himself to complete Hell Week and go on to graduation.

So the instructors kept up the pace. Now that the

students were back by the obstacle course, they were finally allowed to set the logs down. But the logs had to be properly stacked and arranged, and Old Misery was secured separately back in its place of honor. The members of Boat Crew IV had never hated an inanimate object as much as they despised Old Misery just then. Those damned chunks of wood had even managed to make the rubber boats start to look good.

Since the class was already next to the obstacle course, Senior Chief Fletcher thought it would be a shame not to make use of it. But instead of going through the course as individuals, the students would compete as boat crews. Each crew would have to complete an obstacle as a group before they could go on to the next obstacle. So the speed of each boat crew would be determined by their slowest man.

Teamwork was always the watchword pushed by all of the instructors. But maximum individual effort was also needed to get the job done. It was very hard not to do your best when you knew your immediate classmates were depending on you. And the instructors constantly said that it paid to be a winner.

## Chapter Seventeen

Now the boat crews attacked the obstacle course. And even though it was each student's responsibility to complete the obstacles himself, some help was "ignored" by the instructors. When Boat Crew IV hit the Dirty Name, Bob Miller slowed down on the obstacle he always had the hardest time with. The logs that they had to run up and jump up on were just too high for Miller to clear easily. But he was game, and he didn't slack off in his attempt to negotiate the obstacle.

When Miller was trying to clamber over the logs, the instructor nearby didn't notice Jeremy White or Jim Alex shoving him while trying to get over the obstacle themselves. The pushing helped Miller get up on the logs, but the dogged student would have gotten over the log if he'd had to dig at it with his teeth.

On the cargo net, Richard Kozuska paused at the top to reach over and give Rod Shea a hand up and over. The more experienced instructors knew that those students who were putting out that little bit extra to help their fellow students were likely to make it through the week, and maybe the course.

It was late afternoon of the first full day of Hell Week as the first boat crew completed the obstacle course competition. Boat Crew I, following class leader Lieutenant Butterworth, had come in ahead of the rest by a good minute. Their reward was to knock out a quick twenty push-ups while waiting for the next boat crew to finish. Senior Chief Fletcher told them they hadn't completed the obstacles fast enough. But even after they finished, Boat Crew I was able to rest for the few minutes it took for the rest of the crews to complete the course, including Chief Packard's twenty push-up addition.

When all the crews had completed the O-course, the instructors decided there was still time for a quick run down the beach before chow. So, lining up, the students took off after Instructor Burns for an easy one mile conditioning run.

On completion of the run, only a few students were vomiting. Jeremy White was concerned that if he threw up after a run, he would be dropped from the course, even though he had little more than some white foam to toss up onto the sand. But one instructor told him that the reaction showed he was "putting out well." Still, the situation felt anything but good to Jeremy.

There was little time given to any of the students to dwell on the run, or their situation. The instructors wanted them to put on their kapok vests and rig them for land travel. Then it was "Up boats" for another trip across the Silver Strand Highway and on to the Amphibious base. The trip to the middle of the base, and the Enlisted Dining Hall in Building 300, seemed even longer to the students than it had earlier that afternoon. Or maybe it was just the lengthening shadows, indicating that another long, cold night was fast approaching. But at the mess hall there was hot food at least, and meanwhile another shift change of fresh instructors.

The meal, as before, was a comfort, and a danger, to the students. The warmth and food caused them to relax and feel better, if only for a moment. And that made it all the harder to get up and get moving afterward. But the instructors were there to make sure that the students didn't relax too much. Chief Deckert was in charge of the new shift of instructors, and the always smiling, easygoing, and absolutely lethal Instructor Lubi was part of the new shift.

The students weren't given any time to think about what might be in store for them after the meal. They were immediately taken back to their boats and ordered back across the highway. For several hours it was another blur of pain, running, and exercising. Boat drills, push-ups, and running occupied the students. Then came time for surf appreciation.

As they locked arms and walked into the water, Chief Deckert directed the students to gaze off to the west and the setting sun. "Wave good-bye," he ordered the class through his bullhorn. "Everyone wave good-bye to the sun. He was your only friend, and now he's gone."

By this time the entire class was waving at the setting sun. They were too tired to even feel foolish about what they were doing and what it might have looked like. Instead, they heard Chief Deckert's last words as the sun was going down.

"Wave good-bye," Deckert said. "Some of you will never see that sun here again. You'll be gone long before the morning comes around."

Then it was on with the business of Hell Week. And that business was seeing just how far the students could push themselves without quitting. The big exercise for the evening was a long rubber boat paddle down the beach. Then they would have to get up and cross the Silver Strand with their rubber boats and continue their paddling in the waters of San Diego Bay.

Coronado used to be an island facing the Pacific on one side and San Diego Bay on the other. Then Navy dredges and Seabee construction crews filled in the part of the bay that separated Coronado Island from Imperial Beach, beyond. The area had been long, but relatively shallow. Now known as the Silver Strand, the Navy's landfill connected Coronado with the mainland to the south, and supplied an excellent length of beach for prospective BUD/S students to work out on.

The long paddle and cross-beach portage was not the famous "Round the World" tour that the students knew was part of Hell Week. That evolution would be coming later. This particular evolution was more of a sample of what they were in for later. But even as a sample, it stood out as a stretch of misery all its own.

For hours, the boat crews paddled their rubber boats on a southbound course through the Pacific waters along the Silver Strand. The waves and currents slowed the rubber boats, making the several miles of the southbound leg of the trip seem much longer than it was. Finally, the students saw the signal on shore where the headlights of an instructor's pickup truck was facing out to sea. Then they headed inland and across the Strand.

Just as it paid to be a winner, it also helped to pay attention to the details. Jeremy's boat crew was ahead in the competition, until they went in to shore. On land, the sharp-eyed instructor at the pickup truck allowed Boat Crew IV to get ready to move out, pick up their boat, and even start to cross the beach. Then he stopped them and dropped them for push-ups. On land, the leg straps of the kapoks had to be rerigged around the waist, a missed detail that now put Boat Crew IV in second place.

San Diego Bay was much calmer and easier to cross than the ocean side had been. So the boat crews made good time heading north toward the Amphibious base and the finish line at Turner Field. Boat Crew IV managed to pull ahead of the pack again, this time earning a precious few moments rest at the finish line before the rest of the boat crews began to pile in.

Since there still was some time before mid-rats (midnight rations) would be served, the students had time for a little exercise. They were told to down boats and get into the push-up positions with their feet up on the sides of the rubber boats.

Exhausted, the students were barely able to even fake the push-ups ordered by Chief Deckert. They could barely hold themselves up off the ground with arms that had been paddling for miles. Instead of dropping their chests and pushing up with their arms, heads bobbed up and down, and that was about all the "push-ups" consisted of. The instructors, recognizing the edges of collapse coming up on the students, mostly accepted the poor quality of the exercises.

Having grown up around horses during his childhood in Montana, it seemed to Chief Deckert that if he had a horse as swaybacked as the students looked, he would have to shoot it to put it out of its misery.

For the students, the misery continued with the order to up boats and move out to the mess hall. Mid-rats was an extra meal only put on during Hell Week. The cooks had prepared food, up to their usual standards and plenty of it for the incoming students, and after the preparations were done, they and most of the mess stewards left the mess hall for the evening. So the instructors filled in at the mess hall, standing behind the steam tables and loading up the students' trays.

Most of the students' hands were so stiff that they couldn't hold a utensil. Hot coffee, cocoa, and even just a big mug of hot water, were valued for the warmth that seeped into sore hands. Eventually, fingers were forced to bend and the food was consumed. Food equaled heat, and the night was still young.

Outside the mess hall, the students were handed back over to the night shift and Chief Packard. In no uncertain terms, the chief informed the students that they'd had things far too easy for him to be satisfied with their Hell Week. And he would take it upon himself to personally correct that situation.

The night became a blur of activity. Distance swimming in the bay, boat drills, exercises, and running all merged together in a big mess of misery, pain, and movement. Above all, the cold stood out. When the students had to carry their boats across the highway to the training compound, they knew that the cold waters of the Pacific were waiting for them. And Chief Packard took advantage of every cold degree of those waters.

Chief Packard forced the students to soak in the cold water, but before hypothermia had a chance to slip in, he had them get out and roll in the beach sand. This didn't warm the students up much, and the cold night air on their wet skin and uniforms kept them shivering unless they were moving and working hard. When the class lined up to go back into the water, even the most steadfast students quailed at the thought of reentering the ocean.

But they had to go back in, and they did. During the early morning hours, only one more student rang the bell and gave up. Even in his misery, Jeremy White looked on that student's quitting as a means of raising his own morale. He was still there. He was gutting it out. He hadn't quit. That little boost to his motivation helped. It didn't make him any warmer, it didn't cause his muscles to spasm any less from the cold. But it set his heart and mind more firmly on the path to the Teams.

And it was Tuesday. The first full day of Hell Week was over. But none of the students let that thought go to their heads, if their own discomfort left any room for the thought in the first place. It was one evolution at a time. You didn't look forward to the next evolution, just the one you were in the middle of.

One of the other catch phrases of BUD/S was: "The only easy day was yesterday." And yesterday had only been easy because it was over and done with. It was the present that had to be faced.

## Chapter Eighteen
## Tuesday

During Tuesday, nothing stopped, or even slowed down much. Everywhere the class went, it was with the rubber boats on their heads. Or, if it wasn't pressing down on the students, it was on the ground and they were doing some other physical evolution, or they were sitting in the surf, to fully enjoy the brisk Pacific waters.

The instructors didn't limit themselves to just soaking the students in saltwater. There was a swimming pool available on the Amphibious base that was suitable for certain evolutions. The pool drills were something each student would have found hard even had they been well-rested and refreshed, and that was not their condition by the second day of Hell Week.

Pool drills had the students working as boat crews and swimming lengths while holding a towel in each hand, which made it hard for even the best swimmers to negotiate the length of the pool.

The wet towel stretching out behind them dragged through the water. The effort needed just to move a hand forward when there was a towel in it was tremendous. And lifting an arm out of the water for an overhand stroke was next to impossible; the weight of the towel alone would prevent it. But the instructors hadn't said how the swimmers had to cross the pool, only that they had to have a towel in each hand when they did it.

To increase the effort put into the evolution, the instructors made it a competition among the boat crews. There wasn't any question that it paid to be a winner. Even the least reward for a winning boat crew tended to be a moment or two of precious rest. So the competition did raise the level of effort, but not all of the boat crews were equal in size.

Some of the crews had five people, the rest had six. To make things even for the competition, the instructors announced that the race was over for a boat crew when six people had done the evolution. Six was the number of people in a normal boat crew, so the choice made sense. Besides, arguing with an instructor was worse than useless. Arguments were always won by the instructor; fair didn't come into it. And any bitching usually resulted in a lot of extra exercise for the student stupid enough to complain. That lesson had been learned well before Hell Week started.

As a result, in four of the remaining seven boat crews one person had to swim the length of the pool and back twice. If a boat crew had any sense, they chose their best swimmer for the job. Boat Crew IV was one of the lucky three remaining crews to have six people in its ranks, so each man would only have to swim the pool once.

The evolution was run as a relay race. When one student had finished going the length of the pool and back, the next one started out as soon as the first touched the side. The rest of the boat crews were shouting their people on. For those moments, swept up in the excitement of the competition, they forget how miserable they all were.

When Jeremy's turn in the relay came, he hit the water and started out hard, but the towels held him back. He'd seen that the best way to swim while holding the towels was to ball them up in each hand, and he did that. The towels still trailed behind and dragged in the water, but the drag was at least minimized.

It was a long, hard swim, even though the distance was fairly short, considering the miles the class had done in the ocean. As Jeremy's hands grew tired, the towels began to unwrap and trail out through the water. It didn't seem to matter how hard he tried, they kept getting longer. The turn at the far end of the pool was the worst, since it nearly caused the towels to slip from his grasp. But he bunched them up again while maintaining forward motion in the water.

Finally, Jeremy reached the end of the pool, and it was Jim Alex's turn to make a run. Jeremy's arms were aching and there were pains in whole new places, especially in his shoulders and chest. From the locations of his most recent aches and pains, he could see that the towel swim would require serious upper body strength to do it with any speed.

But one of the boat crews had a lot of upper body strength, at least in one person. Richard Kozuska, running the pool twice for Boat Crew II, won the towel race. But that wasn't the end of the pool evolutions. More swimming had to be done, and even stranger objects had to be taken along.

SEALs and UDT men would have to be able to get up on land with the equipment they would need to accomplish their mission. So it wouldn't work to just be a good, fast swimmer. You also had to be able to take the gear in. To simulate this, the instructors had the brick swim.

That was it, nothing fancy. You had to swim the length of the pool and back while taking a brick along with you. And you had to do it as fast as you could.

No matter who the swimmer was, carrying a seven or eight pound brick would make anyone negatively buoyant. Part of the evolution was to just get the job done and complete the swim. Another part was to try and figure out the easiest way to do the swim while taking the brick along. Like most of his classmates, Jeremy White just stuck the brick into his pants and struck out on the swim.

Having a fairly sharp-edged brick in your pants would make most swimmers pause a bit. But Class 78 had already been so beaten up by Hell Week that a little thing like the corner of a brick digging into your groin could be ignored. All the student had to do was swim harder so he could still break the surface and grab a breath of air now and then.

The strangest pool evolution involved swimming lengths while also towing an empty bucket through the water, behind the swimmer. As strange as it looked, this evolution had been developed from combat operations conducted by the UDTs during World War II. During those swims against enemy beaches, the frogmen had towed in packs of high explosives to demolish obstacles. In some operations, individual swimmers were towing as many as five packs connected in a long chain. That kind of swimming took some real skill, and a lot of strength and endurance.

But the students of Class 78 didn't know the background of the evolution. What they knew was that you had to swim while towing a big open bucket. The towels had caused a lot of drag on the arms when they trailed back in the water. The bucket was much worse. The open mouth acted like a scoop against the flow of the water, at least until some of the swimmers thought of plugging it up.

As before, the instructors didn't care how you did something, just that you did it. So some of the students caught on to the idea of pulling the bucket up tight against their bottoms, effectively sealing off the big, water-dragging mouth, while also making for some interesting swimming techniques.

Some of the students used a different technique for crossing the pool with their buckets. Since they were naturally negatively buoyant to begin with, and the extra weight of the bucket helped them sink even faster, they just went down to the bottom of the pool and walked across the bottom. They had to come up for air now and then, but the walking technique was another way to get the job done.

During this and other portions of the pool evolutions, the instructors were more than a little amused to watch the struggling students. Part of their amusement was an act, just like their constant harassment and verbal abuse of the students. The object was to try and weed out those men who couldn't take it, no matter what *it* was. Instructors were Teammates too, and they might very well have to operate with graduates of Class 78 later in their careers.

But there was some real amusement in watching the antics of the students. All the instructors had gone through BUD/S themselves. Everything the students of Class 78 were doing, the instructors had also done. They remembered struggling through the same evolution while their instructors watched and laughed. There was just something inherently funny about watching a guy swim in a pool with a bucket stuck over his ass.

After the evolutions in the pool were over, it was back to the boats to pick them up and start moving around again. When the time came around for mid-rats, it was back to the mess hall and a meal. The students had lost count of their meals. Many of them had already lost count of the days. Hell Week was turning into a big blur. In later years, most of the men who had completed Hell Week wouldn't be able to describe the whole week. Events would run into one another, and they'd remember specific incidents rather than the whole week.

Meals had become even more of a danger, as well as a necessity. Students concentrated only on shoveling food into their mouths. The warmth and comfort of the food and the mess hall, as always, could quickly combine to put an exhausted student to sleep in mid-bite. So it became even more of a fight to keep going and not think about quitting. There was also the strange behavior of the instructors to think about.

As the night before—or was it the night before that?—the instructors were acting as the servers and cooks behind the steam tables of the mess hall during mid-rats. As the students had learned, more food meant more heat, and they wanted everything that could be piled up on their trays. The instructors seemed to outnumber the students as they filled the trays and moved the line along.

As the spaghetti, meat, grits, pancakes, scrambled eggs, and other food piled on the trays, the instructors also added their own tips. "Eat hearty," they said. "Take it all, you'll need it. Because none of you will last out the next evolution."

Whatever was meant by the instructors' words, it didn't do any good to dwell on them. But some of the students apparently did. The portable bell had been sitting in the chow hall, and one of the students took up its offer of warmth and sleep. In front of everyone, three rings of the bell sounded out and another one was gone from their ranks.

None of the remaining members of Class 78 even looked at the young man as he rang out. With bowed heads, his ex-classmates just looked at their food as the defeated man left the mess hall to return to the regular Navy.

For Jeremy White, the man's defeat was, once again, motivation to complete the week, and the training beyond that. He couldn't imagine what had gone through that young man's head as he rang out and quit. Everyone was cold, everyone was tired—more tired than they had ever been in their lives. But what one man had done before, Jeremy knew he could also do. And every member of the Teams had done what they were doing now.

The time for mid-rats was over, and so was the warmth and unbelievable luxury of just being able to sit. Class 78 looked ready to be the stand-ins for a bunch of ghosts who died back during the Civil War. Their shoulders were slumped down from the stress put on them from the boats, logs, and exercises. Limping was common, though a really bad limp would draw the attention of the corpsman and could cause a student to be rolled back or even dropped because of an injury.

Students walking on broken legs were common at BUD/S during Hell Week. Stress fractures would take place in the lower legs, about where the tops of the students' boots were. If the fracture happened late enough during Hell Week, the individual might be able to finish up with his class. But the far more likely result of a stress fracture would be a rollback to the next class. Besides losing the friends and breaking up the loyalties that had developed within a class, being rolled back also meant you would have to do everything again.

Jeremy attributed the sharp pains he felt in his

lower legs to shin splints. He felt he could gut them out, just last and put up with the pain until Hell Week was over. Besides, the cold they were exposed to actually helped make the pain go away. Well, the pain in his shins anyway.

If cold helped Jeremy White, he was about to get his fill of it.

## Chapter Nineteen

One of the memories for many men who went through Hell Week was the steel piers. A line of boat docks and piers extended out into Glorietta Bay, and into San Diego Bay beyond, on the north side of the Amphibious base. With the rubber boats on their heads, the class was headed out from the mess hall to the docks. The actual distance between the enlisted dining hall and the specific pier the students were heading for was relatively short, but the instructors' route did not lead directly to the piers.

With the instructor shift change at midnight, Chief Packard and his band of demons were back. If anyone could have proven at that moment that hell was like a long version of Hell Week, the majority of the students would have quit and joined a monastery. But that fact couldn't be proven, though as some of the students may have been suspected. What would be proven very shortly was just what the expression "colder than hell" could mean.

Past Tarawa Road, which the students had been running up and down for the past two days, was the line of piers extending out into the water. At the end of some of the piers were floating barges whose open decks were covered with grids made of pierced steel planking. PSP, as it was more commonly called, had been developed to quickly build or repair airstrips on enemy islands, or to make a fast roadway across shifting beach sands. The PSP was thick strips of steel, perforated with holes to help keep it light, with edges that interlocked with other PSP strips to make a surface area as large as desired. To the students of Class 78, PSP would be cold and wet, and add to the torture of their next evolution.

The wind never seemed to quit blowing across the water and up among the piers on the north side of the base. In the shallows of Glorietta Bay, the water was five or more degrees warmer than it was on the Pacific side of Coronado. That put it in the low to mid-sixties. And the water was warmer than the surrounding air.

The students either didn't notice or, more likely, just didn't care that the number of instructors on this shift was higher than on earlier shifts. Also, one of the pickup trucks was outfitted with a lot of safety gear, and the chief corpsman sat at the wheel, with an assistant corpsman right next to him. The steel pier was going to be a dangerous evolution due to the exposure to the cold the students would face. Hypothermia was a very real danger, and steps were taken well beforehand to first prevent it from happening, and then deal with it quickly if it took place anyway.

The students of Class 78 knew none of this. They knew that they were ordered to ground their boats and then walk off the end of the pier. The cold water closed over their heads, and they came to the surface bobbing and spitting saltwater. Ordered to tread water, the students began to shiver in the cold water.

Their exposure to the water went on and on. All they could do was keep kicking and try to follow the instructors' bellowed orders. When Chief Packard ordered them to form a beehive, some of the students had almost forgotten what that order even meant. Instructions were quickly forthcoming from the bullhorn in Chief Packard's hand, along with a torrent of abuse for the poor showing by the students.

The beehive was a strange swimming technique for anyone who had not experienced it. Even having gone through it, the formation was still odd. In the beehive, all of the students would form a clump in the water. They would draw together as closely as they could and were not allowed to separate or spread out. It wasn't that they had to link arms, as they would when going in the water for surf appreciation. Instead, they just had to tread water in this tight formation.

It was another technique to make the students more comfortable in the water. It also helped them survive as a group. In the cold waters off the steel pier, all the students wanted to survive was that evolution, and most of them wanted to get up and out.

It pays to be careful what you wish for. Sometimes, you get it.

Now, the shivering, soaked students were ordered

up and out of the water. Ladders along the sides of the barge were the only way for the class to get up to the deck. The limited number of ladders made it difficult to get out of the water quickly, and seemed to enrage Chief Packard.

"You slow, retarded maggots!" he bellowed. "Have you become so useless that you can't even climb a ladder? Just what in the hell are you going to do over the next six days of Hell Week? Drop and on your backs!"

Chief Packard had intentionally given them the wrong number of days remaining in Hell Week. It was just another mental ploy to mess with the students' heads as they became dingy from lack of sleep and general exhaustion. The chief was keeping a close eye on how the students were moving and reacting. Slow and stupid was partially accounted for in the use of the term "dingy" in the Teams. But those same reactions could be the first warning signs of hypothermia.

The students dropped to the steel decking and immediately rolled over onto their backs. The wind blowing across the deck seemed to strip the heat from their bodies. Whatever warmth that might have been in them was sucked away by the pierced steel planks. It was the kind of cold that could drive a man insane, and all of the students had to endure it to continue training.

The shivering started almost immediately, and it was a deep, bone-shaking shiver. Chattering teeth were among the lesser agonies as the major muscles of the body tried to work against themselves to build up body heat and protect the core temperature of the body. All the movement of these muscles was involuntary, and severe. The students couldn't have stopped it if they'd wanted to. And the level of pain deep inside their muscles caused by the shivering caused a lot of them to want the shivering to stop.

The first symptoms of hypothermia included severe pain and heavy shivering. But this was a shaking that could be better described as convulsions, or close to them. As the body's core temperature continued to drop from further exposure to cold, thinking became hard, and speech was slurred when it reached around ninety-three degrees.

At a core temperature of ninety-one degrees, speech became very hard to understand, as the slurring of words blurred everything together and thinking was very difficult. With a core temperature of around eighty-nine degrees, a person became drifty, sluggish, and semicomatose. At this point, the individual could actually start to feel warmer. With a core temperature of around eighty-seven degrees, the individual was barely conscious, if they were awake at all. And even the shivering of the body trying to warm itself would have stopped. At this stage of hypothermia, death or permanent brain damage was a very real possibility.

"So, you think you're a little cold, do you, maggots?" Chief Packard shouted into his bullhorn as he circulated around the students. "Well, we'll just have to give you a little something to help warm you up. Flutter kicks, maggots. Get your feet up off of my deck!"

The students raised their feet six inches up from the deck and prepared to start kicking up into the air. But Chief Packard didn't give the order to start exercising.

Instead, he just let the class lay their while trying to hold their feet up. Legs and feet shook from both the shivering and the effort of holding them in the air. And still Chief Packard didn't give the order to begin.

The tension was agonizing, both from the leg lifts and the cold. Instructors moved about the prone bodies of the students, watching for any of the danger signs of hypothermia and covering their concern with heaps of verbal abuse.

As legs dipped from the strain and started hitting the deck, Chief Packard pounced on the mistake.

"All right, you maggots!" he shouted. "If you can't hold up for a simple exercise, you must have too much weight on you. Recover and remove your shirts!"

Now the entire class got up and stripped off their fatigue shirts. At first, getting rid of the heavy, wet clothes seemed like a good thing. Then the wind hit their wet skins, covered only by a white cotton T-shirt.

Again the class was dropped, and this time the shivering was even worse as they lay on the cold steel planking.

"Legs up," Chief Packard ordered. "Exercise!"

The class started doing the flutter kicks they all knew and hated so well. As they continued lifting their legs in the air one at a time, Chief Packard seemed to get even more angry with them.

"They must be getting heat stroke from all of the exercise," he said. "Cool them off."

Then instructors with fire hoses sent streams of freezing seawater over the students. As they gasped and shuddered with the cold, legs hit the deck. Again

Chief Packard ordered them up and had them remove more clothes. With just a few repetitions, and further rages thrown by Chief Packard over their mistakes, the students were down to wearing their skivvies as they lay down on the steel deck.

This was an agonizing level of cold none of them had ever experienced before. Even Jeremy White, who had grown up with the winters of central Ohio, had never experienced cold as he felt it on the steel pier. Thoughts of quitting, of ending the pain and cold, slipped into his mind. It entered other students' minds as well. In the background, above the shouted orders and rushing sound of the fire hoses, came the sound of a ringing bell. As one student quit, Jeremy hardened himself to keep going.

Then the students were ordered up on their feet and back into the water. Some of them were reluctant, and the instructors shouted in their faces that the only way to stay out of the water was to ring the bell. And some of them did ring out. The rest of the class went back off the end of the pier and into the water.

Jeremy wasn't reluctant to get back into the water. He knew that the water was actually warmer than the air. But that didn't make it any more comfortable. Now they were all treading water again, only this time they were almost naked.

The drown-proofing the students had gone through before Hell Week came into play as they treaded water. When the instructors ordered them to duck their heads under the water, everyone did as they were told. Then they were put back into a beehive.

The beehive formation was for the students' protection, but not the way they might have thought. It kept them all in one place so the instructors could better keep an eye on them. Flashlights in the instructors' hands shone down and illuminated one cold face after another. Then they were ordered back onto the steel pier for another round of exercises.

The shivering almost never stopped. But as the students lay on the deck, one of them was moving very slowly. Nguyen Thanh was still game and not complaining, but he could barely move. And when the instructor went up to him and shined his light in Thanh's face, it was clear that he was hardly shivering at all. Immediately, the corpsmen pulled Thanh off the deck and back to the truck, where they began working on him. Even without knowing exactly what was going on, the students could see that Thanh was in trouble.

Thanh was in the latter stages of hypothermia. When a man passed through the different levels of hypothermia and he got colder, the pain and discomfort lessened and he drew closer to death. But the pain of coming back from the brink was much worse than the cold that had caused it in the first place.

The rest of the class was put through their experience of the steel pier while Thanh was attended to. The instructors knew not to let panic go through the students' ranks, otherwise they could lose them all to quitting, even though they were not in any danger themselves.

As the minutes passed, Thanh recovered under the care of the corpsmen. And he wanted to continue with his class. The instructors allowed the class to give him a ragged cheer as the slight Vietnamese came back among them. But they also knew to keep a sharp eye on Thanh. Once a person has succumbed to hypothermia and recovered, it's that much easier for them to suffer from it again.

And the tortuous cold continued. Icy sprays from the fire hoses kept the students soaked. Then dips in the bay helped to warm them up a bit. The inevitable happened and Thanh again went into hypothermia, almost losing consciousness while treading water with his classmates.

The sharp-eyed instructors immediately ordered the class to get Thanh up and out of the water. The instructors and corpsmen lifted the comatose Asian up and onto the deck of the pier. He was alive and he would stay that way, in no small part due to the expert administrations of the corpsmen. As soon as he was able to speak, Thanh said he wanted to rejoin his classmates. But he was not allowed to come back to Class 78.

The man had all the heart he needed, but his body wasn't built for the level of cold the students experienced during a winter BUD/S class. And Thanh had not completed enough of Hell Week for the instructors to let him roll forward. Instead, he would be rolled back to go through BUD/S again, only this time in a summer class.

In a rare showing of understanding on the part of the instructors, Class 78 was told about their classmate and that he would make a full recovery. That, according to the opinion of Chief Packard, was more than he could say for the shivering mass of humanity that was on the deck in front of him.

That shivering mass was much smaller than it had been before. The steel pier had cost Class 78 nine members from its ranks. Thanh was a rollback and wouldn't be with them at graduation. The remaining eight students had rung the bell and would soon be on their way to the regular Navy.

Now the sore, stiff, shaking remainder of Class 78 was allowed to get off the steel pier and put their wet clothes back on. Stiff fingers tried to work buttons. The wet clothes held no comfort for the students. Just getting dressed was one of the worst things they had ever done in their lives. The cold, clammy cloth draped against the skin caused a new fit of shaking to come over them.

The rage that Chief Packard showed at the students' clumsiness was staged. He used it as a reason to put the students through more exercises, this time away from the salt spray of the hoses and the cold waters of the bay. The students were knocked around from the rock portage of the night before. Their muscles were painful from all of the exercise they had been put through. And now even their bones and joints were stiff and painful from the cold.

The only thing that would warm them up was movement. That, and they had to find it within themselves to shake off the experience of the steel pier and keep going. Tuesday night was over now, and Wednesday morning was well under way. It was time for them to up boats and move out to the training compound again.

Some of the boat crews had been almost wiped out by the students dropping out during the steel pier evolution. Historically, that evolution was second only to Breakout in the number of students it caused to quit. But Class 78 had no way of knowing that. They knew, however, that they didn't have enough people to move the boats lying near the pier.

Quick and expert action by the instructors soon straightened out the boat crews. From the seven crews that had started the night, there were only four full crews left. And only one of those crews had an extra man. George Staverous, the Greek officer and the only foreign student in Class 78 now, had most of his boat crew quit during the evolution. Staverous was now part of Boat Crew I, and Art Logan, the only other survivor from Boat Crew VII, was assigned to fill Tim Beardsley's vacant spot in Boat Crew IV.

Even with the shifting about, there were extra boats to deal with. Those rubber boats were put in the back of one of the pickup trucks, and the rest went back on the heads of Class 78. All of the students were well-rehearsed in how to carry a rubber boat by now, and they settled in with each other quickly. Since the line of boats had shrunk by almost half, the bow-to-stern trip back across the Silver Strand Highway was now a little easier.

Once at the compound, the students were again given a little time to warm themselves as boat crews. The kapoks they put back on added some insulation against the night cold, and the movement and work in carrying the boats produced a bit of warmth in their systems.

As they huddled together as boat crews, they pushed and rubbed, and came closer together than they ever had with any other peer group in their lives. The bonds that were being forged on that beach were constructed from mutually experienced pain and effort. They would last a lifetime.

But training was going to continue. When Chief Packard ordered surf appreciation, just the thought of entering that cold water brought the uncontrolled shivering back for most of the students. But they sucked it up and linked arms to march into the water. None of them noticed that the line of students that made up Class 78 was less than half the length it had been only two days before. The class had been pretty well cleaned of any dead weight or uncommitted students.

The cold of the Pacific was something they would be able to deal with. Then a series of runs, exercises, and sand crawling would start to warm them up and prepare them for the sunrise, which was only a few hours away.

## Chapter Twenty
### Wednesday

Though the days and the events blurred together, the students had to remain as sharp as they could to conduct their evolutions. To go in for a meal, the boat drills had to be conducted perfectly. It didn't matter how tired they were, if they didn't do things right the first time, they would be repeating them over and over until they got it right.

Each group of instructors had their own way of taking the class in to chow. Some, such as Chief Packard, were always hard. His idea of getting ready to do the boat drills that preceded eating was to first do push-ups or flutter kicks, or both, if he was so inclined. It was only after several sets of regular exercises that the tortures of boat push-ups and other drills came into play.

Chief Deckert was just as hard as Chief Packard when it came to piling on the work. But he wasn't nearly as hard about what the students had to do to get fed. Deckert was an easy instructor, but only compared to Packard. Everything was relative, and it was all miserable.

Then there were the instructors who were everyone's favorites. Instructor Hawke had passed out the ice cream at that first meal, and he also liked to pass out big glasses of iced lemonade. That was a hell of a lot of fun to gulp down. And you had to finish it, because the instructor had given it to you.

Some of the students had trouble holding down all of their food. The stress level and amount of exercise were so high, and they had eaten so much so quickly, that a few of them didn't get far out of the mess hall before they lost some of what they ate.

In Jeremy's boat crew, Bob Miller was still eating like a garbage can, and managing to lose weight as well. Everyone was dropping pounds, but no one thought that the Hell Week diet would make it on the national market. "Eat all you want and more and still lose weight!" Too bad the level of exercise, cold exposure, and exhaustion couldn't be applied to a fat farm, Jeremy thought. The instructors would be rich.

Besides being able to eat like an open crater, Miller demonstrated another ability he had during Hell Week: he could vomit on command. It was a party trick that would go over big in some crowds, and the dingy students who made up Class 78 happened to be just such a crowd.

Miller demonstrated his skill after the morning meal on Wednesday. A group of Marines were doing something near the Enlisted Dining Hall when Class 78 was turned over to the day shift of instructors and was moving out for their morning torture. The Marines had left their helmets in a row along the sidewalk outside the mess hall. For some reason, they were upside down, the open side of the helmet gaping up at the sky. Miller accepted the situation as a great time to rid himself of some extra weight, so he proceeded to barf into the open helmets as the class ran by.

It wasn't as if the Marines could do anything to the class, even if they could find them. Most of the students wouldn't have noticed if you hauled off and belted them, other than accepting it as an excuse to grab some rest. And the way the students smiled, the Marines wouldn't have gotten close to them.

The normal level of odor that a wet bunch of BUD/S students had during training was pretty ripe, like a backed-up cesspool. After days of running, swimming, sweating, pissing, and otherwise contaminating their uniforms and their persons, Class 78 stank so badly it could have qualified as a biological weapon.

Even the instructors only wanted to approach the students from upwind now. And the worn and exhausted bodies of the students were breeding grounds for a variety of bacterial infections. Just getting near a BUD/S student during Hell Week could make a person gag. Letting one do something as obscene as breathe on you, and you could come down with several different kinds of lung infections. So the instructors were no longer getting eyeball-to-eyeball with the students. Instead, they were using their bullhorns to get right up into an individual's face.

Now that their morning chow was over, the instructors were using their bullhorns to let the class know what they thought of them. Boats were lifted and the class ran back down the road to the training center. Instead of going out the main gate, however, the class ran up and down Tarawa Street and in and out of Gate 2. This wasn't to make life any easier for the students, but because it was easier for the instructors to maintain control of the group.

The bow-to-stern formation hadn't gotten any easier. And the tired students became more sloppy while carrying their boats. Threats and shouts from the instructors improved the formation for a short time, but it soon spread out again as the students lost speed.

Back on the beach at the training compound, the instructors decided that the problem with the boat crews carrying the rubber boats was simple: the crews were too large. And since they didn't have the extra boats immediately available to spread out the crews, the instructors would do the next best thing—increase the weight of the boats.

As the students continued boat drills, several of the instructors climbed up inside the boats. Now, each of the students was carrying his share of a heavy IBS and a beefy instructor as well. To aid the students in concentrating on what they were doing, some of the instructors walked around in the boats as the boats were sitting on the students' heads.

Senior Chief Fletcher explained in detail what would happen to each of them if a single instructor fell to the ground. The boat drills finally ended when

Fletcher decided that the class was getting too hot. So the boats were grounded in exchange for a round of surf appreciation drills.

Push-ups in the surf hadn't gotten any easier. The students' arms barely had the strength to hold their bodies up as the cold waves bore down on them. The actual push-ups consisted of not much more than heads going up and down with only a little motion of the arms.

Whistle drills finally broke up surf appreciation. When the students had crawled up through the sand to where Senior Chief Fletcher was standing, they received a briefing on their next evolution. The briefing was short, but the evolution was going to be one of the longest of Hell Week.

In their rubber boats, the crews would paddle down along the coast of the Silver Strand. Traveling from the training compound, they would go past the Strand, the state beach, the big circular antenna farm at the U.S. Naval Communications Station, past Imperial Beach, the naval air station itself, and almost to Tijuana, Mexico, just past the California border. There, at the mouth of the Tijuana River, they would first experience the mud flats of Hell Week.

The trip was not considered a long one, as ocean voyages go. The students would be paddling a distance of only about eight miles, though the fact that the rubber boats would have to contend with waves, wind, and currents, would stretch out the distance the students seemed to be paddling.

At 0900 hours the briefing was over and the flotilla

of four rubber boats and crews struck out from the BUD/S training compound to points south. Staying close to shore, just outside the surf zone, the crews paddled their rubber boats, pushing them slowly through the water. And slowly was the correct term. With their tired arms, they had to work hard just to get the rubber boats up to the incredible speed of two miles an hour, or less. The paddling went on all day.

For the first time in a while, the students were almost warm, the sun having been high in the sky all day. In fact, it was the first time during Hell Week that sunny Southern California actually felt like sunny California. Once they fell into a rhythm, some of the members of the boat crews could almost sleep while still paddling. This was quickly becoming another of the skills they would need as operators in the Teams. They not only had to know how to keep going under any conditions, but how to get what rest they could, whenever they could.

There was an advantage to the long paddles in the rubber boats: there weren't any instructors to rag on them. Just the ocean, the water, and the paddle in their hands. That was how Jeremy looked at the long hauls they did with the rubber boats. And his opinion was shared by most of the other students.

When the boat crews were about halfway down to the mud flats, they had their first scheduled stop—to eat a box lunch, which was little more than sandwiches, fruit, and a hard boiled egg. Not quite up to the standards of the Amphibious base mess hall. But it was chow, and that meant fuel for their systems. The students were even given the opportunity for a head break at the toilets at the nearby state beach.

Sanitary arrangements were generally rough during Hell Week. There had been scheduled head breaks, usually after meals. But most of the students just urinated in the water when they were run in for surf appreciation or for any of the dozen other reasons the instructors used to put them in the ocean. There were a lot more chances to get wet all over than there were to use a toilet. But the opportunity to sit for a moment was one they didn't want to pass up. Then it was back through the surf and heading south again.

Finally, by late afternoon, the flotilla of rubber boats reached the destination and moved in toward shore, where the instructors waved them in as they approached the designated landing point. Though the students didn't know it, they had been under careful observation the entire day by instructors on shore. The water conditions were not bad, so there wasn't any expectation of trouble with the rubber boats. But safety was always a prime consideration.

The students were reaching a level of exhaustion that made them progressively more dingy. Some were sharper than others, and they could remain that way throughout Hell Week. But the thought processes of all of the students were getting slower. They could make simple, stupid mistakes, and the instructors were there to make sure the errors were paid for with exercise or cold water, not with serious injuries.

Once the crews arrived on shore, the instructors ordered them to rig the boats for land portage. Paddles were secured inside the rubber boats, underneath the seat tubes. Lines were coiled and properly stowed. Handling the lines on the IBS was one of the few times that Jeremy could make use of the training he'd received in bosun's mate school. And for a moment as he coiled up the bowline of the IBS, he wondered at the fact that he'd been at that school only a few months earlier.

The moment's reflection caused Jeremy to slow, and then to stop altogether, while he was coiling the line. A quick poke from Bob Miller was enough to jolt him back to the present. Snapped out of his reverie, Jeremy finished what he was doing, astonished at how easy it was, despite everything they were going through, to just go away for a moment.

The instructors were familiar with the way students could drift in and out of the situation when the level of physical activity slowed down. It was one of the reasons they tried to make every moment a nonstop flurry of motion and physical output. So now, the boat crews were pushed into moving faster, rigging out the boats for land portage and then rigging out themselves.

In spite of their fatigue, the students were trying hard to pay attention to the details. Leg straps from their kapoks were taken out from underneath their legs and retied around their waists. The canvas straps of the kapoks would be the cause of a number of permanent souvenirs many of the students would have for the rest of their lives. The combination of moment, water, sand, and straps had abraded the skin on the inside of their thighs. By this time in Hell Week, all of the students were walking bow-legged to one degree or another, to try and relieve some of the pain in their legs and thighs. Many would have scars from the straps that would always remind them of what they'd been doing that one long week.

The kapok vests gave a level of support to their necks when they lifted the rubber boats up and onto their heads. The bright orange kapoks also made them easy to spot from a distance, which was why they were that color. But in spite of their thickness, the vests did little to help keep the students warm. The clothes they wore were never given a chance to dry out. On the beach near Tijuana, the students were about as dry as they had been all week. And that was going to change very soon.

The boats were carried to where the rest of the instructors were waiting near the mud flats at the mouth of the river. There, the students put the boats down above the high tide mark.

Instructors indicated where they wanted the boats secured, and the students were given the opportunity to look over their temporary new home at Camp Swampy by the Sea. There were several heavy canvas Army general purpose (GP) tents that had been set up—supposedly for the comfort of the instructors and the students. Inside the tents there were nice, clean, warm field jackets. But the class quickly realized that the tents were just for show. Not one student doubted that they would be spending very little time within their canvas walls.

It was another example of the mental stress the students were compelled to experience during Hell Week. Any anticipation of possible comfort was quickly eliminated by the instructors. If the students were allowed to enter the tents, they were not to slip on the field jackets. Even unspoken threats by the instructors carried a lot of weight with the surviving members of Class 78. None of the jackets would be touched. It was now late in the afternoon and time for the games to begin.

For the balance of the day and the rest of the night, the students would be exposed to the the classic tradition of training—trial by mud. And it wasn't just any kind of mud. It was a particularly nasty black-gray silt that had built up at the mouth of the river for decades. As a farming soil, the mud would have been a great, fertile field. As something to move about in, it left a whole lot to be desired.

Almost all of the Class 78 instructors had done a number of tours in Vietnam. This part of their training applied to their combat days in Southeast Asia. The SEALs had patrolled in areas where no other forces thought of going. They had moved across mud flats that were hundreds of yards wide to surprise the Viet Cong in their strongholds. They surprised the enemy in part because the VC didn't think that the mud at their backs was even passable. If they hadn't been able to cross an area, they assumed there was no way the Americans could do it. But the SEALs were able to cross that terrain, and they first leaned how to deal with it at the mud flats during training.

The mud flats looked innocuous. It was a large open area that shone with the film of water on top. But looks were deceiving. The first warning, even to the students—who all stank at a level they couldn't notice anymore—was that the mud reeked. There was an aroma of rot and decay, methane and sulfides, that lay below the surface of the mud, bubbling up in spots as a warning. For the rest of that day and much of the night, the mud would be their home and workplace.

When Class 78 arrived at the mud flats, it was a still, flat plain. The instructors wanted to see a good mix of the mud, necessary for quality training, and so they ordered Class 78 to lock arms, march into the mud, and churn it up.

The mud was at first fairly stiff and only about knee deep. The boat crews marching around in it appeared to be doing a weird kind of close-order drill under the direction of the instructors. Very quickly, however, the mud was churned up into a thin, silty consistency somewhere between thick pea soup and thin cooked cereal. Now the students were sunk belly-deep in the muck. With the stirring up of the mud came the rise in stink as the trapped gases below the surface were released to spread out in the air.

Now the games could begin. Relay races were conducted, where the students had to run into the mud flats, over an inverted boat, and then back out again. The races were conducted by boat crews, so once again each crew would only be as fast as its slowest man. But the competition helped build up spirit in the students as they tried to slither through the mud as quickly as they could. It didn't take long for them to discover that the best way to make forward motion through the mud was almost flat on the belly and crawling through the muck like a snake.

Boat crew races were continued for hours, some just variations of the caterpillar races the students had done in the bay waters off the Amphibious base. In one race, the rubber boats had to first be pulled across the mud flats, the students flailing and struggling through the mud as they pushed and pulled at the unwieldy boats. The mud was too deep and thin to walk on and too thick to swim in, so the boat crews half crawled and half swam their boats to the far side.

For the return part of the race, they had to form caterpillars to crawl backward through the mud. Each man in the boat crew wrapped his legs around the waist of the man in front of him. As a long, lumpy caterpillar, they crawled backward, pushing at the mud with long strokes of their arms.

Once they got to the shore again, the race wasn't over—the crews still had their boats on the far side of the mud. Individually, they now swam, crawled, walked, and stumbled back across the flats to retrieve their boats. Then, once again, they dragged those unwieldy lumps of rubber and air across the now churned-up mud.

The students were more equal with each other now than they would be with any other group of people in their lives. Not only were they wet and tired, they were coated with a thin layer of muck that covered all traces of skin color, hair, eye shape, or anything else. Even the general features of the students' faces were hard to make out. Noses were just blobs that stuck out a little farther from the face than the rest of the mud lumps. If not for the fact that a person's ears were normally above their shoulders on either side of their heads, there was little difference that could be seen between an ear and a nose of a mud-covered student.

What could be seen was the white of a student's eyes, sunk deeply in the puddles of black that their faces had become. And on a few faces there was a white crescent of teeth that shone through the mud as some of the students smiled when they looked at their classmates, or grimaced in pain as they continued with their exercises in the mud.

If Travis Rappaport hadn't been getting over the racism and prejudices of a lifetime just through the shared stresses and suffering of BUD/S, he would have had a very hard time selecting just who to be prejudiced against in the mudflats. Both Rappaport and Sledge, covered from head to toe with mud, were as equal as two people could be.

"So," Sledge said during a lull in the races, "how's it feel to be black, Redneck?"

Spitting out mud, Rappaport thought about his answer for a moment. "Mostly wet," he said finally.

An instructor coming up to Boat Crew IV spotted something that he reacted to as if it was the worst crime he'd ever seen.

"I don't believe it," Instructor McDonald bellowed into his bullhorn. "Positive evidence that this crew has not been putting out. Chief Deckert, come here and see this!"

The criminal "evidence" that Instructor McDonald

had found was a small patch of red color still visible on the underside of the collar of Mike Zundleman's kapok. Every member of the class was a consistent and smooth gray-black from being completely coated with mud and silt. That there was this one tiny spot of color, not more than an inch or two in size, was a fluke. But a fluke was a good enough reason for the instructors to act.

"Somersaults," Chief Deckert declared. "We'll teach these slackers what it means to get down in the mud."

Boat Crew IV now started back across the mudflats, struggling along a few steps until an order was shouted out by an instructor. Then they ducked forward and rolled through the mud in a somersault. There wouldn't be any freak spots of unmuddied anything on the crew now.

"Somersault races," Chief Deckert announced loudly. "Get moving, the rest of you. Can't you see that they're ahead of you now?"

"It pays to be a winner," Instructor Lubi pointed out through his bullhorn.

The logic of the situation wasn't important to the rest of the class. The fact that there was now a race on and another boat crew was ahead of them mattered a lot more. They all hit the mud and surged forward, rolling about as ordered. The entire class was now literally rolling in the mud.

The ridiculousness of their situation, however, did strike some of the students as funny. Boat Crew IV won the somersault races and got to rest for a moment while the rest of the crews came in. There were a lot more grins shining up from the muddy faces than there had been a short time earlier. The students were starting to get into the feel of things, and the instructors were trying to make a big game of the whole situation.

The night games—or mud Olympics, as some of the instructors called them—turned into a bit of fun for the students. All of the class was more or less dingy by now, and at the point where the instructors couldn't hurt them a lot. Wednesday night was considered something of a turning point in BUD/S, though the students didn't know it at the time. The evolutions would still be hard, long, and cold, but the bulk of the students who would quit were now gone from the class.

One or two students might ring out before the week was over. But now the job of the instructors was to keep the students busy and moving, while also watching out to make sure they didn't do anything stupid to injure themselves or their classmates.

## Chapter Twenty-one

Of course, the students had no idea that things were getting any "easier" for them. They were still working their way through Hell Week, and most didn't even realize that they were halfway through. Many knew that it was Wednesday evening, but that was about all. As far as what time of day it was, it was getting dark, which was all they really needed to know.

The games were hitting their stride. A couple of the rubber boats had been flipped over and set up next to the edge of the mudflats. Now, the hated rubber boats added to the fun by acting as trampolines for the students running up to the flats. Instructors had a lot of fun as well, awarding points for the students who flew out the farthest. Flips and forward rolls became the thing to do as the students hit the rubber and bounced into the air. Tumbling forward, they somersaulted through the air before smacking down in the mud.

Kapok vests absorbed most of the impact of landing. And the students were already so numb that most of them couldn't feel the impact anyway. Fatigue melted away, or was at least temporarily ignored, as the students got into the competition of the moment. It wasn't that they would have enjoyed it as a daily thing, but for the time being it was fun.

With the IBS in place upside down, the instructors were set up for a particular favorite of theirs: "King of the IBS." Everyone was put up on the IBS, and the last man standing would be declared the winner. This wasn't a boat crew event, it was every man for himself. Once you got knocked off, you were down. But you could still knock other guys off as you were falling.

The students got into this game too. They felt no anger toward one another, but the event quickly turned into a free-for-all. The instructors were putting up a single boat crew at a time and letting the crews knock each other around and off the IBS. The crews went up, and then they came off. Most of the time, no one was left up on the IBS by the end of a crew's turn.

When Boat Crew I got onto the IBS, everyone else in the class had already taken their turn. The class leader and highest ranking man, Lieutenant (j.g.) Reginald C. Butterworth III, was immediately picked up and tossed off into the mud by several members of his crew, who found the smack Butterworth made as he sank into the mud quite satisfying. Then they followed him into the muck as George Staverous cleaned the deck.

Staverous was one of the real bulls among the students. For a time, he remained up on the IBS, his arms upraised in victory as he bellowed something in Greek.

The organization of the game started falling apart about then, much to the instructor's amusement.

Richard Kozuska decided that if there was going to be anything Greek on top of the IBS, it was going to be Zeus, the king of the gods. Well, if not the gods, at least the IBS. Kozuska slipped up behind Staverous and surprised him by picking him up and tossing him off the IBS.

Now it was Zeus's turn to be King of the IBS, but it was a short-lived reign. Although they were in his boat crew and had suffered through all of Hell Week with him, Rod Shea and Tim Nelson thought it was an excellent moment to knock their coxswain down a peg or two. During their crew's turn, Shea, Nelson, and Frank Ball had done their best to knock Kozuska off the IBS. They managed to do it, but had fallen off into the mud themselves in the process. Even though they were off the boat and in the mud, Shea and Nelson figured that if Kozuska could get back up on the IBS, they could too.

While Kozuska was raising his hands over his head and shouting "Zeus! Zeus!" Shea and Nelson slipped around the IBS and double-teamed the big ensign. To the applause of the instructors and the laughter of their fellow students, Shea and Nelson surged up and over the rubber boat, knocking Zeus, the King of the IBS, flat on his face in the mud.

The instructors had been betting among themselves as to who would manage to stay on top of the boat. In the end, the winner was nobody in particular, but the entire class benefited from the experience.

It had turned into a kind of fight, but not a serious one. If anything, the event was starting to look like the fight scene at the oil well in the John Wayne movie *McClintock*. No one was hurt, but everyone was muddy. The evolution had degenerated into an excuse for having fun.

By now the mud didn't bother the students, except when they were out of the water for a while and it started to dry. Then the mud caked and it tightened up on a person. And the smell hadn't gotten any better; if anything, it was worse in the area that had been churned up by the students for hours. The methane from the decomposing material in the mud was so thick that the students swore if someone lit a match, the resulting explosion would send them all back to the training compound.

Soon after the King of the IBS event, the mud games were concluded. The instructors lined up the students in boat crews and marched them off to a relatively clean inlet nearby. The water wasn't fresh, it was saltwater, but it didn't have any mud in it. The instructors had everyone get into the water and rinse off, and clean their equipment as well. The students were ordered to take their clothes off and clean them too. Soon, a naked group of shivering students were conducting an impromptu bath and laundry in the cold waters of a Pacific inlet.

Wearing relatively clean clothes, the class returned to Camp Swampy to receive a briefing on the next evolution that night. None of them realized that they had passed the midpoint of Hell Week, that there was now less in front of them than behind them. But it didn't pay to look any further ahead than the next evolution.

A series of push-ups and flutter kicks introduced the students to the night shift as Chief Packard shouted orders through his bullhorn. The cold and stiffness were temporarily driven out of their systems by the exertions. Then the class was told about their next evolution.

Without using his bullhorn, Chief Packard spoke to the class in a loud, clear, but not shouting voice. To the students, it was a big change from the instructor they'd been dealing with every night that long horrible week. Each swim pair would be taken away from Camp Swampy and into the area nearby, the chief told them. There, they would have to conduct an E&E (escape and evasion) exercise, with each team trying to sneak back to Camp Swampy without the instructors capturing them. If they were caught, they would end up in the POW camp, a square area marked by four rubber boats out in the mudflats.

Camp Swampy wasn't going to be hard to find. The instructors had built a roaring bonfire in a pit dug into the beach. Between the relatively quiet voice of Chief Packard and the radiating warmth of the bonfire, some of the students were rapidly starting to nod off. Many in the class could now fall asleep in mid-bite during a meal. Their present situation made it almost impossible to stay awake. So when Chief Packard switched over to his bullhorn and shouted for them to pick out their swim buddies and start the evolution, the jolt came as a shock to the class.

To make sure that the students were in the proper condition to conduct their E&E, Chief Packard ordered a quick few minutes of surf appreciation. Now completely awake, the students broke off into their swim pairs. The instructors then took the different swim pairs out to the nearby Navy helo base and left them there. The distance probably wasn't more than a quarter to half a mile, but it seemed like a very long way to the students of Class 78. Dropping off the pairs of students, the instructors left them with simple instructors: "All you have to do is go that way." And they pointed off in the direction of Camp Swampy.

The evolution seemed to be as much a break for the instructors as it was for the students. And some of the students planned to take as much advantage of the situation as they could. Jeremy White and his partner Jim Alex quickly joined up with another swim pair, Chris Walsh and Barry Fisher. The plan among the four students was to get some rest while continuing with the exercise.

One man from each pair would lay down on the ground, and his partner would lay down on top of him, and the two pairs would stay close and snug with each other. In that formation, the men on the ground would get the heat from the men on top and could manage to get some rest, if not any real sleep. The weight of the men together would cut off the circulation in their arms in just a few minutes. As soon as one of the guys was brought around by his arms turning numb, he would wake up the rest of the group. Then they would all crawl forward a little farther and switch places, with those who had been on top now on the bottom.

The technique worked, even if the "alarm clock" was rough on the circulation in their arms. The guys on the bottom managed to warm up before someone awoke and the procedure went ahead another turn. By the time the group got to Camp Swampy, they figured they had made it all right. Now they had a chance to slip into their tent and maybe get some real sleep.

Crawling into the tent, Jeremy and his fellow escapees thought they had made it without detection. This was the reward for being a winner. There were field jackets in the tent, but they'd already been told they were not allowed to put them on. But the jackets could be rolled up and used as pillows.

Any little comfort went a long way by now, the fourth day of Hell Week. There were already two other pairs of students in the tent, and all eight of them thought they had made it. The evolution seemed to be timed so everyone would reach the tents at about the same time. A few student pairs had been caught by the instructors, and they spent their time sunk in the mud of the POW camp.

It had nearly been daylight when Jeremy and the three others made it to the tent. "All right, we made it," one said, and they laughed as they settled in. And then they saw the instructor silently laying in wait in the back of the tent.

Instructor Holmes snapped on the light in his hands and startled the hell out of the students in the tent.

"Nice to see you guys here," he said with a smile. "Now go hit the mud."

"That's not fair," Bernie Rosencrantz complained. "We made it."

"I'll tell you what's fair," Instructor Holmes said. "Now go hit the mud."

This kind of reward and disappointment had been going on all during Hell Week, and through training as a whole. It was one of the better mental stressers the instructors put on the students, to see who could take the pressure. It was hard to lose and get punished, but it was a lot harder to think you had won and get punished anyway. That mental stress, combined with the anticipation of events, built up and accounted for many of the students who rang the quitting bell. It wasn't that they didn't have the physical ability to make it through, but that they let their minds break their wills.

Especially during Hell Week, the instructors would watch the students who quit, and then conduct a short debriefing with them. For Class 78, the class proctor, Instructor Sanchez, was the one who talked to the students who dropped, to make sure that they weren't going to do something stupid while suffering through their disappointment.

During that debriefing, the exhausted and mentally collapsing students had to be convinced that what they had done—quitting the program—wasn't the end of the world. They were taken care of and watched while they recovered from the rigors of Hell Week. None of the students who were still in class knew any of this, unless they too had dropped out from an earlier class and were back to try it again. A number of individuals had gone back to the fleet after dropping out of BUD/S, only to return later when they'd gotten their heads on a little straighter.

This was the thing about BUD/S that wasn't known by many of those outside of the Teams. The course was the hardest one offered in the U.S. military. In fact, BUD/S was considered one of the hardest training courses in the world, partly because it was so easy to quit. And the mental toughness that it took to get through the pain, cold, and misery was the hardest thing. Some men never did have enough of it.

All of the students in the mud had no idea about mental toughness, they just knew that they were wet and muddy again. And then, to their surprise, the students were all given a sleep period.

Ordered back out of the mud, the students were sent off for a quick roll in the cold but clean water and a quick BUD/S drying off in the sand. Only after that were they allowed to reenter the tents. They still could not put on the field jackets, but they were allowed to at least lay on them, or bundle them under their heads as a pillow. Then came quiet and almost two hours of uninterrupted rest.

Most of the students were so exhausted that they immediately dropped into a heavy sleep. Others found that they just couldn't relax the muscles they had been pushing so hard for so long. In spite of their exhaustion, they couldn't drop off to sleep. But the quiet time continued until after sunrise.

Then came the hardest moment of Hell Week for almost all of the students of Class 78: they had to wake up and get moving again. They had to force their bodies up and out of sleep, and their bodies didn't want to obey. Even at this late point during Hell Week, the rest period had beaten some students' resolutions. They just weren't able to force themselves to get up and moving. That was the lesson of the short sleep period—that you could make your body obey your will, even when it absolutely didn't want to.

Jeremy's eyes were swollen shut, and at first he had to physically force them open with his hands. Like a few of the others in the shelter of the tent, he'd taken off his clothes to try and let them air out a bit. Now he had to put the sandy, smelly, moist and horrible uniform back on.

Some of the people had slept with their clothes on, and some hadn't even taken their boots off. Jeremy could now see that they had the better idea. His feet had swollen badly, and it was almost impossible to slip the worn and beat-up jungle boots over them.

Saltwater had dried in a crust on the students' skin, lips, and eyes. Eyes stung from the salt, and as a result, most of them were hardly able to speak. Finally, after what seemed an eternity of struggle, the students were dressed and ready to continue another day of Hell Week.

## Chapter Twenty-two
## Thursday

The next morning brought another round of mudflat follies. This time the games weren't run with as much fun as they had been the evening before. But everyone had a good chance to get muddy, filthy, and coated with muck.

Eskimo races were conducted where swim pairs raced against each other. It took two men to make a good Eskimo race. One man would grab the ankles of his partner, who would bend down over him and grab the ankles of the first man. In that kind of loop, the two students would roll, like the tread of a tank, turning over and over, and cross through the mud. By the end of the mudflat training, anyone who'd had an aversion to mud, dirt, or filth, was beyond it.

Mud crawls, wheelbarrow races, and other games got students thoroughly caked and coated with the same smelly muck they'd experienced the day before. The wheelbarrow races looked like a particularly good way to drown your partner if you didn't pay attention.

One student grabbed the ankles of his swim partner, and the two of them went across a shallow section of the mud, the man on the bottom with his nose barely above the water covering the mud. If one member of a swim pair didn't pay attention to his partner needing air, the favor could be easily paid back, as the two had to switch places on the return leg of the race.

Now the sun was up and starting to warm Camp Swampy. The boat crews took their rubber boats to the clean water inlet and washed them, and themselves, clean of the last traces of the muck of the Tijuana River. Camp Swampy was over, and the mudflats were in the past, for the time being. There was no ride back to the training compound. The students had the same transport that brought them down the day before: their rubber boats.

The trip north seemed easier than the trip down had been. It was just as long, but the current or tide appeared to work in the boat crews' favor. At a signal from the shore, the flotilla of rubber boats turned in to land at the Imperial Beach fishing pier. The meal was the same as the day before—box lunches.

The sun was out, but the chill factor started to set in when the students were at the pier and trying to eat. Without the exercise of paddling, even the sun wasn't enough to warm them, they were all so tired. Some of them were shaking so much they could hardly unwrap their sandwiches. But food was important, and the box lunch was all each of them had. When Jeremy found that his fingers wouldn't obey him well enough to unwrap the plastic from his sandwich, he did the next most logical thing and tore into it with his teeth.

Plastic wrapping wasn't the best flavoring agent, but by now none of the students cared. Jeremy certainly didn't. And he managed to eat most of his sandwich intact, though some of the instructors commented that getting near him while he was feeding might be a dangerous thing.

Then it was back into the water and on with the trip. When they finally got back to the training command, the boats were put up onto the beach and the class ran through a few exercises and a run to warm things up. The surf wasn't too bad, and the instructors thought it was an excellent chance to spend some quality time with surf appreciation.

Some of the instructors had by now developed a tolerance for being with the students in an enclosed area. Others said they would rather swim through a sewer than be in a classroom with the students during the last days of Hell Week. Even some of the hardened instructor chiefs felt they needed a gas mask when they walked into a room of students. To Senior Chief Fletcher, it smelled like the worst rotten eggs he could imagine. Even if the students were doing very well, and Class 78 was making a fair name for itself, being around the students by Thursday made him want to gag.

Every time the senior chief came onto his shift, the first thing he noticed was that funky smell. And sometimes he would just tell a student: "You fucking stink."

Hearing this, the student would usually wonder what kind of punishment was coming his way. There wasn't any question of what he might have done; it didn't matter anyway. But after his announcement, Senior Chief Fletcher would just tell the student to: "Get out of here, and don't breathe on me, I might catch something."

The confused student would then thankfully run off, thinking he'd lucked out.

The reek didn't come so much from the students' sweat, though they were doing a lot of that. Its source was the marine environment they'd been in the entire week. Uniforms mildewed as the students wore them, and their skin was wrinkled and pale, almost as if they were rotting in place themselves.

Disease was a problem at this point in Hell Week. The students' bodies had been beaten to a physical low, probably the lowest point in their lives. Their resistance was down, and colds or other respiratory infections even pneumonia, were common. The instructors called it "the crud," and they could catch it just by being in close quarters with a student and breathing the same air.

Thankfully, most of the work with the students during Hell Week took place outside, where the open air helped keep the worst of the germs blown away. But it seemed that every time Senior Chief Fletcher went on a Hell Week, he came down with the crud, which lasted at least a few days after the week was over.

The sickness that made the rounds of the students could force them into medical rollbacks. By the last days of Hell Week, the corpsmen were looking for signs of bad infections, and not just in the lungs. The skin and ears could be a mess. A student's entire body could have patches of skin missing from it, due to the abrasion of the sand and exercise. Their exposure to the mudflats and other breeding grounds for germs could cause skin infections that had to be treated by the corpsmen before they turned into something a lot more serious.

But Class 78 had been lucky in that respect. There was only the normal run of mild infections so far, and none of the students had been forced to roll back and then repeat Hell Week all over again with another class.

One of the things Senior Chief Fletcher liked was to see to it that the students who returned from the mud-flats received a particularly strenuous period of surf appreciation. They were not allowed in the barracks showers yet, but there was plenty of good, clean sea-water supplied by the nearby Pacific. And sand could form a reasonable substitute for soap, at least to a BUD/S instructor's way of thinking.

The class linked arms and walked into the surf zone. The cold still bothered them. Some of the students started shivering just at the mention of surf appreciation. But they all did it, and no one quit. They had all begun to learn to shut out the outside world during Hell Week. They would only pay attention to the things that really mattered, such as orders from the instructors. Everything else was ignored as much as possible.

Some Team members who had completed BUD/S referred to this as the "porthole effect." It was withdrawing your consciousness into your mind and looking out at the world as if through a porthole. The cold, wet, and miserable was still out there, but it was on the other side of the porthole and couldn't get to the part of you that had withdrawn.

Others referred to it as learning how to put the mind in neutral while the body remained in gear. Still more referred to withdrawing into their "bubble" where no discomfort or pain could reach them. For Jeremy White, it was in the surf zone that he reached the inside of his bubble.

Sitting in the cold water, he looked up at the sky and imagined himself in the water off a tropical beach. As a young man from Ohio, he hadn't had much experience with tropical beaches. But this trip was only taking place in his imagination, which was all he needed.

In spite of the cold, Jeremy found himself humming, thinking of that warm tropical beach. The students on either side of him wondered what was going on with Jeremy, and he told them that he was looking up at the sky and the sun was beaming down on him and making him warm all over. Then the other students started to hum as well. Soon, the entire line was humming, and that wasn't quite what the instructors expected.

"Stop that humming!" Senior Chief Fletcher shouted through his bullhorn. "If you all have so much energy, we'll have to find some work for you to do."

Then Class 78 was brought out of the surf and back onto the beach and reality. The rest of the afternoon was taken up by beach games, more boat drills, and the normal endless run of exercises and other evolutions. The man with the boats paddled in and out of the surf zone.

The sharp eyes of the instructors didn't miss much. They were there to try and force the students to their limits, and then well beyond. They wanted those who didn't have the heart and drive to make it to simply quit and get out of the others' way. But they didn't want to break young men who could be a credit to the Navy, in or out of the Teams. And they certainly didn't want to cause someone permanent injury and possibly cripple them for life.

Nguyen Thanh had been rolled back to a summer class earlier in the week. It wasn't that he didn't show the heart; it was the opposite. He would have literally killed himself rather than quit. But that was an extreme case. What Instructor Nugent now noticed was much more common. Jeremy White had been limping for days as his shin splints kept getting worse. Now, he was limping fairly badly. It could be something simple, or he might have a broken leg or worse. So Instructor Nugent called Jeremy out of the formation.

"White, get your ass over to Medical," he ordered.

"I'm fine Instruc—" Jeremy began to say.

"I didn't ask you how you were, maggot!" Instructor Nugent bellowed. "I said get your miserable ass over to Medical and check in with the chief corpsman. Now move!"

It was a simple set of directions, and Jeremy hustled over to Medical and Chief Thomson, who was there to check him out. The chief corpsman had plenty of experience with students during Hell Week who were either trying to get a medical reason to quit or to hide a bad situation and go on with their class. Usually, this late in the week, the latter was more common. Just watching Jeremy limp into the room after knocking on the door told Chief Thomson a lot about what might be wrong.

With Jeremy on the examination table, the chief poked and prodded at his leg, and he suspected that a bad inflammation of the muscles along the inner side of his right tibia was causing the young man's shin splints. The muscles were swollen and sore, but so were most of the muscles on Jeremy's body at this stage of Hell Week. There was a possibility of a stress fracture, but that would have been very unusual at that point in training.

Chief Thomson concluded that Jeremy had a simple but bad case of shin splints. The swelling could get worse, however, and start to pinch nerves and blood vessels in the leg. Normal treatment included icing down the leg—which was being taken care of by the student's frequent dips in the Pacific—rest, which couldn't be given now, and anti-inflammatory drugs.

"So, do you want to go to Balboa Hospital and get this checked out?" Chief Thomson asked. "You know you have shin splints, don't you? Once there, you'll get cleaned up and warm again and they'll massage your leg and take care of you."

Jeremy was scared if he went to the hospital he might be rolled back, or worse still, dropped. What he was being offered was a serious temptation, though, an easy way out of training without the shame of ringing the bell.

"Will I be able to come back to my class?" he asked Chief Thomson.

"Nope, you'll pretty much be out of training for a while," Thomson said.

"Then fuck that, Chief," Jeremy said defiantly. "I want to go back to my class."

That was the reaction Chief Thomson had expected. After giving Jeremy a couple of aspirin for the inflammation, he sent the young man back out to join his classmates.

Instructor Nugent was with Boat Crew IV when Jeremy returned. He pulled the young man aside and told him seriously, "I'm watching you. If your leg hurts, I want you to let me know."

"Hooyah, Instructor Nugent," was Jeremy's answer.

A short, ragged cheer came from the members of Class 78, who were glad to see one of their own come back. Then the boats were again lifted up onto the students' heads and they were moved out to the Amphibious base. Jeremy was still in the running with his class. The evening meal was waiting for them over at the base, along with whatever evolution would come next.

The first hot food the students had in over a day was a welcome change from their box lunch meals. The level of exhaustion in the class could be seen by anyone who observed them. They all looked, and smelled, like the walking dead. Even the food servers behind the steam tables felt sorry for the miserable remnants of humanity that passed down the line in front of them. Although a number of the servers had seen BUD/S classes and Hell Week meals for years, it still amazed them that people would volunteer for such abuse.

And the abuse was telling on the students. Sitting down and eating was an even greater danger for them now than it had been—nearly all of them caught themselves slipping into sleep at least once during the meal. Even Bob Miller, the human garbage can, had to concentrate on eating, on actually getting the food up from his tray and into his mouth.

After the meal, it was back out to the boats and more evolutions. This was one of the hardest times many of the students had yet come up against—just getting up and moving from the meal. The shouts and calls of the instructors got them going, but for a few it was a near thing. The bell was still there, hanging in its wooden frame. But to have come so far only to ring out when the end was in sight would have been devastating to the students who were left in Class 78. Still, the temptation of the bell and its offer of warmth, sleep, and an end to the pain and exhaustion of Hell Week was a very hard siren call to resist.

The instructors knew that this was a dangerous time for the students. Normally, when a man made it past Wednesday, you couldn't do enough to him to make him quit. But the relaxation of a meal or rest period could overcome even the strongest will. The constant movement of the class, and challenging them with evolutions, kept them going and not thinking about their situation.

Later that evening, the students would be facing one of the big challenges of Hell Week: the Around the World tour. The students received their briefing in early evening, when the sun still cast enough light to see by. They were back in the training compound then, on the beach often conducting boat races, surf appreciation, and drills. The instructors had gathered them around an easel where a large map of the Training Command, the Amphibious base, and all of Coronado was tacked up.

Chief Deckert was giving the Around the World briefing, while the rest of his instructors were circling the students, making sure none of them dozed off or failed to pay attention.

"You will take your boat crews south," Chief Deckert said, "paddling down past the demo pits."

As the chief spoke, everyone listened carefully, the boat coxswains most of all. This was going to be the longest, most complicated trip conducted during Hell Week. And they knew it would be the easiest to screw up and come in last. The rumor among the students was that the winning boat crews were secured from Hell Week early if they did the tour fast enough. There was no way to tell if the rumor was true, but it did fit the "pays to be a winner" motto.

"Once past the demo pits, you will continue south," Chief Deckert continued. "When you see the headlights of a truck pointing out to sea, you will bring your boats in and land. You will report in to the instructor, who will give you your next check-in point of the tour. Then you will rig for land portage and move your boats across the Strand to the bay.

"Once in the bay, you will paddle north to the dolphin pens outside of Turner Field and report in with the instructor there. Your next point will be farther north, past the aircraft carriers, to North Island, where you will enter the inlet there."

The inlet was the channel that connected San Diego Bay with the open waters of the Pacific to the west. North Island was the naval air station that covered most of the northwest side of Coronado. The students could see that this would be a very long paddle in the rubber boats.

"Once you have reported in at the inlet," Chief Deckert said, "you will continue around the curve of the inlet, following the shoreline just outside of the surf zone. Then you will report in to the instructor stationed on the Enlisted Beach on North Island. The last point will be right back here in front of the training compound."

This was going to be a huge evolution, covering something like sixteen miles. It would be long, hard, and exhausting. And like all the evolutions before it, it had to be completed.

## Chapter Twenty-three

The sun had long since set when Class 78 started their Around the World tour. The lack of instructors hounding them was one of the high points, compared to the rubber boat trips they had done so far. But this trip was going to be so long that even that advantage seemed small next to what they had to accomplish.

Passing out through the surf zone in front of the training compound had gotten easier, after all of the practice they had been getting. Now, they turned south. Their first leg was a relatively short one, but only when compared to the rest of the trip. And they would be working against the currents and winds, as they had when on their way to the mudflats. Though the crews were dingy from lack of sleep, everyone pulled their share of the work and the boats made good progress.

When they could see the headlights of a truck shining out to sea, they went in to land. After paddling for more than an hour, the students were glad to be going in to land. It also meant that the main southbound leg of their journey was over. Now they rigged up for land portage and prepared to cross the Silver Strand.

Instead of having to cross the highway, there was a tunnel near the point where the students came onshore that allowed them to go underneath the road. Then it was on across the inner beach and into the warmer waters of San Diego Bay.

The next point was back up at the Amphibious base. With the base extending out from the shore, the shortest route for the boats was to travel over half a mile out into the bay.

For centuries, sailors at sea had visions while watching the waves, especially at night. The students of BUD/S Class 78 were also sailors, and they were so dingy from four days without sleep and with constant activity that they would have seen visions if they were staring at a brick wall. The lights around the bay, both onshore and aboard ships, only added to their isolation and imagination.

The paddling was easy enough, so the crews took turns trying to grab a nap, with some resting while others paddled.

Bob Miller wigged out aboard Boat IV on the second leg of their trip. He suddenly started yelling, "They're not putting out! They're not putting out!" and dug his paddle into the water even harder.

"Just what in the hell are you talking about, Bob?" Jeremy asked from his place at the number one position, starboard. He was startled by the sudden commotion, as was the rest of Boat Crew IV.

"They're not putting out," Miller complained. "If they don't start paddling harder, Chief Packard is going to catch up to us."

That got everyone's attention. Chief Packard was coming up in another boat? The night shift of instructors was up? Just how late was it anyway?

"Where?" Patrick Neil said from his place at the stern.

"Right there!" Miller said, pointing out at the water. "Can't you see him walking toward us?"

"Walking?" Mike Zundleman said.

"Yes, Zoo," Miller said. "He's right there walking toward us."

"What the fuck are you talking about, Bob?" Jeremy said as he stopped paddling for a moment. "We're halfway out into the bay. Not even Chief Packard can walk on water."

"You sure about that?" Zundleman said with a chuckle.

"No, not really," Jeremy answered, grinning back.

Having gotten through his hallucination, or whatever his problem had been, Miller settled back to paddling with a steady rhythm.

It wasn't the only weird thing different members of Boat Crew IV, and Class 78 as a whole, saw that evening.

Jeremy could only describe the feeling that came over him as being like a psychedelic drug. He'd never experimented with drugs, but he thought that what they were going through must have been similar.

A warm flush spread out over his face as the long evolution continued. Then the lights around the harbor began getting very bright and started to merge together. Jeremy felt very warm and relaxed. It was a natural high that wasn't worth all the work it had taken to achieve. But it was neat, he thought, now that it was taking place.

Things that appeared normal a moment earlier changed as you looked at them. The buoy floating in the water started to sprout arms. As Jeremy continued to watch, the arms reached out to the boat, and toward him specifically.

"Fuck!" he said quietly as he recoiled from the sight.

The others experienced it too: objects would appear closer, and with another glance they were either back in the same spot or even farther away.

The whole trip had a weird feeling to it. But in spite of that, the boat crews all pulled in to the right points along the route of the tour. And the instructors didn't mess with anyone during the check-in. They just marked down the boat number and told the crews the next point they had to reach.

But though the crews weren't messed with, they weren't completely left alone either. At the check-in point near Turner Field, Instructor Hawke had some hard words for the men of Boat Crew IV as they checked in and quickly gobbled down the mid-rats that were waiting for them. They consumed whatever was in the boxes, down to the sugar packets, which were torn open and their contents swallowed. The sugar would give them a little rush of energy, and they needed every bit they could come up with.

While they quickly stuffed the food into their mouths, Instructor Hawke told them his opinion of their progress. "You're way behind the last boat crew that just checked in," he growled. "If you don't get to the next point and check in before I get there, I drop the boom on you. You've got ten minutes to eat, and you've already used five of them. Now paddle your ass off!"

Nothing much could be said to that. The students were too tired to even wonder what "the boom" might be. Boat Crew IV once more hit the water and continued to points north. Now they were getting closer to the lights of downtown San Diego. Even though it was past midnight on a weeknight, the big city shone out across the bay. Passing under the Coronado Bay Bridge was neat, Jeremy thought as he looked up at the lights and bridge. It would have been even neater if Jim Alex in the number one port position hadn't suddenly tried to turn the boat on his own.

"Look out!" Jim shouted as he dug his paddle into the water.

"What?" Patrick Neil said from the back as he tried to hold them on course.

"That building," Alex continued. "We're going to hit it!"

"Building? What building?" Neil questioned.

"That big one right there," Alex said, pointing.

"That's part of the bridge!" Neil said. "It's a couple

of hundred feet away. We couldn't hit it right now if we wanted to!"

"But I saw it move," Alex said as he went back to paddling.

The rubber boats paddled farther north, past houses built along the shore of Coronado itself. On the other side of the bridge was an offshore marina with a few dozen civilian pleasure craft tied up to moorings. As the rubber boats moved past the yachts, sailing craft, and motorboats, some of the crew couldn't help but wonder just how much they cost.

"Damn," Miller said as Boat Crew IV paddled past the last of the large sailing boats. "Why can't I have a dream where I'm on one of those with a beautiful blonde rather than stuck here with you guys?"

"Because you were dumb enough to volunteer for this shit," Jim Alex replied.

That was the last of the banter for a while as the boat continued on its trip. The next check-in point was on a pier beyond where a pair of aircraft carriers were docked. They were now several miles past the Coronado Bay Bridge, almost to the northernmost point of Coronado.

"Haze gray and under way," Jim Alex said as they paddled past the huge aircraft carriers.

"Well, if you miss them so bad," Jeremy said from his side of the boat, "you can always ring out. I'm sure we can find a bell buoy for you around here someplace."

"Knock it off you guys," Patrick Neil said from the stern. "There's the pier." And he pointed off to the north.

The pier he'd spotted was one of the largest on

Coronado, and extended well out from the shore. Landing their rubber boat, the groggy crew checked in with the instructor. Next, they would have to go around the point, through the inlet, and to the opposite side of the North Island Air Station from where they were at the moment. They would paddle almost five miles to reach the instructor, waiting for them on the Enlisted Men's Beach on North Island—or five miles if they could get over or through the jetty at Zuniga Point.

The jetty was more than a mile long, and going around it would add two miles to their trip. It was a rock jetty, and they weren't that experienced in rock portage. But they were all so numb by now that if they did impact on the rock, they probably would never even know it.

For hours, they paddled the rubber boat around the curving point of North Island. When they finally got to Zuniga Point, the tide was almost at its peak. The crew knew that when the rocks were almost awash would be the best time to get over the jetty.

Jeremy took his position at the bow and got ready to jump at Neil's signal. The water was surprisingly calm, since they were in the protection of Point Loma to the west, on the far side of the inlet. The jetty itself was also protecting them from the waves coming up from the south, so the rock portage wouldn't be nearly as dangerous as the ones they'd conducted off the Hotel del Coronado.

When Neil hollered, Jeremy jumped and quickly scrambled into the rocks. The other crew members went over the side as soon as Jeremy had the boat under control. They picked up the rubber boat and carried it across the slippery rocks. Back in the water, they were on their way again with almost two miles shaved off their total trip distance.

It was a happy boat crew that pulled in to the Enlisted Men's Beach and checked in. It was their last point before finishing at the training center. The end of the tour was in sight. But a new problem had cropped up.

Somehow, probably when they went over the rocks at the jetty, they had weakened the bottom of the IBS. Now, the boat that had carried them so far was leaking and taking on water. The tubes were still all well-inflated, but the water level inside the boat was going up. Boat Crew IV wasn't in danger of sinking, but the added weight of the water would slow them down considerably.

Finally, with the sun starting to light up the mountains east of San Diego, Boat Crew IV reached its last point on the beach outside of the training center. The hole in the bottom of their boat had added so much weight that they had a hard time just getting the IBS onshore.

"Motherfucker!" Miller yelled as they tipped the boat up to dump out the water. His outburst was surprising, since he'd rarely sworn during the whole of training up to that point. But everyone was well past being just slightly dingy, and the members of the boat crew weren't responding as they normally would have.

The Around the World evolution was over, and another Hell Week milestone behind them all. Miller wanted to bitch about Boat Crew III having come in first on the evolution. But as he was muttering about their having cheated, Jim Alex turned to him and said quietly, "Shut up, you idiot, we cheated too!"

That was another of the more subtle lessons of Hell Week, and BUD/S in general. The Teams were an unconventional warfare organization. They didn't fight fair. Their numbers in the field were usually so small that they could easily be overrun by numerically greater forces. The Teams avoided these situations by never allowing themselves to get in them, or, to put it simply, to cheat whenever possible. And at BUD/S they learned the rewards that could come from doing that.

There was a corollary to the cheating rule: you could never complain when you got caught. So if Boat Crew III had managed to get ahead of the rest of them through some underhanded means, as well as just working hard, so be it. They hadn't been caught, and neither had Boat Crew IV. And that was a situation Jim Alex wanted to keep in place. So he shut Miller's bitching down quickly. Besides, one of the students' unspoken rules when it came to the instructors was that you never informed on a fellow student who had gotten away with something if it didn't endanger the class or anyone else.

## Chapter Twenty-four
### Friday

After morning chow the students continued with evolutions. Boat crew shuttle races were conducted on Turner Field, the students running across the field with their boats, then running back without them. As soon as the last man in a crew crossed the starting line, they all ran back and returned with their boats. Back to the training compound, by a long route that took them most of the way around the Amphibious base, and they were once again within close reach of the Pacific.

Surf appreciation was followed by a run through the O-course as individuals. A run of whistle drills reminded the students to react quickly and correctly. Then it was time for another paddle down the Strand with the boats, this time to the fenced-in area known as the "demo pit," and also called the "Black Lagoon" by the students because of the dark, stagnant water that could be seen at its bottom.

Isolated from everything else, the students had been familiar with the demo pit for some time. The fence line that surrounded it was one of the markers used by the instructors on four mile runs. Now they would learn just what the pit's primary function was for BUD/S training and Hell Week in particular.

One of the later evolutions during Hell Week was also one of the oldest. "So Solly" day, dating back to the first days of training in World War II, attempted to re-create the atmosphere on an enemy-held beach. It wouldn't do if a man could hold himself together through all the mental and physical strain of Hell Week and then couldn't stand explosions, shock, and violent noise close at hand. That was proven true thirty years before, and the lesson had never gone away.

The students had received a taste of confusion and noise during Breakout, with its blasts, gunfire, smoke, and confusion. And they'd been able to negotiate the mudflats, and were not afraid to completely immerse themselves in the foul dirt and muck. Now they would have to survive both at the same time.

The demo pit was about two miles south of the training compound, centered on the sand between the highway and the Pacific. The area was surrounded by a simple chain-link fence, the same kind that could be found around any household yard. But this fence kept the unwary away from a ten-foot-deep pit dug into the sand, partially filled with seawater and mud.

The pit was about thirty yards long and twenty yards wide. Sand from its excavation was built up in a four-foot-high berm around most of its perimeter. It was dug deeply enough into the beach that saltwater had seeped into it, the pool ranging from a foot or so deep at its edges to about four feet deep in its center section. At the bottom there was several feet of rank, black mud.

The water in the pit was not a clean example of the Pacific. The sludge and organic matter had built up under it to make a rich muck, though not quite up to the standards of the mudflats. Scum and crud made up of things that the students didn't want to know about floated on top. At each end of the pit were two tall telephone poles. Hanging limply from the poles, two heavy hawsers sagged across the pool.

One end of the ropes was secured about five feet apart on the southern pole. The other ends were tied off to anchors at the northern end. As the students came up to the demo pit, the instructors there were securing the end of the lower rope to the trailer hitch of a jeep facing away from the pit.

Instructor Burns was talking about something called the "death trap" as the students came up and grounded their boats. Other instructors were using derogatory terms about "East Coast names," which none of the students understood. Then this attention was commanded by Senior Chief Fletcher, who stood in front of the class and gave them their safety briefing for the evolution. It was short and to the point.

"This is the So Solly evolution, gentlemen," the senior chief said loudly, without using his bullhorn. "It is tough, dangerous, and if you screw up it will kill you. You've come this far and there is still a lot more to go before Hell Week is over.

"Now, you all think you're tired, cold, and want

nothing more than to go home to your mommies. So you've got to want it inside of here, gentlemen," Senior Chief Fletcher said, beating his chest with one fist, "to make it through this course. I've told you that before, and I'll say it again. We throw things at you hard and fast, and you have to react immediately, because if you don't—you will become a casualty. And you won't do the mission or your Teammates any good if you're stuck inside a body bag."

There was more about the direction they would be expected to move around the perimeter of the pit. But some of the students still had the presence of mind to wonder what it was they were about to face. The answer to that was coming up fast, as everything did during Hell Week.

Around the perimeter of the pit, between the berm and the fence line, there were bunches of stretched-out barbed-wire strands. The strands crisscrossed the area, held about a foot or so up from the ground by the posts the barbed wire was anchored to. Growing through the wire and around the area was scrub brush and beach grass. The gate through the fence surrounding the demo pit was on the north end, which was where the students were lined up.

Whistle drills began the evolution. As per Senior Chief Fletcher's direction, the class hit the ground. Two blasts of the whistle, and they started to crawl in a clockwise direction underneath the barbed wire. One blast and they stopped, crossed their legs at the ankles, ducked their faces down, and covered their ears and head with their hands. Then the explosions started.

An ear-splitting shriek of a whistle ended with the thunderous blast of an artillery simulator going off. Then another, and another, detonated in rapid succession. A single blast of a whistle sounded out, and they had to continue their crawl. From the back of the jeep, several instructors pulled out M60 machine guns. Now the rattle of machine-gun fire rang out over the heads of the crawling students.

It was only blanks being fired, but the students continued crawling and covering up when the whistle blew. The explosions weren't as sharp as they'd been during Breakout, since they were out in the open now, not surrounded by concrete walls that reflected sound. But the explosions were closer, and they were plenty loud. Smoke grenades added to the confusion. Some of the canisters poured out thick, white smoke that obscured the area around the students. Others added clouds of green, red, and violet smoke to the roiling confusion.

Then some explosions occurred without the warning whistle. The students didn't know that the instructors were using a mix of both artillery and grenade simulators again, much as they had during Breakout. The bodies of the simulators were just cardboard, so they didn't add dangerous fragmentation that might injure the students crawling by. But the students on the ground didn't know that. One blast of the whistle sounded, and they froze in place, covered up and waiting.

"Holy shit," Instructor Nugent shouted. "Look at that one fuse burning next to Nelson!"

"Oh, man," Instructor Burns added as he ceased fire with his M60. "If that one blows, it'll take his leg off."

Tim Nelson lay on the ground, his head covered and his legs crossed. He heard the instructors talking but just gritted his teeth. He was glad no one could see the tears of frustration, and maybe fear, seeping from his closed eyes. But he held his ground. A grenade simulator went off with a bang nearby, sand pattering down on some of the students. Then two blasts of the whistle quickly followed.

"Go, go," Kozuska shouted to his crewmate as he pushed on Nelson's leg with his hand. "You're okay. Go!"

"Yeah, crawl on there, little maggot," Instructor Burns said with a laugh. "We'll get you with the next one."

The trip around the demo pit seemed to go on for hours. Explosions and smoke, punctuated by the occasional burst of machine-gun fire, dogged every inch crawled by the students. When they had completely circled the demo pit and reached the north end of the area, they were led down into the pit itself. The dark, scummy water meant little to the almost exhausted students now. They crawled down the side of the pit and into the muck, the scum on the surface rolling away from them in oily little ripples.

Now they were in the muck at the bottom of the pit, and the explosions continued. Only the instructors were throwing the simulators directly into the water now. But at least they were throwing the charges away from the students.

The artillery simulators weren't demolition charges or high explosives, but they were loud and powerful and sent out a shock wave and a billowing cloud of white smoke. The students had heard an instructor discussing how he'd tossed a simulator in the base pool once during a drill and the explosion had been enough to crack the tile. They didn't know if this story was true, and they didn't care. The simulator blasts were enough to send shock waves through the water, and the students felt the bang over every inch of their bodies that was below the surface. Which, they reflected, was probably the reason they'd been told not to duck their heads under the water when they first entered the pit.

The burned, rotten smell of the exploding simulators added to the sulfurous stench of the burning smoke grenades. Over it all, a putrid odor rose from the water and muck around them. The pit was low and the smoke heavy, so it lay in the pit, spreading out over the water like a noxious blanket.

Finally, three whistle blasts sounded out and the students stopped crawling through the muck and stood up. The mud reached at least to their knees, and they were standing in waist- or chest-deep water and mud, depending on how far into the pit a student had crawled. The sudden silence was as deafening in its own right as the explosions a minute earlier had been. The students tried to listen to the instructors over the ringing in their ears.

As at the mudflats, the students were now ordered through a variety of exercises, including somersault races, this time across the width of the pool. This churned the mud up, creating a stinking quagmire of black water and even blacker mud. Over the surface of the muck floated bits and pieces of paper and cardboard, the remnants of the simulators that had gone off around them.

New instructors were shouting orders down to the students. When they heard the whistle indicating that a simulator was about to go off, the students were to shout "Incoming," duck down and cover their faces and heads. For practice, the instructors tossed out simulators as the students continued crawling, swimming, and moving through the muddy pit.

Finally, they were all given a reward. Lunch was served. And the meal was coming to them in a particularly unique BUD/S fashion. The class got up out of the pit and each student was given a box lunch, and then they were ordered back into the pit to enjoy their delicious meal. Hard-boiled eggs were being peeled and eaten as instructors tossed more simulators into the pit.

The cry of "Incoming" went up as the students crouched down over their open box lunches. The simulators would sink a bit, then blow. The blast would send a spray of muck and dirty water into the air, and down on the students in the pit. As the meal went on, they were not only swimming and working in the muck, they were eating it too.

The instructors were having a good time around the demo pit, tossing down their explosives and watching the students' reactions. They were careful not to allow any of the charges to come too close to the eaters, who were huddled together on one side of the lagoon. They did not want to injure a student, and the instructors weren't sure that the mental state of the students wasn't so confused that one of their number would jump on a burning simulator to shield his classmates from the explosion with his body.

After a week of the most strenuous work they had ever taken part in, the students were exhausted, more than a little dingy, and mentally confused. The instructors had been on their asses, as they had been all week, while they crawled through this latest obstacle course. The barbed wire, explosions, and gunfire all combined to produce a realistic simulation of combat. Throw in the mental state of the students, and it wouldn't have been hard to convince them that they actually were in a battle.

But they gutted it out. Or in some cases, they gutted it up. More than a few students, overcome by the stress, stench, and taste of their situation, vomited up a portion of their box lunches. But all of them had been throwing up at one point or another during the week. Now, it was little more than the dry heaves and retching after a few minutes.

With their incredible meal over, the students were gathered around one side of the demo pit for the next part of the evolution. They would learn what the overhead ropes were for.

One at a time, each student was to come up out of the pit and try to cross over the water on the ropes. They had to stay on both ropes, they couldn't wrap their arms and legs around one rope and slip across, and they had to make it all the way across. If any student made it all the way without falling off, they were told, Hell Week would be secured right there and then.

The students didn't believe this, but the situation had evolved into an us versus them mentality. On one side were the students, trying to survive whatever the instructors could throw at them. On the other side were the instructors, who were still shouting and suggesting that all one had to do was quit and everything would be over.

The students of Class 78 were now very close to securing from Hell Week, and none of the instructors actually believed any student would ring out on So Solly day. Normally, the instructors couldn't dump enough on a student at this point to make him quit, at least not without taking a chance on really hurting someone. So the instructors were the bad guys and the students the good guys in the us versus them battle of the demo pit.

The thick hawser line that made up the two crossing ropes was tightly twisted manila. The top line was attached to the jeep, while the bottom line had plenty of slack, so the instructors could move it about by hand. It was quickly obvious that not one student was going to make it across the pit, but that didn't stop the class from cheering on everyone who tried, and they all had their turn at the rope crossing.

The instructors were laughing and having a good time watching the students either fall off the line or get catapulted into the air and then hit the mud. The jerking around of the lower line by the instructors forced the students to grip down hard on the upper line to stay on the ropes. Then Senior Chief Fletcher, in the jeep, would gun the motor and pop the clutch, and as the jeep jerked forward, the upper rope pulled tight.

If a student tried to clamp down on the rope with his hands, he quickly discovered that tightening hawser twisted and painfully burned his palms. This forced him to let go of the upper line, but not before it propelled him upward.

Every student started out on the crossing determined to be the one who made it across. And every student either lost his grip and fell or was catapulted into the air. The students hit the water in all kinds of positions, but most often head first. No one was hurt, but several students struggled for a moment to right themselves when their heads were stuck deep into the mud. The instructors found the view of the wildly waving arms and legs hilarious, especially when it was followed a few second later by a spluttering and spitting student turning right side up.

When Kozuska clamped down on the upper rope with his big hands, the twisting hawser made his palms bleed before he finally let go. The general opinion of the instructors was that Kozuska had a possible career as a naval aviator since he could gain so much altitude without any wings to help him. Like his namesake, Zeus, Kozuska flew through the air. He formed an excellent ballistic arc, and impacted head first into the deeper part of the demo pit. That earned him a round of applause from the instructors and the students.

When Jeremy White took his turn at the rope, he only made it about a quarter of the way before his hands failed him and he fell into the mud with a splat.

Very few students were left as Bob Miller climbed into position. His classmates gave Miller, the smallest member of the class, as loud a cheer as they had any of the previous failures.

The instructors figured Miller just might make it into low earth orbit if they snapped the rope when he reached its lowest point in the middle. Not that they ever allowed themselves to get carried away—they knew to an inch just how much they could pull on the rope to toss a student into the air without allowing them to be injured on the landing. The students still had on their kapoks, standard wear for the boat paddle that had brought them down to the demo pit. And that thick kapok also protected their necks and backs from the impact.

As Miller started out on his crossing, the instructors moved the lower rope enough to make him clamp down on the upper line. As he reached the middle of the line, Miller began to get his bearings and was moving well between the two lines. His classmates were cheering wildly, screaming for their fellow sufferer to beat the instructors and get across the lines. That they could get out of Hell Week a little earlier if he had not slipped out of their foggy minds.

As Miller started to pass the halfway point, Senior Chief Fletcher decided to let him have a little more time, then he gunned the motor and slipped the clutch.

The jeep didn't move forward more than an inch before the motor failed and died.

Now Miller had a real chance to get across the rope line. As Fletcher cranked over the motor to the jeep, the students in the pit erupted in screams of "Go! Go! You can make it. GO!"

In spite of his exhaustion, Miller burst into a sprint, moving his feet and hands as quickly as he could. He passed the three-quarter marker before Instructors Nugent and Burns both grabbed the upper line and yanked down hard on it, pulling it from Miller's hands when he was within ten feet of victory.

Everyone in the pit, and more than a couple of the instructors, screamed out their approval and applause at Miller's valiant effort. Their exhaustion and pains temporarily forgotten, the students grabbed Miller up from the mud and soundly congratulated him. The slaps on the back he got threatened to send Miller back down into the mud before the instructors once more took control of the situation.

With the throttle of the jeep more finely adjusted, the students finished going across the ropes one at a time. Then attempts were made to cross with two men at a time, then three.

The students didn't know that the instructors' experience with the evolution had taught them that the more people on the line, the better they snapped into the air when the line was pulled tight. Everyone tried to cross, and everyone failed. But the story of Miller's attempt would stay in the memories of each member of Class 78 for a long time.

Finally, the evolution was over and the students were sent into the Pacific for a quick wash as part of surf appreciation. When they had been rolled around in the shallows long enough to get the worst of the muck and grime off, they were sent out into deeper water to get some of the crud out from underneath their clothes, as well as the sand they had picked up from the roiling water in the shallows. Senior Chief Fletcher was rewarding a well-conducted So Solly evolution, BUD/S instructor style.

Then the students paddled the two miles to the compound and crossed the Strand highway, returning to the Amphibious base.

## Chapter Twenty-five

After the Friday evening meal, the class was sent back to the training compound. Some of the students were trying to remember how the trip had felt back before Hell Week. It was just crossing a road, something they had done most of their lives. Most of them couldn't quite remember what doing it without a rubber boat grinding your head down between your shoulders had been like. But they did remember that they'd preferred it to what they were doing now.

The students were a mess. Class 78 looked like the walking dead, and smelled like them too. Vultures would have turned up their beaks at the thought of such a disgusting meal. And the whole class was dingy. Exhaustion had reached a point where their bodies only functioned because their minds were telling them to. Their bodies ached all over. Everyone had sores, abrasions, and minor cuts and bruises everywhere. Swelling had become so bad in their feet that a number of students had taken knives and cut slits in their boots to relieve the pressure. They looked like the remnants of a train wreck. That they were all still on their feet and moving was a tribute to their personal drive and desire to join the Teams. And that was exactly what the instructors had been looking for.

Now was the time for another traditional evolution, which, in comparison to the others, was the strangest of all. Almost everything they'd done to that point required major physical output. You could not paddle a rubber boat for miles without putting into it everything you had in your back and arms—and not be able to face the other members of your boat crew. Peer pressure, the desire to be accepted by those around you, was very important to the students. It became almost a primal need during Hell Week.

From the biggest to the smallest, everyone in the class had been helped by their Teammates at one point or another. When Kozuska slipped and fell to his knees on one of the boat runs in the sand, it was Rod Shea who reached out and grabbed the back of his kapok, pulling the much bigger man up to his feet. When Butterworth fell asleep during the Around the World tour, his boat crew let him rest and kept paddling on their own.

The students had merged into a team. If they were given an order, they would all get up and move out to follow it. Some would be moving faster than the others, but they would all be on their feet. Being a team, depending on each other, and all giving to the greater good, was a major lesson they had learned from Hell Week.

But the evolution they would face now was one each man had to do on his own. There was no way anyone could help the other. It was time for one of the least known evolutions of Hell Week—the essay test.

Marched into a classroom at the training compound, the students were directed to take their seats. With only four boat crews left, they didn't even fill one of the smaller rooms. On the desks in front of them were pencil and paper. The orders were for each man to write out his life story.

This was actually a rest period for the students, only they didn't know it. The room was warm, and the lights were turned down low as they bent to their tasks. It wasn't enough that a man could just keep going without sleep or rest. He also had to be able to think, otherwise he wouldn't be able to do anyone any good in the field.

However, thinking under these circumstances seemed almost impossible, with Instructor McDonald standing in the front of the class, eating chicken from a cardboard bucket. Noisily sucking the meat from the bones, he made a show of consuming the chicken. As he spotted a student nodding off, McDonald would throw the bones at them to wake them up.

"Anybody want some chicken?" he asked easily. "You can have some of this, all you've got to do is ring the bell."

Only a few students made any show of bravado at the instructor's words. Mostly, they ignored him and bent to their tasks. Just holding the short, stubby pencils they'd been given was a major difficulty. Fingers on hands that had been using paddles for hours didn't want to bend around the slim sticks.

But they'd been told to write their life stories, and the students would make those pencils move across the paper if they had to hold them between their teeth.

To Jeremy, it seemed they'd been in that classroom for hours, though they were only there about five minutes before they all started to nod off. They were allowed to rest for a short time, then Instructor McDonald yelled at them to wake up and keep writing.

None of the students had any idea as to how much time actually passed. Many of the pages were covered with something that could be thought of as writing. Jeremy thought he'd done a pretty good job of writing down his own story. When the students were shown those same pages after Hell Week was over, most of them couldn't read their own scribbling.

When they were ordered back on their feet and out of the classroom, the shock of moving from the warm room out into the cold night air helped to jolt some of the students awake. A quick dip into the surf zone, and an hour or so of beach games and exercises, managed to bring them around to as close to an alert state as they had left in them.

With the boats on their heads, they moved back out to the Amphibious base. The next evolution was almost like another Around the World trip. The boat crews were to paddle north and simulate a mock attack on the aircraft carriers at North Island. The boats would have to go all the way to a buoy marking the water around the carriers, and then they would paddle back. The trip would be over five miles and take most of the rest of the night.

Before leaving on the boat attack, however, the time for mid-rats came up, and after that the shift change for the instructors. It was a major effort now to keep eating and not nod off. Only a few of the students were able to just keep shoveling it in. A number of them had adopted a ceremony of holding a cup of hot water or coffee in their hands before eating. The heat loosened up their fingers a bit, and sipping at the hot liquid gave some relief to their insides. None of them had ever been this cold for this long—it seemed they would never really be warm again.

Then it was time for another shouting session by the instructors to get the class up and moving. It was after midnight and the night shift had come on. Chief Packard ordered a quick set of exercises to get the students warmed up and ready for their boat attack. Launching from the Amphibious base, the small fleet of rubber boats moved out to assault an aircraft carrier.

To anyone else, the idea that a twelve-foot rubber boat with six people aboard could do any real damage to something the size of a Navy aircraft carrier would seem ridiculous. But the students in the rubber boats knew that this was the kind of thing that had been done before, and that the SEALs could be asked to do again. In earlier wars, battleships had been attacked at anchor by boats even smaller than what the students were paddling. But this wasn't war, this was Hell Week, which made it even more serious.

Instead of approaching the aircraft carriers themselves, the order for the evolution had the boat crews paddling to an outer buoy marker near the carriers and then returning. The students wouldn't be safe, especially in their present condition, if they actually pulled up to one of the carriers. The huge ships rarely turned off all of their machinery, and an accident could turn lethal far too quickly for anyone to do anything to stop it.

So the boat crews paddled the several miles to the marker buoy. Boat Crew IV still had a leak in their rubber boat and, still taking on water, it was slowing them up. They had patched the leak as best they could after the Around the World tour the night before, but it looked like they were still going to come in last.

Patrick Neil and the rest of the boat crew thought they had a way of cheating that would ensure that theirs was the winning boat crew in spite of their speed. It was dark, it was some distance away from any other eyes but their own, and who could possibly catch them? So, when the rest of the boat crews made for the marker buoy, Boat Crew IV turned around and started back before reaching the marker.

It was a simple plan, about all the dingy boat crew was capable of. But Richard Kozuska in Boat Crew II spotted them as they turned around.

"They cheated, they cheated!" the scream came up from Boat Crew II.

"No we didn't, no we didn't," Boat Crew IV answered. This verbal argument went on all the way back to the base and the end of the evolution. As far as Boat Crew II was concerned, Boat Crew IV had cheated and they were the winning crew. Boat Crew IV vigorously denied the accusation. Then Chief Packard paddled up in a kayak and shut both of the crews up as well as dropping them to the push-up position.

Chief Packard declared Boat Crew III the winners of the evolution as soon as they came in to shore a few minutes later. Boat Crew I came in a few minutes later, with two boat crews on the ground in the front leaning rest, and another boat crew sitting on their IBS. They wondered just what the hell had happened.

The answer was very quickly forthcoming. Chief Packard had been following the little flotilla at some distance in his kayak. His small boat was silent and almost invisible in the dark water. He'd seen the cheating attempt and decided that both crews had turned back before completing the evolution. Not only had they cheated, but were clumsy enough to get caught.

Boat Crew III, which had fought the hardest to develop into a team, proved itself a good team in the end. They had been plagued with dropouts and problems, but with the last consolidation of the boat crews, they solidified into a group. Two of the original crew members, Redneck and Sledgehammer, had beaten down any prejudices they brought with them, and had learned that everyone worked together in the Teams.

And in the Teams, it paid to be a winner. That phrase had lost some of its meaning at times during Hell Week. The students hadn't noticed any real rewards. The crews that finished first usually had to do whatever exercises the other crews were punished with as well.

But the instructors paid attention, always. And now, Boat Crew III was secured from Hell Week.

The men of the crew were stunned. And the rest of the boat crews were more than a little disappointed, but only for a moment. Their friends, their classmates, their Teammates, had made it, and they were happy for them.

It was almost a quiet bunch of students who picked up their rubber boat and got ready to head back to the training compound. They were more than relieved to have completed Hell Week and to have accomplished what they had. But they were also leaving their class-mates behind. That made them less exuberant than they might have been otherwise.

"Go on," Butterworth said, "and don't use all the hot water in the showers!"

So they turned to go, and another surprise came up: Instructor Hawke had Boat Crew III put their IBS in the back of the pickup truck. They wouldn't have to carry it back to the training compound. It was a very ragged but very happy group of six post–Hell Week BUD/S students who headed back to their barracks and a well-earned rest.

The other three boat crews still had Chief Packard to contend with. He had his own way of dealing with stu-dents who cheated on one of his evolutions, especially those maggots who were too stupid to get away with it. He thought a good warm-up of boat drills, exercises, and his personal favorite, flutter kicks, would be a fine way to work out the kinks in the boat crews.

The instructors couldn't hurt the students badly now—they were too far gone for that. But they could force them to expend whatever they had left in trying to do all of the exercising Chief Packard put them through. When the crews were almost totally spent, they were told to up boats and head back to the training compound.

The night had gone by and the remaining crews were still moving. At the compound, they were gathered around a covered blackboard for their final pre-evolution briefing. The students were attentive as Chief Packard explained that they would be conducting the boat attacks against the aircraft carrier again. They would again have to cross over to the Amphibious base, get into the water, and paddle all the way to the carrier docks. Only this time the attack would be much more real.

Since the boat crews had cheated the first time, they would be expected to actually attack the carrier. They were being sent on as close to a real mission as had ever been done during Hell Week.

This time, the crews would each have to paddle right up to their selected target. They would be given a dummy charge that had to be placed against the hull of the carrier and the switch turned on. Then they had to get the boats back without being detected. However, the chief explained, they would be going up against an alerted crew on board the carrier. And the sailors would be armed with concussion grenades. If a rubber boat was spotted against their hull, the sailors would drop the grenades into the water and knock the rubber boats over.

Chief Packard was adamant that the boat crews pay attention to what they were doing. This wasn't a game, it was deadly serious. If they screwed up on this evolution, they could be killed, or at least seriously injured. And operational security was paramount. They didn't want the crews of the carriers to know which of their ships would come under the attack of Class 78. So on the blackboard behind him was the name of the ship they would attack. And, he told them, they had better pay attention.

As Chief Packard continued talking, Instructors Holmes and Hawke went up to either side of the blackboard and lifted the cloth that was covering it.

In big block letters, it said: HELL WEEK IS SECURED.

"Are there any questions?" Chief Packard said in a normal tone of voice, a grin on his face.

Miller raised his hand and started to ask, "Will those be real concussion grenades, and do we—"

"You all are dingy," Chief Packard said with a laugh as he cut Miller off. The other instructors in the area were also laughing. "Read the damned blackboard, men," Chief Packard said. "Hell Week is secured. Congratulations, Class 78, you made it."

## Chapter Twenty-six
### Secured

That one phrase, "secured from Hell Week," was something almost every member of Class 78 thought he would never hear. During that week, everyone, at least once, thought about quitting—ringing the bell and making it all stop. A lot of their classmates had done just that. But these few still standing at the end—only twenty-three from among all those who had stood in that same spot only a few weeks before—these were the only ones who knew what it meant not to quit.

There was so few of them left that it was almost astonishing. For a long moment, the remainder of Class 78 stared, at Chief Packard, expecting to be told this was just another hallucination. Then it settled in: they had made it. They had really made it.

A ragged but enthusiastic cheer went up from the survivors of Class 78. They had all felt like garbage just a moment before. Chief Packard had made his point about them screwing up, and each of the students had believed him. They were maggots—and now, suddenly, they were men.

Everyone was on their feet, even those students who could hardly stand anymore. First, boat crews were hugging and slapping each other on the back. That quickly spread throughout the class, with everyone congratulating everyone else.

Butterworth's quiet reservedness had been left back somewhere in the mudflats days earlier. He was cheering and carrying on as much as anyone in the class. Redneck and Sledge were dancing around, hugging each. They would never be rid of those nicknames for the rest of their lives, but they'd left behind the foolish prejudices and intolerance that they had both known since childhood. Going through Hell Week was a little like being reborn again, though newborn babies didn't look quite as messy as Class 78 did right then.

The noise was enough that it even aroused some of the members of Boat Crew II, who had been secured hours earlier. Those who woke up roused the others, if they could, and most of them hobbled out on very sore but much cleaner legs, joining in the celebration with their classmates.

"Listen up, you guys," Chief Packard said, still standing up by the blackboard. "I have something to say to you."

The students quickly fell silent and attentive. They were exhausted, but they had still noticed that Chief Packard wasn't shouting at them or using a bullhorn. He was speaking in a normal voice, something they hadn't heard for a week now.

"You guys have done something really serious here," Packard continued. "For the rest of your lives, you're going to measure whatever you do against what you have accomplished here. Training isn't over—far from it. You all have a long way to go, and it's still going to be easy to fail. But right now, you have proved that you have what it takes to get the job done.

"From now on, the training is going to get harder. But we're going to be teaching you skills that you'll have to know to be in the Teams. Right now, you've all shown that you have the heart and the drive to make it. But you're going to need the brains too.

"All this week, you've been doing more than you probably ever thought you could possibly do. That was the object of Hell Week. You weren't trying to prove anything to us. You had to prove something to yourselves, and I think you have."

The class was more than silent now. They were listening to every word Chief Packard was saying. The exhaustion and elation they were feeling a few moments earlier was being replaced by something, more than pride, more than a feeling of accomplishment. Even if they never made it to the Teams, or didn't stay in once they had made it, this group of men, this class, had formed a bond among themselves even stronger, for many of them, than family.

"Now clean up your gear and your boats," Chief Packard said in a sharper tone. "The job isn't done until the gear is cleaned and put away. Move it."

Everyone lent a hand to putting away the gear and hosing down the boats. They weren't going to have to pass an inspection, but they did have to see that everything was in at least reasonable shape before they could see to themselves. Even the students who had been in their racks asleep helped their classmates, so that they too could get to a well-deserved rest.

Once the gear had been seen to, the students were able to see to themselves. One of the first orders of business was a hot shower, something they had all been looking forward to for over five days. It was just sunrise now, and the area was starting to get light.

But there wasn't any evolution that had to be done. They didn't have to go roll in the ocean and then the sand. And to Jeremy, it felt weird, as if something was missing. They had been working so hard for so long, that the absence of that work seemed strange. Then the hot water of the shower drenched down on his sore and abraded skin, and he forgot all about not having to do any evolutions.

All the dirty clothes from the class were tossed in a large pile. Pretrainees who were waiting to class up would have the job of washing them while the students were recovering for a few days. Though when the pretrainees saw and smelled the state of Class 78's Hell Week uniforms, a number of them wondered why they didn't just burn them and disinfect the area afterward.

The showers were hot, and the use of soap was plentiful. The open sores, scratches, cuts, and abrasions stung when they were touched by hot water and soap. But the relatively minor pain couldn't take away from it being one of the best earned showers of their lives.

Everyone was still dingy, and they would remain so

for a while yet. But they were happy as well. The stories making the rounds of the students in the showers were of what they had all just gone through. Most of them were barely coherent as they lathered up and blew off stress at the same time. The words came loud and fast, and it felt great that they didn't have to go back out and into the surf, or under a boat, or anywhere else for a while.

Some of the students were talking about calling their families right away and telling them that they'd made it. The instructors had been through this themselves, both as students years before and with the classes they'd run through BUD/S since. It was easy to imagine just what a family might think, receiving a call from a babbling idiot of a son who couldn't be understood at all. To prevent this, all of the phones had been placed off limits to the students of Class 78 for the remainder of that Saturday.

The restriction hardly punctured their happiness. The students were almost deliriously happy. It was like Christmas and winning the Super Bowl rolled into a single event. They were jacked up, as if someone had just charged their batteries, and were anything but coherent, and the instructors knew that the high would soon wear off and the physical crash of their systems would quickly follow.

Just in case some of the students were too tired to take a shower immediately, there was an instructor on the deck overseeing the shower room. He bluntly told several of the more exhausted students to "wash their filthy asses" before they hit their racks. When the bab-

bling stories got a little too loud, or just too stupid for
that instructor's tastes, he told the class to "shut the
fuck up and get cleaned up!"

After the showers, a corpsman gave all the students
a quick check to make sure there wasn't anything that
needed immediate treatment. Some of the students had
developed ear infections, and these were treated by the
corpsman with special cleaning and ear drops. Jeremy
was astonished to see what boiled up out of John
Rock's ear when the corpsman poured hydrogen per-
oxide into it. The bubbling disinfectant foamed up,
pushing black crud and muck out.

Jeremy and the other students had similar deposits
of mud and muck still in their systems, even after the
long shower. Garbage came out from their noses and
ears for days. But the shower had stripped off the outer
layer of grime, and some skin along with it.

Bacitracin was passed out freely by the corpsman
for everyone to spread on their legs and thighs. The
abraded skin was infected on almost everyone, to one
degree or another, and quick treatment would keep the
infections from becoming serious.

Now the students were able to return to their rooms,
most of which were emptier than they had been the
Saturday before. Jeremy and his two remaining roommates, Jim Alex and Bob Miller, had a stacked bunk to
themselves. Just getting some sleep was the next priority.

The instructors had been watching the class as they
went through their clean-up procedures and started to
return to their barracks. The barracks would be left

open for the weekend; none of the doors would be locked. And each student's room was to be unlocked and the door left ajar. Over the weekend, the instructors would come around to check everyone out, to make sure that were all breathing.

Upper class students also looked out for the post–Hell Week students. If a student was to fall asleep with his legs or arms off of his bed, the circulation would start to pool and swell in the lower extremities. So if a loose leg was seen by an instructor or upper class man, they would lift it up onto the bed and let the student continue sleeping.

Some of the men from the upper classes had slipped in a six pack or two of beer into the barracks while Class 78 had been out on Hell Week.

And Jeremy enjoyed a celebratory beer that he had found in the refrigerator. It didn't matter that it was still early on a Saturday morning. It wasn't as if his body had any idea what time it was anyway. So he sat down on the bed, opened the can, and woke up Sunday afternoon.

He was still tired, and a bit groggy. But it didn't take long for him to realize where he was and what he'd done. Now, he wanted to call his family back home and let them have the good news. His father was at the farm, and answered the phone first. He didn't know what Jeremy had just gone through, but he understood how important it was to his son. Jeremy's mother was more subdued about what her son was going through. It would still be a few days before Jeremy's voice got back to anything close enough to normal that his mother wouldn't be able to detect the strain he'd gone through.

After the call, Jeremy sat and thought for a minute about what he'd done. He found it hard to remember the details. They were blurred and ran together. But his body had no problem recalling just what he'd forced himself through. It was starting to swell up, and he knew he wouldn't be able to put boots on his feet for several weeks.

The aches, pains, and sore spots reminded Jeremy of his accomplishment. He realized that having gotten through that one week, he could get through anything he had to. It was a feeling he would be able to reflect back on for the rest of his life.

There was still a lot of training to go through. It wasn't over yet, not by a long shot. But even the instructors he saw that weekend let him retain that feeling of accomplishment. Jeremy and his classmates had proved to them that they had what it took to make it through the program, though whether they would all actually make it through was yet to be seen.

The recovery period for Class 78 began that Sunday. Jeremy was only one of the students who had bad cellulitis in his legs. It was a bacterial infection of the skin that got through all of the cuts and abrasions so many of the students had received. The infection led to heavy swelling in the legs or feet, but the corpsman were familiar with the problem and its treatment. Jeremy would just be one of the BUD/S students walking around with what were called "elephant feet" for a while.

In spite of bad feet, legs, or whatever, it was hard for the members of Class 78 not to walk with a bit of a swagger to their step that Sunday. That the swaggers were mixed with a variety of limps took nothing away from their feeling of accomplishment. It wasn't the lack of an IBS on their heads that made them walk a little taller to the chow hall that Sunday evening. And it didn't take an instructor barking orders at them to make them walk straight and carry their heads high.

The students of Class 78 knew they had entered a very select fraternity of military men. In all of the military since World War II, among the millions of men who had served in the Navy, there was only a tiny percentage—a few thousand—who had ever completed Hell Week. Even if something happened to an individual now that he was dropped from the program or didn't graduate, he still would have proved that he could take it.

And so the students of Class 78 who went over to chow that first full day after Hell Week had a small chip on their shoulders. They felt that the whole base knew what they'd done. And they liked the feeling of status that gave them for the moment. They deserved the credit for what they'd done individually and, even more important, as a group. They enjoyed the congratulations of the upper class students who knew very well just what they were feeling and what they had done.

## Chapter Twenty-seven

Just because Hell Week was over didn't mean things got any easier for Class 78. The instructor staff didn't pound them with PT the week following Hell Week. Instead they had classes and stretching PT, which had a lower impact on their abused bodies. And a lot of the simple verbal abuse that had been dumped on them was gone. Class 78 had gone from 118 students to twenty-three, which was close to the usual curve for First Phase drops.

The final weeks of First Phase were taken up with hydrographic reconnaissance. The students were back in the water, dropping lines with lead weights and writing down the results on a plastic slate. This was the same technique that had been developed for the invasion on Saipan in 1944. It was simple, and it worked.

Now that they had shown themselves to have the mental and physical toughness to go through training, the students began using their intelligence as well. Second Phase was where they would learn diving, and they would also have to learn the physics and biological effects of working underwater. Teamwork wasn't much of a question anymore. When the mathematics and technical aspects of training were hard for some students, their classmates who didn't have trouble with the subject lent them a hand.

The class grew a bit in size as several students who had been rolled back from earlier classes were added. The diving went well enough, they didn't lose any more people to performance drops, and no one quit. They didn't even lose Bob Miller on one of the night compass dives, though he was the only one to run into trouble.

Swimming across the dark waters of San Diego Bay on an underwater compass course quickly became boring. The students paid attention to the compass that glowed in the water and counted their kicks to keep track of how far along they were. Outside of that, even in the daytime, there wasn't much to see in the relatively shallow bay waters. The only underwater landmark, besides patches of sea grass, was an open oil drum sitting on the bottom.

One night when Jeremy and Bob Miller were swim buddies, the oil drum moved. It hadn't been the tide or currents moving it, but Miller, who swam straight into the open end. His consequent thrashing about rolled the drum.

His classmates were amused and Miller was pumped for information on his swimming technique. Even Jeremy wanted to know how the little student could swim along, keeping up speed and direction with his partner, while apparently being asleep—it was a skill they all thought sounded handy.

Third Phase introduced the wonderful world of explosives to Class 78. PT had been hard all through Second Phase, and it didn't get any easier in Third Phase. For the most part, the students were in the best shape of their lives, and the instructors had to add considerably to the PT regimen to keep them working.

Weapons, explosives, demolitions, and land warfare were the primary subjects of Third Phase. Halfway through the phase, the class was moved offshore to San Clemente Island and the training facility there. On the island, the students conducted patrols and missions, first under the direction of the instructor staff and then on their own.

Weapons were fired on the island's ranges. The CAR-15, the short version of the M16A1 rifle, was the students' primary weapon. They were worn and many had seen time in the jungles of Vietnam, as well as the hands of countless students. But they were more than sufficient to help teach basic weapons handling and marksmanship. M60 machine guns were fired, as well as 40mm grenade launchers. A few live hand grenades were thrown to give each of the students a feel for what it meant to hold live ordnance.

Senior Chief MacKenzie was running the Third Phase training out on San Clemente when he ran into a problem with one of the students. The problem was a relatively minor one. A student cleaning the M60s had inserted the gas cylinder backward on one of the barrels. When the instructors happened to choose that weapon to take with them on one of the training operations, the misassembly proved obvious.

The instructor cadre on the island acted as the aggressors on some of the operations and patrols the students were running. On this particular operation, a couple of the instructors had planned an ambush of the students as they approached another target. The lesson was to expect the unexpected, and when it happened, react accordingly.

The trouble was, because the weapon was misassembled, the unexpected happened to an instructor. When he pulled the trigger on his M60 loaded with blanks and fitted with a blank adaptor, the weapon fired one round and stopped. The gas system didn't work with the piston in backward. The result was the students reacting to the instructor's failed ambush. When the instructor's firepower failed them, the students were able to charge the ambush and break through. The students did the right thing, but they were able to get away with it more easily for the wrong reason. It wasn't until the next day during morning muster that the rest of the problem was brought out.

Senior Chief MacKenzie wanted to know who had torn down the M60s' barrels. The students were supposed to clean all of the weapons, but the weapons were to have been checked before they were secured for the day. Obviously, a student hadn't done his job, and now was the time to make him pay.

When MacKenzie accosted the class about who had screwed up the gun, Washington Sledge stepped forward. The mistake had been a serious one. Had they been in a combat zone, someone might have grabbed that weapon and started using it. Mistakes with weapons were unacceptable, and MacKenzie was determined that Sledge would pay for his error.

That evening, after the rest of the class was secured, Senior Chief MacKenzie called Sledge out to the beach for a little old-fashioned surf appreciation as his means of punishment. The waters of San Clemente weren't any warmer than those off the training compound back in Coronado, and Sledge was just as uncomfortable doing push-ups according to Senior Chief MacKenzie's instructions. Then something happened to warm up the man, if not the water.

Walking down from the rough barracks area of the island, Redneck Rappaport walked right into the surf and fell into the push-up position next to Sledge.

"And just what the hell are you doing in my surf zone?" asked Senior Chief MacKenzie.

"Hooyah, Senior Chief MacKenzie," Rappaport answered. "The student is sticking with his swim buddy."

Within a minute, Lieutenant Butterworth came down the beach and into the surf.

"And your problem is?" the senior chief asked.

"Hooyah, Senior Chief," Butterworth answered from the water as the surf pounded down on him. "I am joining my men."

Before the sound of Butterworth's words had faded, Kozuska was down from the barracks and into the water. The remainder of Class 78 followed close behind him.

"Class 78," Butterworth shouted, "Senior Chief MacKenzie."

"Hooyah, Senior Chief MacKenzie," thundered up from the surf zone.

And the senior chief ran the class through a full set of exercises in the surf zone and up on the beach for good measure. MacKenzie knew that he couldn't hurt these men anymore, no matter what he did. But he wasn't going to lighten the punishment because they were all there. These students had learned the biggest lesson at BUD/S. They were a solid team of their own now. And the senior chief was pleased to run them through the exercises, and the grins on the students' faces told him that they understood why.

Mistakes, even simple ones, couldn't be tolerated on the island. They were working with materials that were designed to kill people. The bangs of the small arms were soon replaced with the bigger booms of live explosives. Safety was always paramount, and Class 78 came through the training with few hitches.

One of the bigger bangs on San Clemente took place when the students conducted a complete beach reconnaissance, located and measured obstacles, then did a demolition swim to blow the obstacles up.

The thundering blast when the haversacks of explosives detonated sent towers of white water into the air. The explosions also punctuated the fact that the class was getting close to the end of its time as a class. Graduation was coming up soon after their return from San Clemente Island.

The beach party the students had their last day on

the island was a relaxed affair. Following a longstanding tradition, the students who could do it best stood up in front of the class, with the instructors behind them, and imitated their favorite instructor. Chief Packard was a big favorite, his "maggots" line being a popular one. Instructor Lubi and his cigar was remembered, as were a number of incidents that covered the entire twenty-six weeks. It was all taken in good fun, and the students, along with the instructors who had been riding them so hard for the last six months, let themselves relax and have a good laugh.

The final day of graduation back in Coronado had some ceremony to go with it. On a spotless grinder with flags flapping in the hands of an honor guard, the students of Class 78 sat together for the last time under a sunny California sky. With the sound of the Navy band playing in the background, the commander of the training compound, Captain Murkowski, addressed the class.

For his own part, Jeremy White sat in the folding wooden chair listening to but not really hearing the captain speak to the class. He was trying to remember how he'd felt over six months earlier when he first set foot on that same grinder. He wasn't the same man as he had been; none of the students were. BUD/S changed a man for life. And he believed that wholeheartedly now.

As each man's name was called out, he stepped up to the podium and accepted his diploma. Stepping a little farther, each student rang the bell that had haunted them so much those first weeks. With a loud *DING, DING, DING,* each student rang the bell three times, signifying he was graduating BUD/S.

When he heard his name called, Jeremy also stood and accepted his diploma. In front of a gathering of many of the students' families and friends, he took his turn at the bell. And like all of the other students, he tried to crack that damned bell with each one of his rings.

I guess they were right, Jeremy thought. You can't leave BUD/S without ringing out.

When Captain Murkowski gave the final order for Class 78 to secure from training, the students cheered and their families and friends applauded. With the formal ceremony over, the students accepted the congratulations from their fellow graduates, friends, and families. Even George Staverous had his wife and two sons at the ceremony. It seemed that some yeoman in the class had conspired with the highest ranking officer available to get their classmate's family over on a military flight.

Butterworth and Jim Alex had big smiles as they looked at the huge Greek picking up his youngest son and setting him on his shoulder. But that wasn't the only family there. A dignified black man in a suit was standing with his wife and a teenage boy as his son came up and introduced his friend, Travis Rappaport.

Standing not a few feet away was a sunburned man, his wife standing next to him. Hard weather had left its mark on a man who lived his life outside, working a Louisiana shrimp boat. The southern man took a few steps and offered a calloused hand to the black Detroit factory worker. A hand used to moving steel met the palm of a hand that had pulled a thousand miles of netting and rope.

"My name's Randall Rappaport," the weathered man said. "My son has written home about training here. Congratulations on what your boy done."

The proud black man shook the other's hand firmly. "William Sledge," he said as he introduced himself. "My son had said some mighty fine things about your boy too."

"It seems the Navy has changed a mite since our day," Randall said with a smile.

"It seems to have been for the better," William said.

The two proud fathers turned and watched their sons, who were talking and laughing with their friends.

## EPILOGUE

Master Chief Jeremy White always liked to be on the grinder when a class graduated from training. It was not only a sign of respect that the master chief would be there when the students finally finished the grueling course, it also allowed him to be one of the first men to welcome the graduates aboard to the Teams.

It was a big change for the men who had been students just minutes before. Now, the instructors who had made them almost quake with fear those first weeks at BUD/S were putting out their hands and welcoming them to their new life in the Teams. It was a strange but always welcome situation for the recent graduates.

The master chief remembered that graduation had been one of the happiest days of his life. Just the acknowledgment of what they had done during training meant a lot to the students. A handshake meant a lot. And for the officers who had just graduated, Master

Chief Jeremy White had a particular tradition of own he had set at the Training Command.

All the other instructors knew to stay to the side as the officers graduated. Master Chief White always liked to be the first enlisted member of the SEAL community to render the officer graduates their first SEAL salute.

After six months of training, where the wrath of Master Chief White had been their worst nightmare, some of the officers had a funny look in their eyes as they received their first salute at the Training Command. But they quickly got over it and returned the honor with a snap.

Master Chief Jeremy White enjoyed giving that bit of respect to the men who had earned it so much. Being the Command master chief was a tough job, but it allowed him to give something back to the community he had come to care about so much. And most of the young graduates in front of him would feel that way themselves some day.

## AUTHOR'S NOTE

Everything in the story you have just read is true. Each of the events that took place in the story happened at one time or another during the hardest training offered in the U.S. military today, Basic Underwater Demolition/SEAL training. Though all of the names of individuals in this book have been made up, except for a few historical incidents, each one is based on a real person. And the struggles and triumphs of these fictional characters have been real.

Class 78 existed. It was used as the class number for this story because it has been the only class at BUD/S to have disappeared during Hell Week. The training was so hard that no one graduated with that class. In each of the well over two hundred classes, the incidents and evolutions on these pages have happened at one time or another during training. Times and events change, but the quality of the graduates of BUD/S has always remained high. It is a compliment to both the instructors and their professionalism, and the students, with their drive and heart, that the SEAL Teams are what they are today: one of the finest special warfare units in the world.